EQUATION OF LIFE . . .
AND DEATH

Bob got up and puttered restlessly around his dark bedroom. He felt strangely distant from everything, isolated, as if the second floor of his own home were a space station orbiting far out in dark regions. He went and looked out each window on the floor in turn, trying to spot FBI agents. In charcoal-gray suburban darkness he saw the side of the Lehrers' house next door; his own shadowed backyard through a crisscross of branches; the peak of the Ranellis' house with telephone wires; and the street, framed in more branches, with a splash of greenish streetlight, cars parked along the curb. The four corners of Bob Wilson's life. Take them away and what would you have? Or drop Bob Wilson into a place where there were no streets or trees at all, no houses or neighbors or cars, only a "phase space" where equations standing for those things swirled, and what would you have? A world where you could do anything you wanted by changing an equation? Was that *this* world?

D1577700

THE HIGHER SPACE

—

JAMIL NASIR

BANTAM BOOKS
New York   London   Toronto   Sydney   Auckland

THE HIGHER SPACE
A Bantam Spectra Book / July 1996

ISBN 0-553-56887-6

Published simultaneously in the United States and Canada

Bantam Books are published by Bantam Books, a division of
Bantam Doubleday Dell Publishing Group, Inc. Its trademark,
consisting of the words "Bantam Books" and the portrayal of a
rooster, is Registered in U.S. Patent and Trademark Office and in
other countries. Marca Registrada. Bantam Books, 1540
Broadway, New York, New York 10036.

PRINTED IN THE UNITED STATES OF AMERICA

RAD   0 9 8 7 6 5 4 3 2 1

FOR
VICKI

No religious system is incapable of a profound and coherent mysticism—not even science. So let the pure scientist, using his electronic computer as the shaman his drum, through rigorous modeling follow the ancient seers to the world of deeper reality.

—M. A. Al-Haq, Ph.D.
Principles of Thaumatomathematics

THE
HIGHER
SPACE

1

"The party's on October twenty-third, three weeks from yesterday, and we can't very well say we have plans because we don't, and they *are* neighbors," said Vicki Wilson from the dining room. "Besides, it'll be fun. You'll enjoy yourself."

Her husband Bob, a large, thin man, was stirring hot milk in a saucepan on the kitchen stove. "I'll enjoy myself sitting around with a bunch of ninety-year-olds at a birthday party for a five-year-old," he said ironically.

October sunlight rested at an early Sunday afternoon angle on the blue-and-white kitchen linoleum, pouring off the Swedish cutting-board counter Vicki had had installed the year before.

"Zachary's going to be six," she said.

"And I'm going to be forty-one." Bob took his simmering milk off the burner.

"If you want to feel sorry for someone, what about me?" said Vicki. "I'm almost as old as you are, and for a woman that's scandalous."

Bob carried his mug of hot milk into the dining room and looked at her—at the long, chocolate-colored eyes, high, theatrical cheekbones, health-club-toned figure in a gray sweatsuit slouched on a chair in front of real-estate contracts spread out on the dining table.

"Don't remind me," he said. "I might break down and cry."

She smiled at the compliment she had been fishing for. "Shall I tell Mrs. Taylor we're coming to Zachary's party?"

The doorbell rang. Bob went out to answer it.

Behind and above the lady who had rung he could see a brilliant curtain of yellow leaves with chinks of pale blue at the top, and thin, chilly sunlight in the street beyond. The lady had large, worried dark eyes in a tired face that might once have been pretty despite the weak chin; one thin hand clutched her cheap coat shut.

"Excuse me," she said in a faint voice. "Is Mrs. Wilson home?"

"Sure," Bob said, and almost forgot to add: "Come in." The lady had the air of someone who expected to be left waiting. "Vicki?"

Vicki came into the living room. Her inquisitive look didn't go away when she saw the lady.

"Mrs. Wilson," said the lady, "you probably don't remember me. I'm Nora Esterbrook. Diana Esterbrook's mother? The girl in your Washington Junior High play last fall?"

"Oh, yes, I remember. How are you, Mrs. Esterbrook?" Pause. "Would you like to sit down?"

Bob hung up Mrs. Esterbrook's coat, mumbled something polite, and took his hot milk upstairs to his detective novel. Real-estate agents did most of their work on weekends, he had learned long ago living with Vicki.

A murmur came up from the living room. It wasn't long before Vicki came up too, and sat on the arm of his wing chair.

"Honey, come talk to the poor lady," she said.

"About what?"

"Her daughter is adopted, and the original mother is trying to get her back. There's something wrong with the adoption papers, and the original mother has lawyers—"

There was a short, whispered argument of the kind not unknown to matrimony. At the end of it Bob was grumpily following her downstairs.

She said to Mrs. Esterbrook: "Here he is. See if you can get anything out of him." She pinched him where Mrs. Esterbrook couldn't see.

Mrs. Esterbrook was sitting on the edge of the Wilson's deep, flower-patterned sofa holding one of the fancy guest teacups.

"Mr. Wilson, I'm awfully sorry to bother you on a Sunday and all," she said tremulously, "but I just don't know what to do. We have a summons to go to court Thursday, and Jayne Wetzel that lives next door to me says not to worry, they can't take her away, but I *am* worried, *terribly* worried—*she* has lawyers, and they say something is wrong with the papers, and Mr. Esterbrook is laid off so we can't really afford one—and I remembered Mrs. Wilson saying you were one, so I—I came to see if you could tell me what to do."

"Gosh, Mrs. Esterbrook, I'm sorry to hear that, but I'm a corporate lawyer—"

"Do you think they can take her from us? We've had her since she was a tiny little girl. Can they take her away?" Her thin, chapped hands clasped the teacup as if she could warm herself on the inch of lukewarm tea in it. Her eyes were anguished.

"I really—"

"Well, do I need a lawyer? Jayne Wetzel—that's Mrs. Wetzel that lives next door—says I don't need one, I should just go in and demand my rights, but I'm worried; I don't have any idea what to say or—Do I need a lawyer, do you think, Mr. Wilson?"

"It sounds like you do. You can call—"

Vicki remarked: "You take those, what do you call them, pro bono cases sometimes."

"Well, of course, but I certainly couldn't take a case like this, even if I knew anything about adoption law, without the permission of the adoptee herself," Bob invented smoothly, his eyes holding Vicki's.

"Oh, well, she's right out in the car," said Mrs. Esterbrook. "We were just on the way home from her computer club." She looked Bob in the face with her scared eyes. "I wouldn't ask you, Mr. Wilson, but I'm desperate, desperate . . ."

While she was out at the car, Bob asked Vicki bitterly: "Are you satisfied?"

"It's just until Thursday," she coaxed him. "Don't you want to help them?" Her eyes were shining with curiosity. "The original mother was in jail *twelve years.* She just got out."

"What did she do?"

"Nora wouldn't tell me."

At first sight Diana Esterbrook seemed too much like Mrs. Esterbrook to be adopted, but after a minute Bob realized that the resemblance was in the anxious, defeated look they both wore; their features were quite different. Diana's eyes, when she glanced at you, were green, her lank hair dusky red, her hands long and narrow. She had a few freckles and was skinny and awkward as a twelve-year-old, though she was going on fifteen. She wore jeans and a shiny green high school jacket.

"I haven't seen you since the play last year. Have you taken any more drama classes?" Vicki made conversation at her when she and her mother were settled on the couch. Diana sat right on the edge too, shoulders slumped, hair almost hiding her face. She shook her head.

"What do you do at a computer club?" asked Vicki curiously, curling herself into the armchair by the fireplace.

Diana mumbled something.

"What?"

"Nonlinear systems programming," Diana repeated angrily, as if people were deliberately not listening to her.

"Diana, be polite," pleaded Mrs. Esterbrook. "You remember how nice Mrs. Wilson was last year, don't you?"

Diana nodded, hair still hiding her face.

"And this is Mr. Wilson, who's going to try to help us." No reaction. "I'm sorry, Mr. Wilson," she said in a confidential voice. "I can't do a thing with her."

"How'd you like to see some photos of that play?" Vicki asked Diana. "I have an album upstairs. It has some other plays in it too. Some with me in them. If you stay here Bob'll just ask you a lot of questions and try to bore you to death."

Diana glanced up gratefully at Vicki, then flushed, as if she had been caught in some illicit desire.

A few minutes later Vicki's enthusiastic voice was coming vaguely down the stairs and Bob was gloomily asking Mrs. Esterbrook questions about her case.

Her story, as it came out in fits and starts, was this: Mr. and Mrs. Esterbrook had never been able to have children of their own, since Mr. Esterbrook had motility problems. They had been married seven years when they signed up on the county adoption agency's waiting list. Mr. Esterbrook had a good job back then, and they had some savings, so they qualified, and after about a year they got a call that there was a two-year-old girl available. They had wanted a younger child but they decided to go see, and they fell in love with her at first sight. For one thing, she was *the* most precious child, and for another she was so pitiful and withdrawn. Her unmarried mother had been convicted of a felony carrying a fifty-year prison sentence. Mr. and Mrs. Esterbrook had filled out all the papers and gone through all the interviews and the adoption had been consummated. For the first few months Diana woke up screaming with nightmares two or three times a week, but that wore off, and she had grown into a perfectly normal, healthy girl, as Mr. Wilson could see for himself. (Mrs. Esterbrook watched him closely when she said that part, as if he might have some reason to disagree.)

"Then two weeks ago I was doing the dishes after dinner, and a woman came to the door with two men—they said they were lawyers—and they wanted to see Diana, and I was afraid she had done something at school, like—" She cut herself off. "Mr. Esterbrook asked what they wanted, and they said the woman was her real mother and she'd come to see about taking her back, and—and of course Mr. Esterbrook gave them a piece of his mind. In the middle of it Diana came out—I tried to get her back in her room but I can't do a thing with her—and when the woman saw her—" Her voice started to shake. "She—she started to—sing, like—and that moment Diana fainted dead away. She fell right down on the floor and banged her head, and I didn't have time to catch her."

"She fainted because the woman started to sing?"

"I don't know, Mr. Wilson. She didn't *sing*, exactly; it was more like chanting, the way they do in those foreign religions, or something like that."

Tuesday afternoon Bob took time out between meetings to read adoption law in the hush of his firm's law library. After an hour he thought he knew enough to win the Esterbrooks' case. It looked open and shut: while a defect in the adoption documents was technically grounds for returning a child to the biological parents, in practice the courts rarely did that. Instead they used a best-interests-of-the-child test: if the child was doing reasonably well in the adoptive home, had been there a long time, and wanted to stay, judges invariably refused to move it, no matter how screwed up the paperwork was. With the biological mother a convicted felon and Diana in her twelfth year with the Esterbrooks, it would take a miracle to get her away from them.

When Bob got home that evening Vicki told him: "Nora Esterbrook called. She's got the papers you wanted, and she gave me directions to their house. It's only about ten blocks."

After dinner Bob decided to walk to the Esterbrooks'. The sky was a dark, windy gray, clouds scudding across a three-quarter moon above the telephone wires, damp, chilly gusts shaking half-clothed trees and rippling puddles on the sidewalk. Suburban windows glowed warmly behind curtains and shades. Bob walked downhill on Cedar, across Wayne at the lights, uphill again, and turned left on Pershing Drive, an elderly street that slanted down under old trees whose roots cracked and humped the sidewalk. At the bottom Pershing dipped steeply to a cross-street lit gray-blue by moonlight, and beyond that an undeveloped plot or field sloped up another hill, overgrown with brambles and vine-draped trees waving in the wind. Across the street from the field, lights of houses glowed. The one with the Esterbrooks' number was tiny, almost trailer-size, with Mrs. Esterbrook's ancient Chevrolet in the drive. A loose wire slapped in the wind somewhere. Bob climbed three concrete steps without a railing and pushed the doorbell button.

The man who opened the door was short but strong-looking, with mud-colored hair and eyes, and a trimmed moustache on a handsome face gone pouchy. He wore brown pants and shiny brown shoes, and the three top buttons of his khaki shirt were open. He was holding a can of beer. "Who the hell are you?" he demanded.

"Bob Wilson. The lawyer Mrs. Esterbrook asked over."

"Oh." He seemed both abashed and suspicious. "I didn't see your car." He called over his shoulder: "Nora? Nora? Your lawyer's here."

Mrs. Esterbrook came quickly across the tiny, dim living room, wiping her hands on an apron. A TV rumbled softly in the corner. The house was full of the smell of recent cooking.

"Mr. Wilson, thank you so much for coming."

Mr. Esterbrook sat down on a worn sofa and pretended to watch TV. He stood up again quickly when Mrs. Esterbrook said: "Did Derek introduce himself? Derek, this is Mr. Wilson, the lawyer. Remember I told you about Mrs. Wilson, who directed Diana's play?"

"I, I didn't see your car." His hand was thick and strong. "I thought you might be one of those other lawyers."

"That's quite all right."

"Give me your coat, Mr. Wilson," said Mrs. Esterbrook. "The papers are right in here. Do you mind sitting in the kitchen? That way the television won't bother you."

The kitchen was tiny, the pattern wearing off the linoleum, but neat and clean. A pile of dog-eared papers lay on a yellow formica table. Mrs. Esterbrook sat Bob in front of them.

"Can I get you something to eat?" she asked anxiously.

"No, thanks."

She sat down opposite him and watched as he turned the papers over, unfolded them, put them in order.

"Here's where the social worker signed," she said, putting a housework-chapped finger by a faded signature. "And here's where we went in for the interview—"

"Just give me a minute."

She sat breathless while he looked over each paper. Everything was there, properly notarized, all the signature lines filled in—except one. The signature of the Director of Social Services was missing on the Certificate of Fitness. The last thing he came to was a Family Court Summons, dated earlier in the month, with an Affidavit signed by Petitioner Armilla Robinson in a peculiar, childish hand. The lawyer's signature under it was large and arrogant, a Barry D. Wentworth III.

"Well, there is a small problem," Bob said finally, leaning back. "But it's what we call a technical defect, and it shouldn't pose any difficulties. This missing signature here." He showed it to her. "Any idea how that came to be left out?"

"No."

"You and your husband had no idea there had been a mistake?"

"Heavens, no."

"And no one has ever challenged your parental rights before?"

"Certainly not."

"Now, Mrs. Esterbrook, I have to ask you this, but don't take it the wrong way—have you or your husband ever had child abuse, neglect, or other parenting complaints made against you?"

She shook her head.

"Anything happen in the last year or two that someone might say either you or Mr. Esterbrook are unfit parents or aren't providing a good home environment for Diana?"

"No."

She said it kind of fast.

"Think carefully, because this is important. The worst thing that could happen is that these other lawyers come into court with some accusations I don't know anything about. No school problems, family troubles, anything like that?"

"Well—Derek got laid off a while back, but he couldn't help that—there was an economic reorganization at his company, and he hasn't been able to get anything else yet."

"Okay," Bob coaxed her. "Think about it, and if anything more occurs to you, give me a call by, say, tomorrow afternoon. Now, I still need to talk to your husband. And I didn't really get to talk to Diana Sunday. . . ."

Her door was in a short, dark hall off the living room. Mrs. Esterbrook knocked and leaned her head close, as if trying to hear what was going on inside. Diana opened the door. The room was dark behind her.

"Diana, Mr. Wilson wants to talk to you."

"Can I come in?" Bob asked.

She nodded.

"I hope your room's not a mess," said Mrs. Esterbrook.

"It's quite all right—this will just take a minute." Bob stepped in and closed the door in Mrs. Esterbrook's anxious face.

Diana sat back down, slouching sideways at a small desk, twining one long, skinny leg around her chair leg and looking up at him shyly between her hanging hair. A pattern of glowing colored lines on a computer screen made shadows of her face, and dimly lit humps of tumbled clothes and an unmade bed. The air was close and warm.

"That's pretty," Bob said to put her at ease, pointing at the screen. He sat on a chair draped with clothes. "What is it, a butterfly?"

"A strange attractor."

"A what?"

"A strange attractor. A phase space map of an aperiodic equilibrium state of a nonlinear system."

"They teach you this stuff in school?"

"No."

Damn kids. "Okay. Well, your mom's told you we're having this hearing Thursday?"

She nodded.

"What do you think of the whole thing?"

She shrugged.

"Would you rather go live with the lady who came over a couple of weeks ago or stay here with your parents?"

"Stay."

"Why?"

She shrugged.

"Have your parents been good to you? Taken care of you pretty well?"

"I guess so."

"What about the other lady? Do you remember anything about her at all?"

Her eyes were down.

"I remember," she said slowly, "being afraid. Waking up and a white face hanging over me in the dark. I don't know if I dreamed it. . . . Then my mother and father coming and taking me away, taking care of me."

Pause.

"Anything else? Any idea why you fainted when the lady talked to you the other night?"

She shook her head.

"I may want you to tell that about being afraid at the hearing. Could you do it?"

She nodded.

Bob stood up. "Thanks for talking to me."

At the door his curiosity got the better of him and he pointed at the computer screen. "What is that thing supposed to do?"

"It's a diagram of someone's life," she said, and there was bitterness in her voice.

"Derek's gone for a walk," Mrs. Esterbrook told Bob innocently out in the living room. "He needed some air. Would you like to wait for him, or—?"

"Well, I have to talk to him," Bob said, irritated. He looked at his watch. "It's getting late. Have him call me at the office tomorrow. And don't forget about thinking of things the other side could use against us."

It was blustery and dark beyond the circle of light from the Esterbrooks' doorlamp. A roof of clouds now covered the moon, and a few raindrops came on a wind with a smell of vast, distant countryside. Bob pushed his hat firmly onto his head and started up the sidewalk.

In the darkness on the other side of the street a short figure stood silhouetted against the swaying bushes and weeds of the empty field. Bob hesitated, then crossed toward it. No use coming all this way without talking to Derek Esterbrook.

But it wasn't Derek Esterbrook. It was a little old man in a black raincoat, white hair sticking out from under a black ski cap.

"I beg your pardon," Bob said. "I thought you were someone else."

"Who was it you were looking for?"

Bob hesitated. "Mr. Esterbrook."

"I saw him go up the street." The little man had sharp, pale eyes under scraggly eyebrows. "What name shall I say when he comes back?"

"Bob Wilson."

"And what shall I tell him you wanted to discuss?"

"He'll know. Sorry to have bothered you."

"A fine family, the Esterbrooks," the little man called after Bob as he started up the street. "Good night."

Bob was walking up Cedar before he realized that the little man was following him, crossing Wayne under the traffic lights swaying in the wind, skirts of his black raincoat flapping. Bob hurried. By the time he reached his own block the little man was out of sight. Maybe he hadn't been following him after all, just coincidentally walking in the same direction.

Vicki was in the dining room drinking tea with a small, fiftyish lady wearing tennis shoes and what used to be called a leisure suit.

"This is Mrs. Sanzone," she said when Bob came in. "She and some other ladies are circulating a petition."

"It's terrible, Mr. Wilson," said Mrs. Sanzone. "I was just telling your wife. I don't know what they're doing with our tax dollars if we can't get sufficient protection. First there are all these robberies you read about, and now this. It's too much, I'm telling you, and we have to do something."

"I agree," Bob said, and tried to escape to the kitchen for a cup of hot milk.

"Tell him what it is so he won't have to strain himself being funny," Vicki said, getting hold of his hand as he went by. "Honey, listen to this."

"I was just telling your wife," said Mrs. Sanzone, "that it's an outrage against people who just want to live in their homes without being terrorized. Why can't the police do anything, I want to know?"

"I don't know. What's 'it'?"

She counted on her fingers. "Wild animals prowling around in Sligo Creek woods. One ate Mrs. Jefferson's poodle, who lives down the block from me. Howling sounds in the ravine at night. And strange movements in the fog, like eddies and little whirlwinds that come from nowhere."

"Whirlwinds in the fog?"

"There, you see? If you say that, the police think you're a loony-tune. But everyone on the block has seen them, and if all of us are crazy, then what ate Mrs. Jefferson's dog?"

When they had signed her petition and gotten her out of the house, Vicki followed Bob into the kitchen. "Isn't that horrible? Do you think any of it's true?" Her eyes were bright with interest.

"I was down by Sligo Creek woods tonight, and I didn't see any whirlwinds. Of course, there wasn't any fog. Do you think there's something wrong with Diana's father?"

"I never met him," said Vicki thoughtfully. "He was the only parent who missed the reception for the play last year, as I remember. Why?"

"Maybe he's just nervous about lawyers. What was Diana like last year?"

Vicki twirled one of the dark ringlets that hung over

her shoulders, thinking. "A little strange," she said slowly. "Preoccupied, maybe. Kind of gawky for a water-nymph part. The other kids didn't pay much attention to her. She's not, you know, very *developed* for her age."

Bob looked at her lithe shape leaning against the refrigerator. "You, on the other hand—" he leered.

Behind him, his milk boiled over onto the stove with hisses of steam and frothing.

"I've told you a thousand times," Vicki scolded him. "Now you have to change the aluminum foil, because I'm sick of doing it."

Next day at work the New England Gas Light case boiled over without warning like a saucepan of superheated milk, and Bob spent twelve hours teleconferencing, marking up drafts of pleadings, meeting with the litigation team, and faxing letters to opposing counsel. By evening things were under control, but he was so tired and distracted that he didn't remember until he was in bed, listening to Vicki's slow, even breathing, that Derek Esterbrook had never called him.

Well, it doesn't matter, he thought. *Whatever he has to say, it's an open-and-shut case.*

2

Nora and Diana Esterbrook looked like two timid prey animals huddled in their best clothes against the Information desk in the county Circuit Court building's huge, bustling lobby at nine forty-five the next morning. Bob Wilson, in his best dark suit, was nervous too.

"Where's your husband?" he snapped at Mrs. Esterbrook's anxious welcoming smile.

"He's parking the car. We couldn't find a space, and I was afraid we'd be late—"

"You okay, Diana? Ready to do battle if necessary?"

She nodded, looking desperately nervous. That made Bob feel better. There was nothing to soften a judge's heart like a shy high school girl, hair in a neat ponytail, awkward and gangly in a gray skirt and pink sweater. Her mother's eyes followed Bob's with pride, and she brushed a stray hair from her daughter's shoulder.

"Okay, let's go. Derek will have to get directions." Bob led them through the throngs of tough-looking juvenile defendants and their three-piece-suited lawyers, indignant small-claims plaintiffs clutching court papers, policemen, bail bondsmen with mock-sympathetic smiles and big diamond rings, lost housewives and senior citizens trying to find the jury room. It was a big, new building with marble floors and lofty ceilings, murals and skylights, but already muddied with the smell of fear and elation, the atmosphere of backroom deals and suppressed violence that hangs around courthouses.

They rode the escalator to a sublevel hall and found a heavy wooden door marked "Family Court Hearing Room 3." After the echoing bustle outside, the hearing room seemed hushed and dignified, its indirect lighting refined. It was empty. Bob led Diana and Mrs. Esterbrook past the spectators' benches and through the swinging gate, and they sat at the wide, shiny respondents' table. Bob's watch said six minutes until the hearing began. A uniformed bailiff came through the curtain behind the judge's dais, smiled at them, and started checking the lawyers' and judge's microphones.

"I hope your husband is coming," Bob growled at Mrs. Esterbrook.

She started to say something but the hearing room door opening cut her off.

It wasn't Derek Esterbrook. It was a woman and two men. The men were obviously lawyers; they wore dark suits and one carried a briefcase. By the look in Mrs. Esterbrook's eyes, the woman was Armilla Robinson.

Bob had represented felons just out of prison in a couple of pro bono cases the firm had taken on; he realized now that he had unconsciously expected the Robinson woman to be one of them: frowzy and wary-eyed, mouth permanently tensed to emit the anxious, streetwise mumble that would never give you a straight answer. Somebody a judge would decide was an unfit parent in about three seconds. But the woman who came demurely down the aisle between her lawyers was nothing like that. She was slender and erect, with fine features, long, delicate fingers holding a handbag that matched her tailored gray suit. She had curly auburn hair and serious emerald eyes. She was maybe in her early thirties. The bailiff had stopped fiddling with the judge's microphone and was staring at her too. Armilla Robinson was the kind of woman you stared at, that you could imagine living in a big house on a hill, but not in a jail cell.

One of her lawyers held a chair at the petitioners' table; she gave him a soft, purely articulated "thank you." As she sat, her eyes sought Diana's and her thin, shapely lips got a sad smile on them. Her fingers moved in a small, sisterly wave. Diana looked away hastily.

The bailiff said: "All rise. The Honorable Gerald Cramer, Senior Circuit Judge."

Everyone stood up. Bob caught a glimpse of an old man with sharp blue eyes before the click of the hearing room door made him turn. To his relief, Derek Esterbrook was coming down the aisle.

He wasn't relieved for long. Derek was wearing a neat zippered jacket, his hair carefully combed, but as he came closer Bob caught a strange glitter in his eyes. His face was flushed. He gave Bob a jaunty, arrogant smile, as if he had outsmarted him at something. He smelled strongly of liquor.

"Be seated," said Judge Cramer.

Thinking fast for a corporate lawyer, Bob nudged Derek to a chair at the far end of the respondents' table. If the Robinson woman's lawyers got a whiff of him, there would be a feeding frenzy.

Nora Esterbrook wouldn't meet Bob's eyes.

Judge Cramer read the case number into the record, and the lawyers stood up and gave names and business addresses. Barry D. Wentworth III was the large, hard-bitten, athletic type with thinning hair who had held Armilla's chair. The sneering associate carrying his briefcase had a name too, but Bob was too busy trying to think over the pounding of his heart to catch it.

"This is an adoption annulment proceeding, as I understand it," said Judge Cramer when they were done with the preliminaries.

"Yes, your honor," said Wentworth. "You could also call it a child abuse proceeding, I guess."

Derek Esterbrook snorted. He was sitting with his hands clasped on the table, the flushed, arrogant smile still on his face. He ignored Bob's warning look.

"That doesn't appear from the record, Mr. Wentworth," Judge Cramer said. He put on a pair of reading glasses and turned over some papers. "The Social Services Department indicates that the child has lived with respondents for twelve years, is doing fairly well in school—though she could do better"—his stern, kindly eyes glanced at Diana—"and there have been no complaints or reports filed with the Department indicating the parents are unfit." He closed his file with a snap. "Frankly, Mr. Wentworth, you're going to have a hard time persuading me to move her from a home that appears to have provided a stable environment for twelve years merely on the basis of a technical defect in the adoption papers. You may proceed, sir."

Wentworth stood up. "Thank you, Your Honor.

"Your Honor, I don't have to tell you that an absence of reports to the Social Services Department doesn't necessarily mean a family that's doing well. You've been on the bench over thirty years now, and I'll bet you've seen some pretty innocent appearances that have hidden some pretty ugly realities. Now, I don't wish to judge the Esterbrooks or condemn the Esterbrooks. All too often, people don't seem able to help themselves. Alcoholism is an incurable disease, they say, and child abuse, even sexual abuse, is rationalized—"

Bob hadn't spent much time in court, but he knew enough to realize that Barry D. Wentworth III was overplaying his hand. He stood up to cut the legs out from under him.

"Your honor, I object to Mr. Wentworth trying to win his case by innuendo and slander. Nothing in the record supports his statements, as you yourself have observed. If Mr. Wentworth has any *facts* to bring to the court's attention, let him do it. For starters, perhaps he could explain why he thinks a felon just paroled from a *fifty-year sentence* in the state penitentiary for a heinous crime—and that's a matter of official record, Your Honor, not some outrageous *insinuation*—will be able to provide a more stable, nurturing, *moral* environment for Miss Esterbrook than the parents who have raised her for twelve years."

He sat down, portraying disgust.

Wentworth's face was dark—after all, Bob had called him a liar. He purred: "Your honor, I thank Mr. Wilson for making that request. With your permission, I'll skip my introductory statement so as to address his concerns more quickly. Maybe the best way to begin"—his associate took out a folder and passed some papers to Bob and to the bailiff, who passed them on to the judge—"is to review the affidavit of a Mr. Jimmy Watkins, Mr. Derek Esterbrook's supervisor at his most recent job—which Mr. Esterbrook left almost two years ago. At that time Mr. Esterbrook was assistant floor manager at Stahl's Department Store. Let me read to you from the affidavit: 'Derek L. Esterbrook was dismissed from his position as Assistant Floor Manager as a result of severe alcohol-related problems that disrupted the functioning of the store, including chronic lateness, inappropriate sexual advances to other employees, a physical assault on another employee, abusive treatment of customers—' "

Derek Esterbrook stood up. "That's a goddamn lie," he snarled.

Bob dropped the affidavit he had been trying to skim, jumped up and put his hands on Esterbrook's shoulders. "Mr. Esterbrook, please sit down," he hissed in his ear.

" '—and drinking on store premises,' " Wentworth went on. Bob saw now what he was trying to do—had he smelled Esterbrook all the way over there? " 'When asked to enter a treatment program as a condition of keeping his job, Mr. Esterbrook flew into a rage—' "

"That's a goddamn *lie!*" roared Esterbrook over Bob's shoulder.

"Sit down, Derek, or we're going to lose the case," Bob gritted in his ear.

"Is it, Mr. Esterbrook?" Wentworth asked. "It's perfectly consistent with another affidavit signed by the personnel director, and with a long history of lost jobs and complaints by employers—"

"Let me tell you something, fat-ass," snarled Esterbrook, pushing to get past Bob, "they laid me off—because of a—an economic reorganization, and I don't like your lying face—"

"Mr. Esterbrook, I'm going to ask you to *sit down*," snapped Judge Cramer icily.

"Just a minute! Just a minute!" said Esterbrook plaintively, "I just want to—"

"I mean it, Derek," Bob hissed. "You'll lose your daughter."

Derek's dark, crazy eyes met Bob's with sudden fear, and he stopped trying to push past him. He drooped back into his chair.

Wentworth struck again with surgical precision. His voice was regretful, decent: "And I guess to get it all out on the table, Your Honor, and to get to the heart of the matter, I have another affidavit here, signed by a Mrs. Jayne Wetzel, the Esterbrooks' next-door neighbor."

Nora Esterbrook's eyes were suddenly horrified.

"That lying bitch," muttered Derek.

Copies were distributed.

"I don't want to make this any uglier than it has to be," said Wentworth, "so I won't read this one, but just summarize what I believe you'll find it says: that Derek Esterbrook, in his alcoholic frenzies, has repeatedly abused his adopted daughter—"

"That's a lie!" roared Esterbrook, knocking his chair over. Bob jumped in time to get him by the arm.

"Mr. Esterbrook, sit down!" shouted Judge Cramer, pounding his gavel.

"I have one thing to say to you, fat-ass—!" yelled Esterbrook up at him.

"Your Honor, I apologize—my client is distraught because of Mr. Wentworth's completely false—"

"Your client is *drunk,* Mr. Wilson," snapped Judge Cramer.

"So wha-at? So wha-at, fat-ass?" yelled Esterbrook, straining at Bob's hand. "If you don't like it why don't you come down here and do something about it?"

"Your Honor, I request a recess," Bob yelled desperately as the bailiff began to approach them and Judge Cramer banged his gavel angrily.

Diana Esterbrook had been sitting frozen in her chair, staring at the ground. Now she stood up in front of her father.

"You—" she started.

He slapped her viciously across the mouth.

"I told you *never, ever* to talk back to me," he shouted. *"Never, ever."*

"I move for a recess," Bob pleaded again. A little blood ran from between Diana's lips. She sat down suddenly, shocked, hand over her mouth. Armilla Robinson had a hand over her own mouth, eyes tearing.

"Motion granted. This hearing is adjourned until further notice," snapped Judge Cramer, red-faced. "Wentworth, Wilson, I want you in my chambers. Bailiff, take Miss—the young lady to the first aid station and have the nurse look at her." He banged his gavel and strode out, black curtains waving angrily behind him.

Derek Esterbrook seemed suddenly to run out of steam. He stood staring at Diana sobbing quietly and hysterically, Nora and the bailiff leaning over her. He slowly and stupidly lifted his hand and looked at it. His lips moved. He reached tremblingly out toward his daughter then, but she was stumbling away up the aisle between her mother and the bailiff.

Bob Wilson's large frame was soaking in a steaming bath that afternoon when the phone rang. Vicki brought it to him.

"Mr. Wilson, you were wonderful," Nora Esterbrook's thin, effusive voice came over the line. "It was just like you said about how that horrible man provoked Derek—"

"Nora," Bob broke in wearily. "Nora. Your husband's an alcoholic. He's been arrested twice for public drunkenness and lost a whole series of jobs. Once a month he kicks up a row that has the neighbors calling the police. I've been reading about it in the papers Wentworth brought to the hearing." Judge Cramer had made Wentworth give Bob copies of all of it—police reports, employment files, affidavits—with the air of someone helping the mentally challenged. Bob eased his shoulders further into the hot water to relax the kinks the posthearing conference had put into them. "And what I can't figure out is, why did you lie to me? Probably none of this stuff is bad enough to warrant taking away your daughter, but after that scene today there's a good chance they'll take her. I've just about made up my mind to withdraw from the case, but what I can't figure out is, why?"

There was silence, and then her trembling voice said: "He lost that job because of an *economic reorganization,* Mr. Wilson, I swear he did—"

"Maybe he told you he did."

"—you *can't* drop the case—*they'll take away my little girl—*"

"You should have thought of that Tuesday night. When Derek had to go out for a breath of air." His voice echoed bitterly on the steamy pink bathroom tiles.

"What can I do to—? I didn't know—I *told* him—But Mr. Wilson, I'll do anything, *anything*—"

"Then do this," Bob snapped, sitting up so that water sloshed out of the tub. "Remember the list I asked you to make, of nasty things the other side might bring up? Well, it's a little late now, but do it anyway. If I come over this afternoon, say, around three, and you've made a full list of everything—and I mean *everything*—and if I decide you're being completely honest this time—and remember, I have Wentworth's file, so I can check you—maybe I'll stay on the case, at least long enough to turn it over to some other lawyer who's dumb enough to take it, if there is any."

"But how can I do all that by three o'clock?"

"It's up to you." Bob slammed the phone down, sank back into the hot water, and shut his eyes.

Vicki came into the bathroom and sat on the edge of the tub, studying him. Finally she said quietly: "Honey, I'm sorry. This is all my fault."

"No it's not," he said bitterly, hunching in the water.

"Why *don't* you drop the case?"

He shook his head. "I can't."

"Why not?"

"I just can't. Stop badgering me."

"I'm not badgering you, I'm trying to figure out why you're too stupid to do what I should have let you do in the first place."

"Because I'm supposed to be a lawyer, okay? If word gets around that a slimeball like Wentworth ran me out of court, I'll be a laughingstock. Even if I'm not, *I'll* always remember it." He mulled that over for a minute. "Besides," he went on sheepishly, "I already asked to withdraw, at the posthearing conference. I was upset, you understand. The judge turned me down. He said it would be a lesson to me never to come into court unprepared. He said my performance virtually amounted to malpractice." He winced at the memory of Judge Cramer's red, angry face and sharp voice, sank deeper into the water.

"Didn't you tell him what happened? That they lied to you?"

Bob shook his head, closed his eyes. "Couldn't tell him that. He's practically decided against the Esterbrooks already. Wouldn't have helped if I'd called them liars, on top of everything."

After a while the bathwater turned lukewarm. Bob dried off and sat in the bedroom armchair, finished reading through Wentworth's file folder. What he found didn't lift his spirits. There was a letter from the warden of the Jonasburgh Correctional Facility Women's Wing saying Armilla Robinson had been a model prisoner—in fact had undergone a religious conversion in prison. That was confirmed by the mother superior of a convent forty miles north of the city: her letter said that Armilla was "of the highest moral character and deepest religious conviction." The icing on the cake was a set of probate papers showing that a distant great-uncle had died two years ago leaving Armilla over half a million dollars in cash and property. It was amazing. Judging by the information in the folder, Armilla Robinson was the only paroled felon in the country who could beat out Mother Teresa of Calcutta in a custody fight.

And all of it was stuff a minimally competent lawyer would have found out on the first day, Bob thought angrily. He had been lulled by Nora Esterbrook's protestations and the fact that Armilla was an ex-con. Maybe he'd been practicing softball corporate litigation too long. Maybe Judge Cramer was right about him.

As he stood up to get dressed something slipped out of the folder onto the rug: a three-by-five photograph. He picked it up and studied the best argument of all for Armilla Robinson's character, staring at him levelly from clear green eyes, a face so pure it was almost sensual, like a carving of some medieval maiden-saint. He looked at it for a long time.

3

It was clear and windless and just a little warm when he pulled up across from the Esterbrooks', long yellow sunlight illuminating the neighborhood in overripe hues like a 1940s color photograph. The stillness of the street and the Esterbrooks' thin, neat lawn and swept concrete driveway gave the house a mausoleumlike atmosphere, which wasn't dispelled when Nora Esterbrook opened the door to Bob's ring and whispered: "Come in."

"Mr. Esterbrook isn't feeling well," she whispered as she took Bob's coat. "He's resting."

"I've got to talk to him," Bob whispered fiercely.

"Oh, you can, of course," she said a little louder, and led him onto the crackling linoleum of the kitchen.

"Did you make that list?"

"Well—yes," she said uneasily. "But really, I couldn't think of—"

"Let's see it."

"—I really think that awful man has thought of everything anyone could possibly bring up—"

"Then if you'll give me back my coat—"

"—and he's made up a lot of other things. Why don't you sit down, Mr. Wilson? You better let me read it to you, because it's in my own handwriting."

Bob sat at the yellow formica table and she sat opposite, fidgeting. The smell of cooking was fainter than it had been the night before. A bar of sunlight gleamed on the windowsill over the sink. She took a paper out of her apron and unfolded it.

"It's so silly, really," she said faintly. "I don't think I'd even care to—"

"Nora," Bob said in the voice of a person trying to wake someone from a dream, "the judge only agreed to let Diana stay with you until the next hearing if I promised to be ready for final arguments by then. That's ten days away. And as of tomorrow, Social Services Department people are going to be crawling all over the neighborhood, your daughter's school, your and your husband's employment records, everything. I need to know what they're going to find."

"But Mr. Wilson, it's not fair! I don't know why Jayne Wetzel said what she did, but it's just not true!"

"Don't worry about Jayne Wetzel. Her affidavit's not as bad as Wentworth made it sound: just that in the middle of a bad fight Diana ran over to her house crying hysterically about something Mrs. Wetzel interpreted as sexual abuse. I'll go talk it over with her and see if I can get her to retract it. She isn't too crazy about your husband, I gather."

"Well—"

Bob decided to try a different tack. "Look, I still think we can win this case," he pep-talked her. "It's not a sure thing—your husband really shook the judge up today—but the way I figure it, no matter what problems you have, a convicted felon has got to have something worse. What did Armilla do, anyway?"

"Something—something about kidnaping."

"Kidnaping." He whistled. "We ought to be able to make a stink out of that. And if Derek, say, signs up with Alcoholics Anonymous this weekend, and shows the judge he's working on his drinking problem—"

"Oh, he's going to. He's already made up his mind."

"So what do we have to worry about? Come on, read me that list."

She looked down at the paper, cleared her throat.

"Well, it's silly, really," she said. "But the first thing is—well, some trouble Diana had in school. It's so silly, really—" She coughed nervously. "They had a special computer come to her school, something called a 'work station' that they circulate around the country from the MIT up in Boston. She loves computers so, and she needs a lot of computer classes for the college major she wants. Have you ever heard of 'thaumomathematics'?" she asked him, as if a new worry had occurred to her.

"No."

"Well, I don't understand exactly what it is myself. They only offer it at some institute place in New Mexico, and she wants to study it. I don't know why. Just a passing stage, I imagine. She's such a normal, healthy girl."

"You were telling me about some trouble she had in school."

"Well, she loved this MIT computer so much that she got permission from her math teacher, Mr. Pin, to play with it after school. It was getting late in the evening and Mr. Pin came into the computer room to check on how she was doing." Nora stopped and swallowed. "He said she had taken off her clothes and was standing on the computer with her hands in the air and singing something— The—the—school psychologist said it was stress, and they had me keep her home for a week. It could happen to any normal, healthy child under stress, the school psychologist said."

"My God. What kind of stress?"

"Well—he didn't know. She went into some kind of trance, the school psychologist—that's Mr. Rappozio—said. But he said it could happen to any—"

"Has she had any other school problems?"

"Well, no. Not really."

"What does that mean?"

"Well, no, not at all."

He studied her, then let her go on. The rest of her list didn't sound too bad. Derek had gotten into a drunken yelling match with Mr. Karis, the next-door neighbor, about property boundaries. Derek had been ejected from a movie theater for yelling. Their new car had been repossessed because they couldn't make the payments on what Mrs. Esterbrook earned at her bank teller job. When they got to the end Nora swore there wasn't anything else. He couldn't be sure she wasn't holding back, but he didn't think she was. He lectured her a little more, then had her take him to Derek.

His door was in the dark hall off the living room, opposite Diana's. Nora knocked and opened it softly.

The room was about twice the size of Diana's, which didn't make it big. A queen-size bed, small dresser, and sagging armchair were all squeezed together. A sour, sweaty tang mingled with the smell of stale cooking that pervaded the house. Derek Esterbrook sat in the armchair in a sleeveless undershirt, a bar of sunlight falling across a blanket covering his legs. He sat very still, not looking up when Nora and Bob came in.

"Derek? Derek, honey, Mr. Wilson needs to talk to you."

He nodded slowly. His face was dark and creased, old-looking. Bob noticed that his chest and arms were thick and hairy.

Nora leaned over him and ran a hand through his dark, curling hair, kissed him gently on the forehead. When she straightened up there was pain in her eyes, and memory, and for a second Bob thought he saw a flash of the Esterbrooks as they had been long ago, in their courtship: Derek loud, confident, and gallant, Nora shy, quiet, and adoring. Then it was gone and Nora went out, closing the door softly.

Bob sat on the edge of the bed. Derek sat perfectly still, staring at the wall.

Bob cleared his throat. "Derek, I'm not going to bother you long, but I need to ask you about your drinking."

"I'm never going to drink again," Derek said in a low, miserable voice. "I hit my little girl, I—" He choked and curled his right hand into a trembling fist, looked at it helplessly, then dropped it into his lap. He closed his eyes and began shaking his head. "I'm never going to touch it again. Never."

"That's what I wanted to hear. I want you to go sign up with AA this weekend—"

"I'm going *tomorrow*," he said angrily, looking at Bob with dark, bloodshot eyes. "What do you mean this weekend? *Tomorrow*."

"That's even better. Tomorrow," Bob said nervously. He caught himself picturing Derek's large, grimy fist, as if that was a metaphor for the man himself, for a violence that lived inside him. He made himself ask: "I have your word on that, then? You'll go to AA tomorrow?"

"Tomorrow," Derek said, rocking his body back and forth miserably. "Tomorrow."

Bob could hear Nora moving around in the kitchen as he came out, shutting the door quietly behind him. A voice inside Diana's room answered his knock.

Diana was sitting in front of her computer screen again. As he opened the door a disk drive chattered and a shape like a glowing spider's web was erased. Daylight filtering through closed curtains showed the tiny room more clearly this time: a riot of clothes, books, magazines, and bedcovers, like one of those newspaper pictures of tornado disasters.

"Hi," Bob said. "How are you feeling?"

"Okay." She looked around at him. One side of her mouth was swollen.

"Did you need stitches?"

"No."

He shuffled his feet awkwardly. "Vicki wanted me to ask if you'd like to come over for dinner. She found some more pictures of her Walter Carlyle play. I'll drive you back afterwards if you want."

Her eyes flickered up gratefully. "Yes, please," she said.

"Okay. But I need to talk to you for a minute first. I'm sorry about this morning."

She shrugged.

"How do you feel about your dad right now?"

"I hate him."

"Well, I guess I can't blame you for that." Awkward pause. "Look, I have to ask you something, and I promise whatever the answer is I won't tell anybody. Is that a deal?"

She nodded, flushing.

"Has your dad ever—is there any truth to the accusation the lawyer made this morning that your dad has sexually abused you?"

"No," she said. Then she surprised him by adding: "Maybe it's because he's always too drunk to."

"He says he's going to stop drinking," Bob told her lamely. "He seems really sincere."

"He always says that."

"I think he really means it this time."

"He won't."

"Why not?"

"Because he won't," she said angrily.

"He's going to sign up with Alcoholics Anonymous tomorrow. Don't you think we should give him a chance? Wouldn't it be wonderful if he never drank again?"

She shook her head. "Conditions aren't favorable."

"What do you mean?"

She turned vindictively and typed on her keyboard.

"I'll show you," she said.

A glowing dot flew over the screen in a complicated pattern, filling in a shape with intricate multicolored detail until Diana hit a key to stop it. It was the same crude butterfly shape Bob had seen on his last visit.

"This is a phase space mapping of a system with three independent variables," she told him. Her shy, sullen eyes were suddenly alive. She typed and the shape rotated slowly, showing that in three dimensions it was more like two lumpy balloons tied together. "It's defined by a set of nonlinear equations. The equations describe my father's drinking. I've been watching him, gathering tuning data."

"This describes your father's—How do you mean?"

"This dimension," she moved a finger back and forth across the screen, "is anger/guilt: as you go from left to right, the ratio of anger to guilt increases. My father is more likely to drink when he's feeling more angry than guilty. This dimension," she gestured vertically, "is time of the month. The full moon is in the middle; new moon is extreme top and bottom. This," she moved her hand out of the screen, "is self-confidence—into the screen is low self-confidence, toward me is high self-confidence. The two lobes show drinking behavior—the left lobe is not drinking, the right lobe is drinking."

"Where did you learn this stuff?" Bob asked cautiously, trying to follow her explanation and at the same time figure out if she was pulling his leg. It was hard to believe this was the same tongue-tied fourteen-year-old who answered his questions about her family with shrugs.

"From a book. *Principles of Thaumatomathematics* by Dr. M. A. Al-Haq. He's at the Los Alamos Institute. Now see this? The place all the lines go through when they go from one state to the other?"

That was the narrow place where the two butterfly wings/balloons were attached together.

"That's where he goes from drinking to not drinking." Her finger moved from the right wing of the diagram to the left. "See, it's got to be within a few days of the full moon, he has to be not too angry relative to his guilt, and he has to be not very self-confident or un-self-confident, but just kind of medium self-confident.

"This afternoon he's feeling guilty, so that's good, but

his self-confidence is low—he stays in his room when it's low—and besides, we're too far from the full moon. That's why I told you conditions aren't favorable for him to stop drinking."

She glanced at Bob.

"When conditions *are* favorable," she went on before he could think of anything to say, "sometimes a shock, like what happened today, will knock him from one side to the other. Like what got him started drinking was when he had a car accident when I was a little girl, my mother says. It's not totally predictable. But lately he's been drinking more and more, staying sober less and less. That means the pattern in his brain that makes him drink is getting more stable, and the pattern that makes him stay sober is getting less stable." She typed a long command; the butterfly disappeared and was rapidly resketched, but this time distorted so that the right wing bulged, engorged with a heavy pattern of intertwining lines, leaving the left thin and wobbly. "So he can still be knocked over to not drinking if conditions are favorable. But it's harder, and he doesn't stay sober as long. And"—she typed again and the screen started on a new pattern—"if it keeps up, there won't be any not-drinking state left. When that happens, he won't be able to stay sober at all."

The pattern taking shape on the screen now was a single misshapen blob, an impenetrable thicket of lines leading endlessly around and around, like the vortex of some profound misery.

In the living room the telephone was ringing. Bob vaguely heard Nora answer it.

"Well, what—what can be done about this?" he asked, shaken in spite of himself.

"I don't know," Diana said, and for the first time ever he felt that she looked straight at him, and he was surprised at the anguish in her green eyes, as if his question had tormented her for a long time.

There was a knock and Nora Esterbrook stuck her

head in: "Oh, Diana, I hope you're not making Mr. Wilson look at your computer games. I just don't know what to do with her, Mr. Wilson. Mrs. Wilson called to invite Diana to dinner, and it's so nice of you, but I'm *sure* she's being a bother—"

"Not at all."

While Diana was getting ready to go, Bob said to Nora out in the living room: "There's one thing I forgot to ask you; is there someone around here—a friend or neighbor—who'd be willing to vouch for your and your husband's character? Someone who's known you for a while, preferably? They wouldn't have to go to court—just sign an affidavit."

Her eyes got vague. "Well, we haven't kept up with too many of our friends. I would have said Mrs. Wetzel that lives next door, but—"

"What about that little old man who lives around here somewhere? White hair, kind of short, maybe sixty-five or seventy?"

She looked blank.

"I thought he was a neighbor. I met him on the sidewalk Monday night. He said you were a fine family."

"I can't think who that would be," she said slowly.

"Ask your husband—maybe he'll know," Bob said as Diana came out of her room wearing jeans and an oversize sweater. Her mother kissed her and told her not to bother the Wilsons for too long, and let them out. She didn't forget to thank Bob effusively for everything he was doing.

After the close smell of the house the long, yellow sunlight and chilly air of a late autumn afternoon were cheerful. Diana seemed to feel it too—she walked next to Bob with fast, springy steps. His car was parked across the street by the empty field. As Diana walked around to the passenger side her breath made a sound, and she stared at the ground.

"What is it?"

"A footprint." She crouched down intently.

Bob walked around the car and leaned over her. "Good God."

Two rainy days earlier in the week had left the ground muddy, fallen brown and yellow leaves mushy and disintegrating. In this soft surface was a paw print that looked like something big had made it—something big with long, curving claws.

"What do you think *that* is?" Bob asked nervously. He straightened up and glanced around. The neighborhood looked reassuringly quiet in its sea of yellow trees, pale smoke from a chimney up the hill tanging the cool air with the smell of firewood. The field, its tangled vines and riotous bushes drab in the last rays of afternoon, sloped down to meet the clump of woods the subdivisions had left around Sligo Creek.

"Probably a dog," he answered himself doubtfully. "Big one. We better get going. Vicki's expecting us."

4

When they pulled up in front of the Wilson house, evening was beginning to tint the afternoon chilly blue, hints of dusk gathering under the trees that arched above the leaf-daubed street.

"Hi, sweeties," Vicki said when they came in. She threw a curled-up script onto the couch and kissed Bob. It was always amazing to him that a real-estate agent could look and smell so good, but of course she was an actress too, which was how he had met her, being a community theater buff.

She tousled Diana's hair. "Let's make dinner before we look at those pictures."

Bob went upstairs to check with the office, and when he came back down Vicki and Diana were chopping vegetables, Diana listening with an embarrassed smile to Vicki's lewd commentaries on theater men, and looking almost like the normal, healthy girl her mother wanted her to be. Soon the three of them were eating salad, canned mushroom soup, boiled carrots, and baked potatoes with cheese. The phone rang.

Vicki answered it in the study. "It's your mom," she called to Diana.

Diana pushed her chair back and went to get it, anxiety coming into her face.

"I think something's going on over there," Vicki whispered when she came back into the dining room.

"Like what?"

"Shh." She put her hand on his and strained her ears at the door. Bob put a spoonful of soup quietly back into his bowl.

Diana mumbled something in the study, then was quiet for minute.

"No," she said angrily then. "No, I won't."

Pause.

"Because I won't, that's why," she hissed. "I don't care." And she hung up.

Vicki and Bob were innocently eating soup when she came back and sat down, pale but trying to smile. When the phone rang again she burst into tears.

Vicki got up and went to her. Bob got the phone.

"Mr. Wilson? This is Nora Esterbrook." Her voice, thin and anxious as usual, was also shaking. "Mr. Wilson, I have to ask you a favor—I tried to get Diana to ask, but I can't do a thing with her—"

Bob thought he heard a deep voice yell something in the background.

"Could Diana stay at your house tonight?" Nora hurried on. "Derek is—terribly upset about something, and—"

"Nora!" Derek roared in the background.

"Coming, honey! I think it would be more comfortable for Diana not to—"

"Is he drunk?" Bob demanded.

"Well, he's—very upset about what happened today, and he's—"

"Is he drunk, Nora?"

"A little."

A loud crash from her end had breaking glass in it.

"I'll be over in two minutes," Bob said, and hung up. Back in the dining room, Diana was sobbing, Vicki standing with her hands on her shoulders and saying: "It isn't your fault. You should have seen my parents."

"I'm going over there," Bob told Vicki, making gestures meaning Diana should stay. "If he's drunk tomorrow morning when the social workers show up, we're dead."

Diana looked up, her face red, wild, wet. "I'm coming with you."

"No you're not," said Vicki, holding her shoulders. "You're staying here, young lady, and I'm going to make up the guest room for you. We'll make some popcorn and put on a movie—"

"But my computer!" she screamed, her face turning a frightening crimson. "He'll break my computer! He's always trying to—!"

"I'll bring your computer back with me," Bob soothed her. "I'll have your mom pack it up for me and I'll have it to you in half an hour. Okay? You stay here with Vicki."

The darkness was chilly, the clear sky faintly luminous at the horizon. Crickets trilled. The streetlight across the street was lit, but there were enough leaves left on the trees to throw deep shadows on the sidewalk. When Bob walked out to his car, he dimly saw someone standing in them—a short figure in what looked like a black overcoat, a fringe of white hair poking out from under a black hat or cap. Bob thought suddenly of the little man outside the Esterbrooks' Monday night.

"Excuse me," he called. "Sir?"

He started across the street. The figure turned and ran.

Bob ran after it. "Excuse me!"

The figure ran fast. When Bob rounded the corner at Shope and almost knocked down Larry Abercrombie, he was gasping for breath.

"Whoa! Who's that?" boomed Larry, grabbing Bob's arms. "Wilson? What the hell! Running for exercise?" He laughed his loud, deep laugh.

"Larry—sorry. Did somebody run past you just now?"

"You chasing somebody? No, I didn't see anybody. Heard something in the bushes over here, but I thought it was the Taylors' dog or—Not a burglar, was it?"

"I don't think so," Bob said, trying to catch his breath, going over to the tall unkempt hedge that overhanging branches from the Taylors' yard almost touched.

Larry followed him, lighting his pipe, the streetlight casting his big, bony frame in shadow on the sidewalk. "Well, who was it, then? The gas meter reader?"

"A witness, maybe." Just around the corner was a gap in the hedge that someone could have pushed through. Bob stuck his head through it. Yellow glow from the Taylors' windows showed unraked lawn under the arching darkness of still trees. The yard looked empty.

"A witness, eh?" Larry said, running a hand over his bald head. "What is it, some kind of Mafia trial?"

"Worse than that," Bob said ruefully, "but I can't tell you about it. I have to meet a client, Larry. Sorry I bumped into you."

"My pleasure," said Larry, puffing curiously, wreaths of aromatic smoke rising above him into the dark air.

Bob almost went back into the house to warn Vicki, but decided against it; it would take too long to explain, and besides, he guessed he had chased the little man away—for now, anyway. He got in his car and headed for the Esterbrooks'.

All the lights were on in the tiny house, but everything seemed peaceful. Bob had a moment of hopefulness as he climbed the steps to the front door and rang the bell. Before he could take another breath Nora Esterbrook had opened the door, stepped out onto the stoop, and closed the door quietly behind her.

"You shouldn't have come, Mr. Wilson," she said accusingly.

Inside the house somewhere, Derek Esterbrook bellowed: "Nora!"

"He's got to sober up," Bob said angrily. "The Social Services people are coming tomorrow morning, and if he's drunk or even hung over you've as good as lost your daughter."

"If he sees you, it'll set him off again. I've got him quieted down some. If he sees you, he'll start up again."

The front door came open suddenly, pouring bright light and warm, stuffy air out onto the stoop.

"Mr. Wilson," said Derek Esterbrook. He held out a large, thick hand with grave enthusiasm. "Bob Wilson."

Bob Wilson, six inches taller than Esterbrook and in reasonably good shape, was afraid suddenly, irrationally. It was part courage, part reflex that made him take Derek's hand. The hand was warm, dry, powerful. Derek shook for longer than was comfortable.

"Come in," he said, pulling Bob by his hand. "Why didn't you invite him in, Nora?" His bright, enthusiastic eyes turned onto her face as if he was really curious to know. "Come in," he said again, and pulled Bob into the living room, then stood shaking his hand some more. His face was ten years younger, his eyes unnaturally bright, dark hair carefully oiled and combed, but a little disturbed, as if he had been waving his head around. Except for the grimy, sleeveless undershirt, he looked like an orchestra conductor in the middle of a particularly inspired performance. He smelled discreetly of liquor.

"What are we going to do about this adoption business?" he asked Bob earnestly, finally letting go of his hand and looking him closely in the face. "I'm ready to do anything I have to. I'll do whatever you say to kick those bastards' ass." His voice was louder than it needed to be.

"I'm glad to hear you say that," Bob said. "I thought you told me this afternoon you were going to stop drinking."

"Drinking? Who says I've been drinking?" He leaned forward truculently. Bob's heart started to pound. Suddenly Derek burst out laughing and slapped him heartily on the shoulder.

"Drinking isn't the problem," he said. "A drink now and then doesn't bother me. But drinking like I was—when was it—this morning—phew!" He rolled his eyes. "I was plastered, and I'll tell anybody I was. I'm not going to drink like *that* ever again. I swear." He was suddenly grave. He held up his hand. "You have my solemn word on it."

"I think they're going to want you to lay off it altogether," Bob said. "They're coming tomorrow morning—"

Derek's eyes flashed. "Who's coming where?" he blustered.

"The Social Services Department. They're sending social workers here to talk to you. If you're drunk—"

"The hell they can tell me what to do in my own house," Derek thundered, leaning forward, eyes protruding.

"Derek—" said Nora.

"You shut up," he said, pointing a thick finger at her.

Bob's head whirled with sudden anger, as if the demon of rage coiled inside Derek Esterbrook had jumped onto him to play for a while.

"Derek, you listen to *me*," he grated, putting his own finger in Derek's face. "They're going to take your daughter away. Do you have enough brains left to understand that? Judge Cramer is going to take Diana away because you were drunk this morning. If you're not stone cold sober tomorrow when the social workers get here, Diana's gone—like that." He snapped his fingers under Derek's nose. "You'll never see her again. Do you care about that at all?"

Derek was suddenly meek. "I care about that," he said, waving his hands as if to fend off Bob's anger.

"They're coming tomorrow? In the morning? I'll—I'll go sober up right away. I'll be stone cold sober by tomorrow morning."

"I want you to be stone cold sober," Bob repeated loudly, a thrill going up his back at his own strength of character, the forcefulness that had pacified this out-of-control alcoholic.

"I will. I will," said Derek excitedly. "I'll go take a cold shower right now. Nora, go get all that stuff out of my room."

"Yes, Derek," said Nora in a voice like ashes.

Bob looked at her in surprise. Derek was already half-way to the bathroom.

"You'll see," he yelled over his shoulder. "I'll be sober as a judge."

The bathroom door banged behind him.

Bob stood looking at Nora, trying to read her face.

"Will they really take her?" she rasped, "if he's—"

"I'm afraid they will."

Two large tears rolled out of her eyes, and her weak chin trembled.

"You don't think he'll—do what I asked?" Bob said anxiously.

A sob came out of her thin, worn body.

"Why do you stay with him?" Bob demanded angrily. "Why do you put up with it?"

Her eyes darted toward the bathroom, where the shower was running now, and got a faraway look. She smiled; a very small, sad smile.

"If you had known him before the accident," she whispered.

They stood awkwardly for a minute, and then Bob said lamely: "Well, do the best you can to sober him up. Oh, and I promised Diana I'd bring her computer back with me."

"She does so love to play with it," said Nora, momentarily happy as they unplugged and untangled wires laced through piles of papers and rumpled clothes in Diana's room. "She won it in the math competition at school two years ago. And Mr. Wilson, I really appreciate you and Mrs. Wilson keeping her for a few days. She gets so upset when Derek is—like this."

"Quite all right," Bob said, the phrase 'a few days' echoing in his head. "But remember what I said about Derek. Tomorrow is crucial. If we can sneak him past the social workers and get him into AA before the next hearing, we have a good shot at keeping Diana with you. But if they see him like this . . ."

They carefully set the computer case, monitor, and keyboard, and all their associated wires, into a large cardboard box Nora brought from the kitchen.

"And here's her book." She put a heavy gray tome into the box too. "She has to have it when she's playing her computer games. Oh, and let me get her schoolbooks together, and a few clothes." She started digging through Diana's wreckage.

Bob carried the computer into the living room. When he turned around, Derek Esterbrook was standing there, his face red and ugly. He still had on his brown shoes, pants, and his grimy undershirt, and he didn't show any signs of having taken a shower.

"Where the hell are you going with that?" he said, pointing to the computer. "You put it right back where you found it."

"Diana wants—"

"Diana wants!" Derek bellowed, his face turning a deeper red. "What about what *you* want?"

He unbuckled his leather belt and pulled it out of the beltloops.

"Put it back," he commanded, pointing toward Diana's room.

"Derek—"

Derek whipped the belt down on top of the television set with a frightening bang.

"Put it back!" he shouted. Short as he was, he suddenly looked huge.

Nora Esterbrook hurried into the living room with an armload of clothes. She stuffed them into the box Bob held.

"Go," she murmured urgently. "Go."

"Hey!" Derek screamed as Bob headed for the door Nora opened. His feet pounded on the flimsy living room floor.

"Derek!" Nora yelled in a voice Bob barely recognized, iron-hard and desperate.

Derek's belt slashed down on Bob's shoulder, hardly stinging through his coat but making a loud noise.

Bob half turned in surprise and rage.

"Go!" pleaded Nora, and pushed him out of the house.

Derek was laughing loud and crazily.

The door slammed shut and Nora's furious screams mingled with Derek's insane bellowing, making the place sound like a lunatic asylum.

As Bob walked shakily to his car in the cool, still air, a curtain in the house next door moved aside and somebody—Mrs. Wetzel the neighbor lady, he guessed—looked out.

He had parked across the street again, by the empty field. The closest streetlight was halfway up the hill, so it was dark. Crickets creaked loudly, drowning out the Esterbrooks' voices. He had unlocked his trunk and put Diana's stuff in, when there was a sound.

A silence, rather. The crickets in the field had all gone quiet at once.

He froze with his hands on the trunk lid, eyes and ears straining into the darkness. The field seemed empty; but why was the hair on the back of his neck acting so strangely?

Bob slammed the trunk and got to the driver's door, the crunching of his feet and fumbling of his keys loud in the silence. His heart didn't slow down until he was turning the car around, headlights showing only bedraggled bushes and vines.

When Bob carried the box Nora Esterbrook had packed into the Wilson's first-floor guest room, Diana was sitting under the bedcovers wearing one of Vicki's flannel nightgowns, a book open on her knees and a mug of hot chocolate on the night table. Her eyes went anxiously to the box.

"One computer," Bob said casually, setting it down by the door. "Not a mark on it."

Diana seemed to be fighting the urge to get out of bed and go to her machine, so Bob said good night. He was closing the door when she spoke up anxiously: "Mr. Wilson?"

"Bob."

"Bob—I'm sorry I was so stupid tonight."

"Not at all."

"Were my parents—was my father—very bad?"

"Not too bad," he said comfortingly.

"He hit me with his belt," he told Vicki when they were in the upstairs bathroom getting ready for bed.

Her eyes widened. "What? Where?"

"My shoulder. I told you, they're crazy."

"I think I see a swelling," Vicki accused him, peering closely at his bare shoulder.

"It's the other side. It didn't hurt, but I've never been strapped by a client before."

Her eyes were pained. She clasped her hands around the back of his neck. "Honey, I'm sorry. I should never have volunteered you for this."

"True. But you know, much as I hate to admit it,

they're beginning to interest me. You don't see people like this in the corporate business."

It wasn't until they were in bed, Vicki taking the slow, even breaths of sleep, that he realized he had forgotten to tell her about the little man watching the house.

5

Bob rolled back and forth for a while worrying about the Esterbrook case. He whispered "Are you asleep?" a couple of times, but Vicki didn't wake up. Finally he put on his robe and tiptoed downstairs for a cup of hot milk. At the bottom of the stairs he saw a faint light under Diana's door and heard the chatter of a disk drive.

He tapped softly and put his head in. Diana was sitting against her pillows, keyboard on her lap, the monitor propped on the bed next to her lighting the room dimmest blue.

"Hi," Bob said softly.

"Hi," said Diana. "I couldn't sleep," she explained as he came in.

"It's late." The clock on the bed table said almost midnight. "Don't you have school tomorrow?"

"Yes." She looked up at him innocently.

A fiendishly complicated pattern glowed on the monitor, like vortices of tightly curled fern leaves sprayed out in a firework pattern, surrounded by multicolored traces that roughly followed their contours.

"Still trying to figure out when your father's going to stop drinking?"

"No. This is something else."

"What?"

"Me," she said, looking at it absently, as if the vortices

drew her attention away to depths beyond the screen. Her profile was very pale in their light.

"Diana, is this stuff for real? You're not just pulling my leg, are you?"

"No."

"You learned all this from books?"

"One book."

"It's incredible. How could you—?"

"It's not so hard. You just have to have what Dr. Al-Haq calls unbending determination."

"Unbending determination? It looks to me like you have to be a genius." Her eyes flickered up bashfully and she might have blushed in the dim light. "Describe it to me," he said. "How do you do it?"

"Well," she began shyly. "You start by—you watch yourself or whoever it is you're trying to figure out for a long time, and keep notes. Like every day I write down what I eat, how much sleep I get, what my heart rate is, whether I had a fight with my parents, how I do on my schoolwork—all kinds of things. I have forms I fill out. After a while, after you gather enough data, you graph it on the computer different ways to see if you can find patterns, relationships. Like, there's a relationship between how much sleep I get and how I do on my schoolwork."

"Is that what this is?" Bob pointed to the screen.

"No. This is a lot farther along in the process. You have to turn whatever relationships you see into a useful form. My favorite way is to draw cognitive maps—they're like flowcharts, with mathematical relationships between the nodes. Like 'Percent eight hours sleep' in one node with an arrow to 'Percent perfect grades' in another—except when you're done drawing, your grades will depend on a lot of things, and so will everything else. Cognitive maps are good because you can link a lot of them together—like simultaneous equations, sort of. The hard part is 'tuning' them—adjusting the links so that the whole 'supermap' gets as close as possible to really predicting things in your life—I usually use neural nets for that, and feed them data as I go along."

She looked up at Bob suddenly, as if wondering if he was following her.

"Neural nets?" he said doubtfully, gazing at the pattern on the screen. There was something hypnotic about it, mathematical and at the same time organic, so that you could almost believe it was a cross between a computer program and something alive.

"That's not what this is," said Diana. "I'm looking at a boundary region between two attractors in one of my submaps. You have to do some more math to get this—I guess it's kind of hard to explain," she concluded meekly.

Bob felt old and stupid. "So this—thing tells you what's going to happen in your life?"

"I'm—it's getting better," she said humbly. "I'm still collecting data and trying to make everything fit together right, but—but I've had some good results. Almost paranormal. Dr. Al-Haq says it can take a lifetime. He says it's like a poem or a symphony." Her eyes sparkled with wonder. "He says to perfect it you have to model the people around you too—your mother, your father, your friends and neighbors, anyone who influences you. And to be really accurate, you have to include all the people who affect *them,* all the people in the world, really, and everything else: the weather, the seasons, the animals and birds, the tides, the moon, the stars—the whole universe in a net of equations going on and on. . . ."

The dim monitor light made her awestruck face almost otherworldly. And strangely, looking at her, an exaltation seemed to come over him too, an intuition of the vastness of the world, the infinite possibilities—

A noise came from outside the window, like a low growling.

"What's that?" Bob said, making her jump. "Did you hear that?"

They listened. A few seconds later it came again, a

deep, guttural sound. Bob went to the window and pulled the curtain aside. There was nothing but the faint reflection of his face on blackness.

"I wonder what that is?" he murmured. "I better go check. I'll be back in a second."

He was half hoping she would volunteer to go with him, but she didn't. He shuffled along the flagstone walk at the side of the house in his slippers, breath steaming in damp, chilly air that smelled of wet fallen leaves, cold stars shining in a vast, empty sky above the darkness of the backyard.

"Hello?" he said into the dark. "Anybody there?"

There was a stirring in some dead leaves under Diana's faintly lit window.

"Rudolph?" said Bob with sudden recognition. The part of the stirring that was a large tail wagging intensified. The Great Dane was a big, dark shape against the lighter blob of the leaves. Bob bent down and scratched the wiry fur on the back of his pony-size head.

"What are you doing lying outside people's windows and growling?" Bob asked. "You better go home now. Go on. Go home. Go home."

Bob pointed off in the direction of the Taylors' house, where Rudolph lived, then bent over and got his arms around the dog's barrel chest, tried to pull his vast bulk up. Rudolph grunted contentedly and pawed at Bob with a huge, sandpapery paw.

"You want to stay there, I guess," Bob concluded. "You're guarding Diana's window, huh? Okay, but be quiet. Shh. Shh."

Diana's room was dark when he poked his back head in.

"It's just a neighborhood dog," Bob whispered to her. "He's friendly."

He drank his cup of hot milk and fell asleep as soon as he got back in bed.

A brief din of snarling, struggling barks from the

backyard woke him during the night. He went to sleep again at once, hoping Rudolph hadn't caught whatever cat or squirrel had been unfortunate enough to cross his path.

Next morning at the office Bob worked hard to catch up with his lost Thursday. There were twice as many phone messages as usual on his chair and new memos on a desk already covered with untidy piles of paper. By noon he had made a good start, and he was irritated when Lois broke his concentration after he had told her to hold all calls.

"It's Vicki," she said. "She says it's important."

"Honey, something weird happened just now," Vicki said as soon as he picked up. She sounded shaken.

"What? Are you okay?"

"Yes, I'm OK. But it was so *weird*. I was making a sandwich for lunch and the doorbell rang. It was this little old man. I thought he was a street person or—"

Bob's hand tightened on the telephone. "What did he look like?"

"He was all dressed in black, with a black cap. Why? Do you know him?"

"I think I've seen him."

"It was so weird. He asked me did we have any old newspapers, because he was in the recycling business. I went down in the basement to put some in a bag for him—I figured he was some poor old guy trying to make a living. But when I came back up he was gone.

"I thought maybe he had gotten tired of waiting. I shut the door and went back to finish my sandwich. But then I heard a noise in Diana's room. I went in there, and there he was standing on a chair by the window with his hand up on top of the window molding.

"I got scared and started yelling. I told him I was going to call the police, and he left in a hurry. But the weirdest part is"—she took a breath—"what do you think

I found when I climbed up on the chair and felt around on the molding where he had his hand?"

"What?"

"Guess."

"Honey!"

"Garlic," she said. "He left cloves of garlic on top of the molding of both of Diana's windows. What do you think of that?"

"Did you call the police?"

"I wanted to talk to you first. What—"

"I think I saw the same guy hanging around outside the house last night. Yeah, you better call them. I was hoping I could use him as a character witness for the Esterbrooks, but this is getting strange. Did he seem dangerous?"

"No, but what was he doing putting garlic—"

Bob told her everything he knew about the little man in black. When he was done she got off to call the police. He was pondering, staring blankly out his window over the buildings and traffic of downtown, when the phone rang again. Nora Esterbrook was on the line.

"Nora, did you ask Derek about the little man in black?" Bob asked her. "The one I told you I met outside your house? Did you find out who he is?"

"No, I—Mr. Wilson, I forgot all about it, what with the social workers coming and having to clean up the house for them."

"Did the interview go well?"

"Well, they were very nice," she said in her breathless, anxious voice. "But Derek wasn't here."

"Where was he? I told them he would be there for the interview."

"He was—he was in no condition to be seen, Mr. Wilson. I sent him out of the house before they came. I told them he had gone on a walk and I was terribly sorry. And that was the truth, both parts of it. Only—only I don't know when he'll be back."

Bob thought that over. "Well, maybe it's just as well under the circumstances. I just hope he doesn't get himself arrested or something. What happened to AA? He said he was going to sign up today."

"I don't know."

"Another thing, Nora, do you have any savings? Any money in the bank?"

"Well—yes, a little. Mr. Wilson, I know we can never repay you—"

"That's not why I'm asking. We need to hire a private detective."

"A private detective?"

"Yes. We need to play the same game on Armilla Robinson that she played on us at the hearing, and I want to know how long we can hire one for. The Code of Ethics doesn't allow lawyers to pay their clients' consultants' or investigators' fees." *And thank goodness for that,* he thought.

Then Nora started up with: "Do you think we really need to hire someone? I could go around and find out anything you want to know. A lady I work with at the bank used to be at the courthouse, and she knows all about how to look up where people live and where they work. . . ."

Bob provided fugue counterpoint: "Nora, this is a serious matter. What we turn up investigating the Robinson woman will probably determine whether your daughter is still with you two weeks from now. It's important that we use a professional. They know all kinds of tricks you and I would never think of. . . ."

After a while of this he eased them onto the topic of how much was in the Esterbrooks' bank account. About $1,200, he finally got Nora to admit, her voice tight and strained, as if the thought of spending it was giving her constipation. It was a tug-of-war to get her to agree to spend all of it, if necessary, on a detective. As soon as Bob got her off the phone, he had Lois bring him the Yellow

Pages. He felt a little excited as he found the "Detective Agencies" section.

He dialed the first entry there: AAA Investigations.

It rang five times, and then an old woman's voice answered: "Hello?"

"Hello," Bob said smoothly. It wouldn't do to let them know he was a novice at this. "Could I speak to the detective on duty, please?" He had read enough crime novels to know there was always a detective on duty.

"Who?"

"The detective on duty."

"There's nobody like that here."

"Is this Triple-A Investigations?"

"The what?"

"I'm sorry, I must have the wrong number." He hung up and dialed AAA Investigations again.

After two rings, two voices answered at the same time, apparently on different extensions. One sounded like the old woman he had just spoken to.

"Is this Triple-A Investigations?"

"What?" asked the old woman.

"Ah, yes it is," said the man's voice, smooth, quiet, and businesslike.

The other extension hung up.

"This is Triple-A Investigations?"

"Yes it is."

"I'd like to speak with the detective on duty."

"You're speaking with him."

"I have a matter that requires a confidential investigation," Bob said casually. "I'd like to inquire as to your rates and terms."

"Okay, we charge five hundred dollars a day plus mileage plus out-of-pocket expenses. That's based on a ten-hour work day."

"Five hundred?" Bob tried to compose himself. "Is that your absolute lowest rate?"

"Well, what kind of work do you have in mind? If it

doesn't require carrying firearms, we can sometimes go as low as four hundred a day."

"Four hundred?" Bob said doubtfully. He was picturing a confidential investigation lasting exactly three days. And that was if the detective didn't incur any expenses.

"Well, possibly we could let you have one of our lesser-experienced detectives, in which case three hundred a day would be the going rate," the voice on the other end of the line said. Then he added: "Of course, he would be a very qualified individual. We take pride in our work here at Triple-A Investigations."

There was something rehearsed about the way he said it that made Bob a little suspicious. "Let me get back to you," he said.

"How much do you want to spend?" the detective asked hastily. "We're in a slow period right now—I could give you a deal on a detective—say two fifty a day—and we'll throw in the expenses."

"Let me get back to you," Bob said, and hung up.

He pored over the Yellow Pages, trying to figure out how to weed out the fly-by-night outfits, of which apparently there were some. AAA Investigations only had a line entry, he saw now, without a corresponding banner ad on the page above it. He finally settled on a half-page ad for "National Security Systems—Confidential Investigations—Divorce, Criminal, Civil, Industrial, Employee Screening, Security—Since 1962—Our References Are the Best in the Area," with a picture of a stern-looking man smoking a pipe and holding a magnifying glass. He dialed the number, got put on hold, and finally learned from a hard-sounding woman that National Security Systems' base rate was a $700 per diem plus mileage plus expenses plus contingency on some types of cases, and that they required a $5,000 cash advance.

Bob dialed Confidential Investigations, Inc., Roger Reiner Associates, and Plimpson's, Ltd. The lowest rate any of them had was $600 a day, and that was for employee reference searches. Roger Reiner Associates wanted an automatic bonus of $2,000 if Bob won the case. Bob sat at his desk staring at the wall and chewing his lip for a while, then dialed AAA Investigations again. The smooth, businesslike voice he had talked to before answered.

"I called earlier," Bob said, "and you quoted me a price of two hundred and fifty dollars a day."

"Yes sir." Bob thought there was an unprofessional eagerness lurking just below the professional drawl.

"How do I know I'd be getting competent detective services for that? Does your firm have references?"

"Our references are the best in the area." Bob's eyes sought the National Security Systems ad in the phone book. "What kind of case are we talking about?"

Bob described it.

"Hm. Well, Mr.—"

"Wilson."

"Mr. Wilson, I think we happen to have an excellent person for your matter right on hand, as it happens. As it happens, we can let you have him at two fifty a day, as a kind of introductory offer."

"Including expenses?"

"What did I say before, including expenses?" He pretended to weigh the matter. "Okay, I guess we can do it just this once. Now I need your address and—"

"Hold on. I haven't hired you yet. I'll need to see your references, and the person you're planning on using. And what is *your* name, sir?"

"Alvin Corrant, Jr."

"This is an urgent matter, and I'd like you to begin work on it today, if possible. Where are your offices located?"

"That's 3101 Locust Avenue, but I can send the man over to you."

Bob still had a lot of work to get done by the end of the day. "Okay, we'll do it that way. But I haven't hired you yet, and I may not if I decide your agency isn't suitable."

"No obligation," Alvin Corrant, Jr., said cheerfully. "I'll have the man over there this afternoon."

Bob worked like a horse for an hour. Vicki called to say that the police had promised to put the little man in black on their suspicious persons list, and to send a car down Cedar Street a few times a night. After she hung up, Emma at the front desk buzzed him. "There's a man out here to see you. He says he's a detective."

She sounded doubtful.

6

He certainly didn't look like a detective. He was maybe in his late twenties, smallish, with short-clipped hair and quick, alert eyes. He wore a light jacket half zipped over a dark shirt, dark pants, and deck shoes. The only thing unusual about him, Bob noticed as he shook the man's hand, was that the chocolate-brown back of it was striped with pale scars, giving it a tigerlike appearance. He carried a folder in another scar-striped hand.

Bob led him back through the firm's plush, winding hallways to his office. When he was behind his desk and the man was in one of the visitors' chairs, Bob said: "Okay, Mr.—I'm sorry, I didn't catch your name."

"You can call me Max."

"Max—"

"My instructions are to discuss your case before I show you references." Max held up his folder. "We don't want to reveal names of past clients unnecessarily. I'd like to start by asking you some questions." He got a small pad and a ballpoint pen from an inner pocket.

"Okay."

"As I understand it, this is a background investigation to dig up information for a custody battle."

"An adoption battle. The petitioner is the biological mother. I represent the adoptive parents."

"What makes you think there's something to dig up?"

"Well, she's been in prison for a dozen years, for one thing."

Max looked up. "The mother? What for?"

"Something about kidnaping. That's one of the things I want you to confirm."

"That's not enough for you right there? I mean, kidnaping is a bad offense. Isn't that enough to win your case right there?"

"Well, it might be if that were all there was to it." Bob explained a little about Armilla Robinson and the Esterbrooks, without using names.

"So she looks like a little angel now," said Max with satisfaction, writing. "You have a picture of her?"

Bob hesitated, then slipped the three-by-five glossy out of Wentworth's folder, tossed it onto the top of his piled-up In box near Max.

Max picked it up and whistled.

"What a babe," he said finally. "I should be working for *her.*" He laughed until he saw Bob's unamused face. "You feel the same way?" he asked shrewdly.

"Certainly not," Bob snapped. "And I didn't give you that picture to drool over."

Max tossed the picture back. The passionate, innocent eyes made Bob's heart jump. He looked at it for maybe a second too long.

"I know what you're thinking," Max laughed. "You don't have to tell me."

Bob put the picture back in the folder, irritated. "Now you tell me what *you're* thinking," he said. "What would you do on this case if I decided to hire you?"

Max swallowed his laughter and licked his lips. His forehead creased and his eyes widened nervously.

"Well—" He cleared his throat.

"Yes?"

"The first thing I'll do is—just tell me this, was she incarcerated at Jonasburgh?"

"Yes."

"Then I got some friends I can ask about her. I know plenty of people in Jonasburgh."

"She was a model prisoner."

"That doesn't mean anything, Mr. Wilson. Sometimes all it means is they're the ones running the prison. Don't you think all those mob bosses they got in there are model prisoners? I'll ask my girlfriends what her play was on the yard. A girl like that had to have something. Institution life doesn't bring out the best in people."

Bob was a little impressed in spite of himself, but to keep up appearances he grunted: "How come you know so many people in prison?"

"I used to run with them, is all."

Bob kept looking at him.

Max held up the scar-striped backs of his hands for Bob to see.

"Back twelve, fifteen years ago I was in a street gang downtown called the Tigers," he said, studying his hands as if they were the relics of an ancient civilization. "A lot of the kids I ran with didn't amount to anything but criminals."

"Hmm. What else would you do on the case?"

Max shrugged. "*You* got any angles on it?"

Bob put his hand on Wentworth's file folder. "Maybe. But I want to see your references first."

Max handed his folder across the desk. Bob opened it. It was empty.

"Mr. Wilson," Max said solemnly, "you are our first customer."

Bob stared at him openmouthed. He had heard of brazen bait-and-switch schemes, but—

Max waved his hands. "Mr. Wilson, I know what you're thinking. But I guarantee you if there's anything on this Armilla Robinson—"

"How do you know her name is Armilla Robinson?"

"It's written on the back of that picture. Like I say, if

you want to stop worrying about this Armilla Robinson and get back to your New England Gas Light case—"

Bob stared at him in surprise.

"—which your receptionist told me you're handling, I'm the man that can help you. Look, Mr. Wilson, a girl doesn't look the way she does after being in the institution twelve years. Not normally. And I'm probably the only person who can find out what went on in those twelve years—what really went on."

"I ought to report you to the licensing board for misrepresenting your qualifications."

"There isn't any licensing board, Mr. Wilson. In this state anybody can be a professional investigator." Max leaned forward. "I need the work, Mr. Wilson. I don't want to end up back at the McDonald's. Look, how much do have to spend on a detective? A thousand? Two thousand?"

Bob maintained his indignant expression and didn't answer.

"If you had more, you wouldn't have called me back. You checked with some other agencies, right?"

"That was you on the phone?" Bob was outraged again. "When the state Consumer Protection Board hears you've been using false names to misrepresent the size of your *agency*—"

"My name is Alvin Maxwell Corrant, Jr.," Max said with dignity. "People call me Max. Now look, Mr. Wilson, your clients don't have much money—if they did, why would they use an electricity lawyer for their adoption case?—and they can afford what they can afford. The other agencies in town won't even answer the phone for a thousand dollars. So it's between hiring me and hiring nobody. And I'm telling you, Mr. Wilson, *I can do the job*."

Bob began to smell a deal coming down the road.

"But to pay two hundred and fifty dollars a day to someone with no experience, no moral standards—"

"I know what you're saying. I'll give you my special rate: two hundred a day, including expenses."

"One hundred a day."

"One seventy-five. Plus expenses."

"One hundred."

"Mr. Wilson, that's not fair! I can make more than that at the shoeshine stand on the corner down here. I'll give you one seventy-five a day, including expenses, and I can't go any lower than that."

Bob stood up slowly, looking down at his stubborn, anguished face.

"You've got yourself a deal," he said, and stuck out his hand. Max stood up and shook it.

"Mr. Wilson, you won't regret it. I don't care if that woman's the Virgin Mary, I'll get something on her'll make the judge scream."

"If I'm not satisfied in a couple of days, I'm going to fire you," Bob warned him. "I can't afford—"

"You'll be satisfied. You'll be satisfied. You'll be satisfied, because the next time I give that folder to somebody, it's going to have your name in it."

Bob handed the empty folder back to him, and handed him the Wentworth file. "Look over this stuff tonight and call me at home tomorrow morning. I want you to start on it tomorrow. We only have ten days." He looked at Max doubtfully. "I hope I'm not making a mistake."

"You're not. You're not. Mr. Wilson, I'll have something for you by Monday. Say by Tuesday. By Tuesday."

When Bob pulled up in front of his house a couple of hours later, deep blue-gray dusk was rushing with a fresh wind that smelled like rain, scattering pale, almost fluorescent leaves and bringing clouds scudding across the sky. The house was dark. Bob jogged up the sidewalk, fumbled with his keys, and banged the front door open.

"Vicki?" he called anxiously in the dark living room.

A door opening made him jump.

"She's gone to rehearsal," said Diana. "She'll be back late."

"Oh, it's Friday," he remembered, relieved. Diana was framed in her doorway by dim monitor screen light, hair scattered untidily on her shoulders. "How are you doing?"

"Okay." She sounded preoccupied. Something banged faintly against the side of the house in the wind.

"Are you playing—working on your computer?"

"Yes." She backed into her room and Bob followed, curious to see the patterns on her monitor again. The clothes and books Nora Esterbrook had sent over, plus some things Vicki had supplied, were scattered around the room in a state of maximum entropy. Diana sat cross-legged on the bed and typed on her keyboard.

A sound hung over her, something different from the rush of the wind outside and the occasional chatter of her disk drive: this was an edgy whine, like the violin section in an avant-garde symphony. Looking for the source of it, Bob saw for the first time that there were speaker grilles in her monitor. An intricate, symmetrical arabesque curled on the screen, unwinding a maze of detail from vortices that slowly shifted position as the arabesque deformed itself; and as it did the whine from the speakers changed too, grew shriller, more charged with tension, like the sound track of a suspense film.

"What's that noise?" Bob asked, watching Diana's taut profile in the screen's glow, hair tucked untidily behind her ears.

"Audial patterning. Values in the map associated with musical tones." Her voice seemed to be shaking a little.

Wind gusted outside. Something—maybe an acorn from the backyard oak—hit a gutter downspout with a dull *clunk*. Leaves whirled past the windows. Bob put his hand on the girl's thin, slumped shoulder.

"Diana—"

She looked up with a start. She was very pale, dark circles showing under her eyes.

"What's the matter?"

Her lips were trembling. "I don't—it says—" she pointed at the screen.

The arabesque was stretching and twisting agonizingly now, edges coiling into tortuous deformations. Against the gusting of the wind and a distant boom of thunder its urgent screeching was eerie and ominous.

"What's the matter?"

She took a long, shuddering breath. "It disintegrates," she quavered. "Falls into a Fatou dust. Dies."

"Your computer thing? Diana, honey, you can't let yourself get so—"

"It's my life," she sobbed. "Look."

The tormented arabesque was shrieking now like an insane thing. As Bob watched, it came apart with a snap and a sighing, overstressed lines curling back upon themselves in detached coils that separated into smaller, writhing lines, these quickly disintegrating into dustings of separate points.

The room was dark now, the deep glow from the tumultuous atmosphere outside almost gone from the windows, the monitor screen ominously blank.

"You see," rasped Diana. "It ends."

There was a quick spatter of raindrops. Far away, the wail of a siren wavered on the wind.

Bob sat down on the bed next to her. "You don't really take it that seriously, do you? You told me yourself you were in the early stages of—doing whatever you do with the equations and all. You know: it's not accurate enough to predict anything."

"It shows the same behavior over a wide range of parameters. Dr. Al-Haq says—"

"Well, maybe Dr. Al-Haq is wrong. Who says a computer can predict what's going to happen to a living, breathing person?"

He interrupted her opening mouth: "But I'm willing to believe he's right and the computer's right, and something is coming down the line for you. In fact, I know what it is. It happened to me and Vicki and your parents and a lot of other people. It's called adolescence. It is sort of like the end of life as you know it. It makes perfect sense that the patterns you've found so far are going to end. In fact, you're a late bloomer, so really you're overdue for the change. The difference between you and most people—everybody else I've ever heard of, in fact—is that you're smart enough to see it coming, whereas most people your age are just—well, kids."

She was watching him suddenly, her eyes in the dark alive with thought.

"I'm afraid you'll have to start from scratch with your equations, and gather your data all over again."

He had no idea whether any of this could be true, but it seemed to have its effect. Diana turned shyly to type on her keyboard. The disk drive chattered and another arabesque scribbled itself onto the screen.

"A phase transition structure," she breathed, as if thinking out loud. "Julia sets fall to Fatou dust when they cross the boundary of the Mandelbrot set. In fact, that's when they enter the domain of the attractor at infinity." The thought seemed to excite her.

The wind was getting less now, and rain was pattering steadily at the panes.

"I better go make sure the windows are closed," said Bob, standing up. "You okay?"

She nodded distractedly.

He climbed the stairs. The bedroom window that faced out over the backyard was open a little. He went toward it.

A pair of hands loomed from the outer blackness toward the glass.

Bob jumped backward with a yell.

Diana's door opened, and her voice came anxiously up the stairs: "Mr. Wilson? Bob?"

He crept toward the window. Somebody was out there, bobbing unsteadily in the air—somebody small, clinging to one of the branches of the backyard oak, now inching backward into the darkness—

Bob ran downstairs past a wide-eyed Diana, grabbing the flashlight from the front coat closet. His shoes squished in mud and leaves along the side of the house. The flashlight beam made white streaks of the rain as he shone it up into the oak tree.

"Come down from there!" he yelled at the figure that was now slowly and cautiously doing just that among orange leaves fifteen feet above him. "What are you doing up there?"

There were squishy footsteps, and Diana ran around the side of the house at the same moment as a wet, bounding shape hit Bob's hip with an excited panting.

"Rudolph, stop that. Sit," Bob commanded, not displeased. Two hundred pounds of friendly dog might come in handy if he had to chase this crazy old man all over the neighborhood again.

"Diana, go back in and call the police," he ordered her. "No, wait."

As the figure in the tree came lower, carefully sliding down a thick branch to a fork in the trunk, it looked less like the old man; for one thing, it was smaller, and for another, it had red hair—

"Zachary!" Bob cried in surprise. "Zachary Taylor, is that you?"

Zachary didn't answer. He slowly felt for a branch with his foot and lowered himself onto it, hugging the trunk. His dog Rudolph rushed back and forth under the tree, whining ecstatically and bounding clumsily into the air.

"Zachary, what are you *doing* up there?" Bob complained, crestfallen, wet, irritated, and afraid Zachary would fall. He went and stood where he could catch him if he did, shining the light up to help him see, squinting against the raindrops. "Don't you know how dangerous that is? Does you mom know you're out here? It's just a little boy from down the street," he told Diana. "He does funny things sometimes. He's—what do you call it—autistic." Zachary continued with his slow, methodical climbing, and in a minute was close enough for Bob to lift him down, a chubby little boy of five or six, his clothes wet, dirty, and disheveled.

"Now look at you," Bob scolded. "What a mess. What is your mom going to say?"

Zachary ignored him, staring into the flashlight. Rudolph was snuffling at him excitedly, tail going like a fan blade.

"Are you all right, Zachary? You scared me to death. What were you doing up in that tree? Huh?"

"Tree," Zachary repeated seriously.

"Come on." Bob grabbed his hand. "Your mother is probably worried stiff. Come on, Rudolph. Come on, let's walk them home," he told Diana. "Can you get an umbrella out of the coat closet? His house is down the street."

They walked squeezed together under the umbrella, Rudolph crowding back and forth between their legs. The deserted, tree-arched sidewalks and the rain sparkling in the streetlight on parked cars made the neighborhood seem slightly surreal; maybe that was what made Bob feel peculiar. He was walking between Zachary and Diana, holding the umbrella, and for some reason he couldn't shake the feeling that there was a faint electric current running between them through his body, prickling in the hand he held Zachary with and in the opposite arm that pressed against Diana. It made him light-headed. Some weird perceptual illusion, he guessed.

They reached the Taylors' yard, climbed three cracked cement steps between the tall untrimmed hedges and went up the walk. Rain pattered around them in earthy-smelling vegetation. They climbed wooden steps to the dimly lit front porch, and Bob knocked at the door.

It flew open and old Mrs. Taylor's wide eyes sought out Zachary.

"Zachary! Where have you been?" She gathered him quickly up into her arms. He put his fat arms around her neck. "Mr. Wilson—Ed? You don't have to call, dear, Mr. Wilson's found him! Oh, *Zachary*—Well, come in, come in! Not you, Rudolph, you're wet."

Mrs. Taylor was a thin, gray old woman and Zachary was big for his age, but she held him almost effortlessly, balanced on one skinny hip like a baby. He put his head on her shoulder. She closed the door behind them, Rudolph lying down on the porch with a sigh.

The Taylors' parlor was dim, musty, and warm, a sagging sofa and some bookshelves lit by a frilly lamp on a low table, an elderly brown rug of indeterminate pattern on the floor. Old Mr. Taylor came in from another room. He was thin and stooped, with brown spots on his bald head, limping from his war injury. Bob had never dared ask which war.

"Well, Bob Wilson! You found him, eh? He always seems to turn up. Where was he?"

"In the oak tree in my backyard."

"Oh, *Zachary*—!" said Mrs. Taylor.

"Climbing trees in a storm. Good way to end up like a keebob." Mr. Taylor took hold of Zachary's foot and swung it back and forth. "But he's an adventurous fellow. Nothing stops him, once he's got something on his mind. No use trying." He swung the foot back and forth some more.

"He's shivering," said Mrs. Taylor, feeling Zachary's chest with the flat of her hand anxiously, as if to detect the palpitations of pneumonia. "I'm going to put him in a hot bath." She whisked him out of the room.

"Hot bath'll do him good, mother," Mr. Taylor called after her, winking at Bob and Diana through his thick glasses. Everyone in the neighborhood knew that the Taylors' daughter had adopted Zachary a few months before dying in a car crash; old Mr. and Mrs. Taylor had referred to themselves as his father and mother ever since. "She worries herself sick about that boy," he confided to them. "Doesn't realize he leads a charmed life. I've never seen the tree he could fall out of. Sit down, sir, sit down. And I haven't met this young lady, I don't believe."

"Oh, I'm sorry. Mr. Taylor, this is Diana Esterbrook, a—friend of Vicki's and mine who is visiting for a while."

Diana blushed and Mr. Taylor shook her hand gravely. "Well, sit down, sit down. You're making me dizzy standing there. Mrs. Taylor will have the hot chocolate on in a minute."

"Thank you very much, Mr. Taylor, but we have to be going." Despite Mr. Taylor's jaunty air, Bob had the feeling he wanted to go sit with Zachary too. "It's nice of you to ask."

Mr. Taylor opened the front door for them. Rudolph, chin on paws, wagged his tail mournfully.

"We appreciate you bringing him around," Mr. Taylor told them in almost a whisper as they went out. "I guessed he had just snuck off to climb something, but what with these animals prowling around, we naturally wondered—"

"Animals?"

"Yes. Haven't you heard? A couple of the folks on the block saw 'em last night. Art Johnson over here two houses down said there was one in his bushes when he took out the trash. 'Bout scared his pants off—'scuse me, young lady. The police are checking with the zoo to see if there've been any escapes."

7

Bob had been lying in bed and thinking for an hour or two when Vicki snuck in, leaving the light off so as not to disturb him, and started fumbling quietly with her dresser drawers. Bob listened for a few minutes before he said: "There's something weird going on."

She gave a little scream and a drawer thumped.

"You scared me," she accused him. "What are you doing still up?"

"Thinking. Honey, something weird is going on."

"What? The little man?"

"That and other things. Something strange happened tonight."

"What?" She got in bed and snuggled against him under the covers in the slightly chilly air of the bedroom, the softness and smell of her woman-flesh engulfing him. Her hands and feet were cold.

"Zachary Taylor climbed up in our oak tree."

"Zachary—he didn't fall—?"

"No. That kid can climb like a squirrel. But he was groping around outside the upstairs windows when I came home—almost gave me a heart attack. Diana and I got him down and took him home, but I had a thought when we got back, and after Diana went to bed I opened the window and felt around outside. Sure enough, there was something stuck onto the window frame out there—a little plastic box with holes in it. Guess what's inside."

"What?"

"Guess."

"Honey—!"

"Garlic. A clove of garlic."

Vicki rolled over fast and turned on the bed lamp.

"Let's see it," she demanded, wide eyes on his face.

"I don't have it," he said, squinting in the light.

"Where is it?"

"I put it back out there."

"Why?"

"Honey, did you ever see those old movies where people are afraid of vampires, and they get these old wise women to hang something in their windows to keep the vampires out? Remember what they hang in the windows?"

She was staring at him as if he was crazy.

"Garlic," he said. "Strings of garlic."

"You're crazy."

"I am or somebody is. Somebody's been working awfully hard to get garlic up on our windows. First that little old man, and now Zachary. And Zachary must have been busy before I caught him, because there are little plastic boxes outside all the other windows on the second floor too."

"You think that old man told Zachary to—?"

"I don't know how anyone could tell Zachary anything. All I know—"

"And you didn't take them down because you're afraid of vampires?"

"Mr. Taylor told us some of the neighbors have seen big animals lurking around at night."

"My husband's crazy," said Vicki ruefully, as if to an audience in the bedroom. She rolled over mournfully and switched off the light. After a minute she asked: "Did you call the police?"

"And tell them what?"

She reflected on that.

"The only way I can figure it," Bob went on, "is that that old man has some kind of fixation on Diana. He saw me outside the Esterbrooks' and followed me home. He must know Diana is staying here. He's been hanging around on the street, and today he comes in and starts putting garlic on the windows. You catch him, so somehow he gets Zachary, who is just as crazy as he is—"

"Zachary's not crazy, he's autistic."

"—to hang garlic outside. Why? Does he think he's protecting Diana from something? I wonder if he's got garlic up over the windows at the Esterbrooks' too. Maybe I *should* call the police again."

"Call them tomorrow," Vicki yawned. "We have protection tonight. Rudolph's lying outside the front door. He almost knocked me down on my way in."

"He's been spending a lot of time over here lately."

"He likes you because you're crazy. He's used to Zachary."

She lay against him and scratched the back of his neck drowsily. In a little while he fell asleep.

There was a ringing sound that wouldn't stop. Bob finally realized it was the telephone and woke up.

Vicki was still asleep, well tucked under the covers, only dark curly hair and a peek of white forehead showing. The phone was down in the study, and seemed to be on about its fortieth ring. Bob staggered up, shrugged on his bathrobe, and stumped unsteadily downstairs to get it. Dripping gray daylight came through the windows, and the clock on the rolltop desk said 8:02.

"Hello?" he managed to croak into the phone.

"*Good* morning, Mr. Wilson," came an offensively cheerful voice over the line. "Max Corrant calling to discuss our case, per your instructions."

"Max—auch."

"Pardon me, Mr. Wilson?"

"Don't you—couldn't you call back sometime a little later, when I'm awake?"

"Well, sure." Max sounded disappointed. "I just figured since you're paying a daily rate you'd want to get the most for your money. Start early, turn in late, that's our motto at Triple-A Investigations."

Bob sighed. He was all the way awake now.

"Okay," he said. He shut the study door so he wouldn't disturb anybody else, sat in the armchair next to the window, and rubbed his feet on the nap of the Oriental rug. "Will it take long?"

"Long as you want," said Max. "First let me tell you what I've done already, then I'll tell you what I'm going to do."

"Okay."

"Okay, first thing I did was float a line into Jonasburgh—"

"'Float a line'?"

"That's detective terminology, means I'm opening a communications channel into some people I know there, in the women's wing. I should be able to ask some questions in a few days."

"You did this yesterday?"

"Yes, sir, last night after I read your file, which I'm getting to."

"I hope you're not thinking of charging me for anything you did yesterday," Bob said. "My understanding was that yesterday was strictly informational, and I never authorized—"

"Absolutely free, absolutely free of charge," said Max cheerfully. "Not that I'd do it for just any customer. Next I got Armilla Robinson's address—"

"How did you do that?"

"It's on her affidavit, the one her lawyer gave you. Then I went over there."

"You went over where?"

"Over to Armilla Robinson's. But don't worry, I was disguised—I had on my gas company outfit. I told her there had been a gas leak in the neighborhood and I needed to check her lines to make sure it wasn't in her basement. She didn't suspect anything. And I'll tell you, she's a honey. That picture doesn't—"

"You gained admittance to her residence under false pretenses?" Bob cut him off furiously. "How am I going to use you as a witness if she recognizes you? We'll both end up in jail, you—"

"She won't recognize me, Mr. Wilson. I had on my—"

"I never gave you permission to go near her, much less break into her house—"

"It's standard procedure, Mr. Wilson—"

"I should have used a reputable agency. I knew it. If the judge ever finds out about this—"

"No one's ever going to find out about it. Will you listen for a minute, Mr. Wilson? It's standard procedure in a case like this to get access to the subject's residence. Just a routine surveillance measure. You never know what you'll find out. And she left me alone in the basement for over five minutes, and I got an impression of her basement door key that she left in the lock. Now if we ever want to get into the house, all we have to do is—"

"You *what*?" Bob yelled. "You committed a felony in violation of my express instructions? Look, Corrant," he tried to calm himself, "I don't want you to ever do anything like that again, is that clear? I want you to throw away the impression you made of the key. And in the future, before you go off on your own tangent, I want you to check with me, tell me what it is you want to do. Is that clear?"

"You want me to throw away the impression?" Max was horrified. "It's not doing any harm just sitting—"

"Throw it away," Bob gritted. "I'm willing to believe

you didn't know the law when you did this, but next time we talk I want it to be gone. Is that clear?"

There was a choked silence on the other end of the phone. Bob relented a little bit. "Look, Max, why don't you try something simple, like going to the courthouse and finding the records on Armilla's kidnaping trial, or digging up clippings on it from the newspaper? That stuff could be really useful. Why don't you stick to that for a while, and we'll discuss the James Bond stuff later? Okay?"

The house was silent, the daylight somnolent gray, brown and yellow leaves dripping in a heavy drizzle outside. Bob slouched barefoot and grumpy into the kitchen, put a saucepan of milk on the stove, and pulled open the drapes on the sliding glass door to the backyard deck. When he turned around, he saw a sheet of paper on the counter with two cloves of garlic lying on it.

He guessed it was the garlic Vicki had found on Diana's window moldings. He picked up one of the cloves—reasoning that the police couldn't get fingerprints off garlic anyway—and examined it curiously.

It seemed, somehow, a tiny bit heavy for a clove of garlic. Bob joggled it in the palm of his hand, then held it up to the light and squinted at it microscopically.

Was that a tiny slit in its concave surface?

A rising hiss behind him was his milk boiling over. He yanked it off the burner. Then, very carefully, he pushed his thumbnails into the slit in the clove and split it apart.

He jumped then, dropping the clove, because the inside was infected by an ugly insect.

But it didn't move when the clove hit the floor, or when he poked it with his toe, or when he picked it up again and looked more closely. The smell of raw garlic filled his head. The thing stuck into the white flesh of the clove wasn't an insect at all, he saw. It was a tiny, flat, complicated-looking object made of metal or silicon or

plastic or all three, a maze of tiny circuits with small
L-shaped arms reaching out from each side. It had apparently been gouged into the garlic, leaving only a nearly
invisible slit.

Bob picked up the other clove with fingers that shook
slightly from excitement. It felt a tiny bit heavy for a clove
of garlic and seemed to be slitted on its concave side too.

An idea came to him. What if the circuit thing was a
listening device? What if the old man in black was a spy
hired by Barry D. Wentworth III to bug the Wilson home
for material he could use in the Esterbrook custody hearing? If Bob could prove such a thing to Judge Cramer,
Barry D. Wentworth III would be history, and so would
his case.

Vicki was still asleep. Bob put on some clothes in a
hurry, wrapped the little circuit device in a tissue, grabbed
a coat and umbrella from the front closet, and hurried out
into the drizzle. A few minutes later he was ringing the
Abercrombies' doorbell.

Larry answered in a worn Oriental bathrobe with
what looked like flying herons on it, the few gray hairs on
his head standing straight up, his cheeks and long, fleshy
nose ruddy.

"We-ell," he said heartily. "It's Perry Mason. Come on
in. Kind of early to be chasing witnesses around the neighborhood, isn't it?" His eyes gleamed with curiosity. Maybe
he could tell Bob was excited.

"Larry," Bob said when they were in the dim front
hall, Bob taking off his coat, "you're an electrical engineer,
right?"

"Well, I'll admit that much," Larry said with his
booming laugh. "But don't try to push me much further
than that."

"What do you suppose this is?" Bob pulled the tissue
out of his pocket and unwrapped the device. Larry took it
between a large, tobacco-stained thumb and forefinger.

"Larry? Who is it?" called a female voice from the in-nards of the house.

"Bob Wilson," Larry called back, preoccupied, squint-ing closely at the thing.

"Hi, Marybel," Bob called, squinting at the thing too.

"Hi, Bob. Come in and have coffee."

"Huh. Looks like a device," said Larry, flummoxed. "Let's take a closer gander . . ."

He led Bob into a breakfast room with a glass wall that looked onto a cozy, autumn-frowzy garden with dripping lawn furniture. Marybel Abercrombie, in her robe, sat with a coffee cup amid a welter of newspapers.

"How *are* you?" she asked Bob. "Where's Vicki?"

"He's here on a professional visit," Larry told her. "So don't discuss anything foolish with him."

Bob said "No, thank you" to an offer of coffee, and Larry led him into the next room, which had a glass wall too but was small and cluttered, with a drafting table, sol-dering iron, circuit boards, and other odds and ends lying around. Larry sat at the drafting table, slipped on a pair of bifocals, and turned on a donut-shaped florescent lamp with a magnifying glass in the middle.

"Sit on anything that doesn't look like it'll bite," he said. He picked up a worn, empty pipe from among the clutter, clenched it between his teeth.

"Don't you light that," warned Marybel, out of sight in the next room. "Don't let him light it, Bob. He's not al-lowed to smoke in the house anymore."

"I'm not going to light it, Mother," said Larry amiably, adjusting the magnifying light on its extendable arm and squinting through it.

"I heard you and Vicki have a houseguest," Marybel said.

"Interesting," mumbled Larry, and moved his pipe to the other side of his mouth. "Fascinating."

"Yes, a little garlic—little girl," Bob said, crowding

Larry and trying to look through the magnifying glass too. "What is it?"

"I'm not sure," Larry said, sucking on his pipe. "A device of some kind." He got hold of it with a pair of large tweezers and turned it to different angles, concentrating. "Where did you get this thing?"

"A relative?" asked Marybel.

"Friend," Bob said to Marybel. "The daughter of some people who are—having problems."

"I'll be damned," muttered Larry.

"What is it?"

"Everyone's having problems these days," said Marybel.

Larry looked at Bob over his glasses. He took his pipe out of his mouth.

"Where'd you get this thing?" he asked softly.

"Well, I—what is it?"

"It can't be what I think it is," Larry said. "But if it is— Look, I'm going in to the office for a while this afternoon. If I can take this thing with me, I'll have a couple of the guys run some checks on it." Larry worked at the Naval Research Lab, on government projects so secret he could never talk about them. "But they'll want to know where it came from."

"Larry, I—I don't feel I can tell you exactly where I got it."

"One of those Mafia cases you're working on?"

Bob nodded.

Larry sighed.

"Okay, but if I find out what it is for you, can you at least tell me *something*?" he complained. "You have no idea how boring an electrical engineer's life can be."

"Well—I guess so. Sure, it's a deal."

Marybel poked her head around the door.

"What are you two talking about in here?" she demanded. "You're being mysterious, and I don't like it."

8

When Bob got home, Vicki and Diana were in the kitchen. While he was hanging his raincoat in the closet, he heard Diana saying: ". . . it says my father won't stop drinking this time for at least another—"

A panic took him. He rushed into the kitchen.

"Shh! Shh!" he hissed, finger to his lips.

Vicki and Diana were sitting at the kitchen table drinking tea. They looked at him wide-eyed.

"So there you are," scolded Vicki. "What did you do to the stove again?"

"Shhh!" he hissed, unfortunately spraying her with saliva.

He picked up the second garlic clove from the counter and made vigorous gestures at his mouth and ears meaning they shouldn't talk in front of it.

Vicki put her teacup down. "What are you—?"

He opened the cupboard and hunted noisily for a jar, popped the garlic into it, tightened the lid, wrapped the jar in a dishtowel, shoved it into the cupboard, and shut the door. When he turned around, Vicki and Diana were staring at him.

"We're being spied on," he explained.

It took him a little while to tell them everything. Vicki seemed inclined to believe he had lost his mind until he took the garlic back out of the jar and carefully split it open on the kitchen table.

Vicki and Diana, leaning over his shoulder, gasped.

"It's a—you think it's a—?" Vicki half whispered, until he shushed her with a finger to his lips.

"But who—?" asked Diana plaintively.

Vicki leaned closely over the tiny device, studying it intensely.

"I know what this is," she announced excitedly after a minute. "I've seen this before."

"What?" Bob exclaimed, forgetting to be quiet.

"I've seen this exact one," she said. "Or a picture of it. You're sure this is the one the old man left? It's not a spy microphone, you idiot. It's an Indian charm. See that pattern of lines and dots? I've seen this exact one before."

"No, honey, Larry Abercrombie says—"

"Larry Abercrombie's crazy. Look, I'll show you. See that?"

Bob squinted closely. It looked exactly like the one he had left with Larry, but now the tiny, intertwined pattern of lines and faintly colored dots *did* seem vaguely familiar, like one of those ancient Mayan carvings that prove extraterrestrials visited South America three thousand years ago.

"It's just a coincidence," he soothed her. "Larry said definitely—"

"I'll *show* you," she insisted. "There's a store downtown that has a picture of *this exact one.*"

"It can't be *exactly*—"

"But where did you get it?" asked Diana. "Where did it come from?"

Vicki and Bob both stopped talking at once and looked at her. Bob put the garlic thing back in its jar, closed the lid, and wrapped it in the dishtowel again.

"Diana," he said carefully, "do you know a little old man, say in his late sixties, kind of short, sharp blue eyes, white hair, wears a black overcoat and black cap?"

Shocked recognition came into her eyes. She swallowed.

"No," she said.

"Are you sure?"

"I just told you *no*," she said angrily.

"Honey, she just told you she didn't know anybody like that," Vicki scolded him. "Don't you believe her? This crazy little man brought these into the house," Vicki explained to Diana. "We think he's dangerous and we're trying to find out who he is before he hurts one of us. We've already called the police. He probably thinks garlic stuck full of magical amulets will put a curse on us or something. We thought you might know him because he's been hanging around your parents' house too. I just hope the police get him before he murders someone." She gave a shudder.

Diana got very pale.

"Excuse me," she said faintly, and got up. She went out and they heard the door of her room close gently.

"She'll tell me sooner or later," Vicki murmured. "But honey, that thing's not a spy microphone. Why would anybody put a spy microphone in a piece of garlic?"

That was an interesting point.

"I have to show some houses at two. Let's go downtown first and I'll show you the picture of it I saw at the Indian store. Spy microphone." She looked heavenward wearily. "I bet that little man is a nutcase who thinks he's doing magic on us. But first you have to clean up the stove."

An hour later, showered, breakfasted, and somewhat calmed down, Bob shared the front seat of his car with an excited Vicki and a subdued Diana. The morning was almost twilight-dim under dark, puffy clouds, and a thin, steady rain blew in gusts against the windows. They headed for Old Town. Vicki passed the time by spinning wild theories about how Zachary Taylor could have gotten involved in putting garlic with Indian charms in it on people's windows and by pumping Bob about the Esterbrook case.

"You got a *detective*?" she exclaimed excitedly when he reluctantly told her about Alvin M. Corrant, Jr. "Why don't we have him find the little garlic man?"

"Because he's off doing things we need to win Diana's custody case," said Bob, hoping uneasily that it was true. "Besides, you're probably right—the garlic man's just some nut, and the police'll catch him sooner or later."

"I'll bet he's not," said Vicki. "I'll bet Diana's an Indian princess kidnaped at birth, and he's her spirit guardian."

Diana smiled wanly. A small car thumping with rock music slid past in the right lane, two boys a little older than Diana in the front seat, two girls with non-Earth hairdos elegantly holding cigarettes in the back. Diana's eyes followed them wistfully.

"*You* don't believe in magic, do you, Diana?" Bob asked, feeling sorry for her.

"Yes," she said seriously.

"What? A brilliant scientific mind like yours? How's that?"

"Well, something that's like magic, anyway. Thaumatomathematics."

"Meaning what?"

"The first part is from *thaumaturgy*, which means 'magic.' It's from a book by Dr. Al-Haq, the one my mom gave you to bring me. *Principles of Thaumatomathematics*."

"I thought that was computer stuff."

"Well—it is."

"What are you guys talking about?" demanded Vicki.

"Thaumatomathematics," said Diana. "Dr. Al-Haq invented it at the Los Alamos Institute, this really neat place where they study complex systems. Not many people have picked up on it yet."

"Tell us about it," said Vicki.

"It's kind of complicated," Diana murmured.

"Try us," said Vicki. "We're pretty old and stupid now, but we both went to college once."

Diana looked at her in surprise. "Well—it's a way of producing what Dr. Al-Haq calls an 'epiphany state.' Great scientists—especially mathematicians—get them. You get it by—by optimizing your brain functioning as a result of penetrating mathematical truth, Dr. Al-Haq says. It lets you see a deeper level of reality. And if you can see it, you can change it, and that's doing magic." She was flushed with excitement suddenly in spite of her shyness.

"This Dr. Al-Haq," Bob said. "Does he accept donations?"

"Oh, shut up, honey," said Vicki.

They were on the narrow, hilly streets of Old Town now, the uneven brick sidewalks carpeted with yellow leaves from the old trees, the big patrician houses, subdivided now into upscale condos, dull and dark under the heavy clouds, as if their occupants were still asleep. They parked on one of the market streets and crowded under Vicki's umbrella through the greenish, luminous light of the rain toward a sodden wooden sign that said "Indian Craft Shop."

A bell clanked dully as they went in. The shop was small and dim, with a display counter that held silver and turquoise jewelry, shelves lining the walls crowded with embroidered pillow covers, brightly painted pottery animals, carved hardwood, books, and polished stones. A couple of potted cactuses leaned by the door. There were no other customers. Behind the display counter sat a woman with powerful cheekbones, braided black hair, and slanted black eyes.

Vicki went straight to the book section, picked one out, and started flipping through it. After a minute she said: "Here it is!"

She held a page for Bob. It had a close-up photograph of an object with L-shaped arms held in the palm of someone's hand. It did look a lot like the thing wrapped in tissue in Bob's pocket, but bigger, about the size of a quarter—and *old:* corroded and dusty, as if it had been buried in the ground. The caption read: "This ancient charm was used for protection against Black Shamans."

"What do you think now, Mr. Big Shot Lawyer?" Vicki asked triumphantly.

"Huh," said Bob doubtfully.

"Here, show it to the lady," said Vicki, putting the book on the counter. Bob reluctantly pulled the tissue out of his pocket and unwrapped it. Vicki put the tiny object on the page next to the picture and turned the book around so the lady could see it. "Miss, can you tell me if this thing is the same as the one in the picture?"

The woman glanced at the object disinterestedly, then took a longer look, her eyes and nostrils widening.

She looked up at them. "Where did you get this?" Her voice was strong and local-accented.

Vicki and Bob glanced at each other.

"We—found it," said Vicki.

"I'd like to have this," the woman said. "I'll trade you for it." She slid the book to one side to expose the silver and turquoise jewelry in the display case.

"No, thank you."

"Some of these pieces are worth over a thousand dollars."

"Thank you, but we really don't want to part with it."

"This is a sacred object of the Powhatan Indian nation. You should not be in possession of it," said the woman reproachfully, taking it in her hand. "Its rightful owner is the Powhatan Tribal Authority."

"I'm sure you're mistaken," said Bob. "I don't think it's an Indian artifact at all. If you'll look at the difference in size—"

The woman was staring at the thing with focused concentration. Softly, she began to chant, strange words in a strange music rising like heavy incense in the air.

Then another voice began to chant along with her. It was a light, clear, dreamy voice that started off faint and grew stronger, and the melody of it brought to Bob's mind high, barren mountains echoing the tinkle of icy streams into a deserted sky. It was Diana, her wide, blank eyes staring into space.

The woman dropped the garlic thing onto the display case in shock. Her own wide eyes were fixed on Diana.

Bob stared too. Vicki recovered faster.

"Thank you," she said politely to the woman. She picked up the garlic thing. "And we'd like to buy this book, please."

When the woman didn't answer, Vicki looked quickly at the price, threw twenty dollars on the counter, and stuffed the book into her bag.

"Shall we be going?" she trilled to Diana and Bob.

"What is going on around here?" Bob asked in amazement when they were out on the sidewalk huddling under the umbrella against the blustery rain. Diana was still singing faintly, but seemed to be snapping out of it, looking around her as if remembering where she was.

"Like I told you," said Vicki. "Magic."

Glancing back at the Indian Craft Shop as he unlocked the car, Bob saw a figure struggling with a raincoat under the awning.

"I think that lady's coming after us," he said. "You probably forgot the tax on that book."

They U-turned and headed downhill on Wisconsin Avenue. No suspicious cars followed them, but several normal ones did, and Bob couldn't swear the Indian Craft Shop woman wasn't in one of them.

"What do you think now, Mr. Big Shot Lawyer It's A Spy Microphone?" Vicki asked him. "Diana, honey, are you all right?"

"Yes," said Diana unexpectedly. "But who was that lady?"

"I don't know." Vicki looked curiously into her face. "Why did you start singing like that?"

"I don't know. I mean, I remembered the song when *she* started singing it."

"Remembered it from where?"

"From when I was a little girl, I think," Diana said slowly. "Or sometime a long time ago. Or—yes. It reminded me of—sometime a long time ago, when I was—" she wrapped her arms tightly around herself.

"What?" Bob asked.

"I don't know." She started to hum again abstractedly, her eyes distant.

Bob opened his mouth but Vicki frowned at him.

They got home without more talking. Diana went into her room, closing the door quietly.

It was a little after one o'clock. Bob sat at the kitchen table and Vicki fried potatoes and eggs.

"Am I going crazy?" Bob complained. "To start out with, all we had was a weird custody case. Then we had an old man who snuck around putting garlic on people's windows. Then we had a little boy climbing trees to put garlic on people's windows. Then we had a mysterious Indian snake charm circuit board. Now we have a chanting Indian lady and a reincarnated pubescent computer genius."

"You're silly. My guess is that the little man has been after her for a long time—and probably some of the other neighborhood kids, like Zachary. *He* taught her that song when she was little—it goes along with his Indian magic. Ugh." She shivered. "I hope he's not some kind of pervert. Maybe that's why Diana didn't want to tell us about him."

They ate and then Vicki had to go to her real-estate appointment. Bob sat in the bedroom armchair and read the shaman magic book for a while in the gray window light, about men in feather-and-bone costumes who could extract arrowheads from injured bodies without cutting them open, disappear and travel long distances in an instant, and turn into animals. The book wasn't any help in explaining how an Indian talisman could look like an electronic device, but it did say that talismans were sometimes used with garlic to accomplish their magic. Bob hadn't slept well the night before. He lay down on the bed and closed his eyes for a few minutes, and when he woke up it was after five o'clock and getting dark.

He got up dizzily, splashed water on his face in the bathroom, and went downstairs. He hesitated by Diana's closed door, wondering if he should tell her he was going out to interview Mrs. Wetzel. He decided against it; somehow the idea of talking to her with no one else in the house gave him a slight case of the creeps.

The rain had stopped but there was a wet, blustery wind, half-naked branches of trees waving at the dark, overcast sky. The Esterbrooks' house was lightless as Bob pulled up across the street, the narrow driveway empty, prompting him to hope that Derek had gone to AA after all. Warm yellow light leaked from behind Mrs. Wetzel's curtains next door. Her house was identical to the Esterbrooks' but looked in better repair.

Bob was halfway to her front door when a thought struck him. He changed direction, walked to the Esterbrooks' house instead, and around the side of it. Grass grew long against its cinderblock foundation, to which big silver propane cylinders were connected by pipes. A TV aerial wire slapped against its aluminum siding in the wind.

He stood looking up at a dark window that was probably Nora and Derek's bedroom. Sure enough, something half the size of a kitchen matchbox was stuck onto the siding above it. To get at it he had to climb on top of the propane cylinders and lean far out, holding himself by his fingertips. The tiny box came off easily. He jumped down and examined it.

It was made of plastic, with holes at the bottom. Inside was a withered clove of garlic.

He put it in his raincoat pocket, heart thumping.

Barely twenty feet away, from a window in Mrs. Wetzel's house, a face watched him with intense curiosity. A curtain dropped in front of it the second she saw him looking.

He sighed, imagining her dialing the police. He marched across her yard, climbed the concrete steps to her door, and knocked.

It opened at once, with a chain on it and Mrs. Wetzel's face behind that. It was a soft, pinkish face with suety cheeks, big round eyes, and a long, inquisitive nose.

"What do you want? I saw you peeping in the neighbor's window. I'll call the police if you don't go away."

"I'm the Esterbrooks' lawyer."

"I know you are. I seen you going in and out."

"You're Mrs. Wetzel, aren't you? I'd like to come in and talk to you if I could."

"Mr. Little told me I didn't have to talk to you."

"Mr. Little?" Then he remembered: the kid carrying Barry D. Wentworth III's briefcase at the custody hearing.

"He said you'd be around bothering me. He said I didn't have to talk to you at all."

"You certainly don't. But you know Mr. Little and his boss are trying to take Diana away from her parents and put her into the hands of a convicted kidnaper."

Mrs. Wetzel stared. "They want to turn her back to her real mother."

"Who is a convicted kidnaper. She just spent twelve years in the penitentiary for kidnaping."

"Mr. Little said you might try to tell me terrible lies. He said she was wrongly accused for—for something."

"Kidnaping."

"Well, I just don't believe it. I know lawyers are supposed to try to trick people."

"May I come back in a day or two and bring you some material that'll prove it? Will you talk to me then?"

She stared at him without answering.

"Another thing, Mrs. Wetzel: did you ever see Diana with a little old man—a little man," he eyed her own white hair, "with white hair, kind of short, maybe wearing a black overcoat?"

"That's old Mr. Thaxton. Why, what's he been doing to her?"

"Who is he? Does he live around here?"

"He's old as the hills. I can't think he'd do her any harm. He's a little wrong in the head, but I've never heard of him doing anybody any harm."

"Well, we don't know that he's done her any harm. We want to find out. Do you know where he lives?"

"I've always said it was better for her to spend time with old Mr. Thaxton than with that drunken, vulgar father of hers. He lives down Sligo Creek somewhere."

9

Beyond the circle of light from Mrs. Wetzel's doorlamp the rush of wind somehow seemed to make the night darker, obscuring the waving, nodding, fluttering, and leaning shapes in the overgrown field across the street. As Bob was unlocking his car a sudden gust knocked his hat off; he caught a last glimpse of it tumbling over tall weeds and bushes into darkness.

He ran around the car and plunged into the field after it. It was a hundred-dollar hat from Woody's, barely a month old. Deep mud almost sucked his shoes off. He climbed onto a tussock, cursing. Brambles clung to his raincoat as he pushed forward, and riotous bushes shunted him to the left and right. He seemed suddenly far from civilization: there were no lights in sight, and the only sound was the wind in branches and leaves.

Or was there a deep growling too?

He froze, listening.

No, that was silly. It was the wind muttering some deep harmonic.

He thought he could make out his hat fifteen feet farther on, being worn jauntily by a waving bush.

He stumbled forward over roots and branches, hummocks and swamp.

Another growl froze him, close enough now to hear clearly in the wind, the gurgling of a huge, savage throat.

A big, dark shape moved behind the bush where his hat was.

A powerful, stinging smell filled his head.

Bob ran, forgetting his hat, forgetting everything until he was squealing his car up the hill toward Cedar Avenue. The smell was still strong around him, and that made him drive irrationally faster until he realized that it was raw garlic and was coming from his raincoat pocket.

He pulled out the tiny box he had taken from the Esterbrooks' window. The smell got strong enough to break the windows.

Halfway home he remembered to turn on his headlights. Sprinting up his front walk he realized he was missing a shoe.

He banged into the study, turned on all the lights, dialed 911. After the woman at the other end had taken his name and address and the location of the incident in slow motion, and told him to calm down, and he had insisted he was perfectly calm, he got to tell his story.

"Now, what *kind* of animal was it, Mr. Wilson?" the woman interrupted him for the third time.

"It was a—I don't know exactly. It was huge! Huge! Look, can't you get someone down there right away? It's going to escape while we're talking here!"

"You're sure it wasn't a person? You couldn't have made a mistake in the dark?"

"A person? How could it be a person? Now this is—I demand to talk to a real policeman! It was growling and snarling and—gurgling, sort of."

"And it attacked you? Are you hurt in any way?"

"No, no, I ran away when I smelled the garlic, and it was right on my heels probably."

"The garlic?"

"The—look, forget the garlic. I had it in my pocket. What I'm telling you is, there's some kind of huge animal in that field, and it was right behind the bush with my hat on it, and I ran away and it didn't get me. But it's a menace, I'm telling you!"

"The reason I'm asking, Mr. Wilson, is because we've had a number of calls about strange animals in Sligo Woods recently, but we've been all through the area with dogs and we haven't turned up anything except some claw prints our forensics people say have to be fake. We think probably some kids in a gorilla suit or something have been scaring people. So I'll send a car, but I wouldn't be too concerned if I were you."

Bob thought he had made enough noise to wake the dead, but Diana's door was still closed when he came out of the study. He tapped on it. "Diana?"

No answer. He tapped again, opened it an inch, and then wider. The room was dark and Diana wasn't there, but her computer was turned on. The monitor screen on her bed was a cauldron of the quasi-organic shapes he'd seen before, seething and unfolding and antivortexing, throwing weird shadows among the rumpled bedcovers.

He went upstairs, peeled off his muddy clothes and took a hot bath, then made himself a cup of hot milk and got in bed. He didn't hear Diana come back in, but he wasn't in the mood to worry about it. He turned out the lights to wait for Vicki, and fell immediately into a deep, exhausted slumber.

Sometime during the night he dreamed. He was back in Diana's room and her computer screen was boiling with shapes and patterns he recognized as fragments of his life floating up from its depths, but dismembered, distorted, barely recognizable. Soon the fragments started to fall together, and a picture formed. It was a picture of the street in front of his house. He was standing there in the quiet sunlight, a few birds singing, the distant hush of traffic from Thayer Avenue mundane and reassuring. He barely had time to reflect that this was the most familiar place in the world to him when another feeling came: a sudden, intense vertigo, as if he were tottering on the edge of a precipice.

Then, suddenly but without any abrupt transition, he was swimming; swimming through a vast, cool ocean, the sun at its zenith burning the waters a transparent zircon blue around him, so that he could see into their fathomless depths, and on their horizons nothing but the mist of distance. His vertigo intensified, until he saw that he was swimming not in water but through the swells and troughs of an endless space, the blue distances of it opening above and below and around him to infinity, and all vibrating with a sound; a sound so deep and powerful that he felt rather than heard it. And then he realized that it was the sound of space itself flowing in a tremendous cataract off the edge of the world—

"Aaah!" he yelled, and banged his head.

Vicki faced him in lamplight, sitting on the edge of the bed in her real-estate suit.

"Honey! Be careful." She rubbed his head where he had hit it on the headboard. "Are you okay? How did your clothes get covered with mud? And what's that horrible smell?"

He sat up and told her about the animal in the field. Her eyes got wide.

"—but the weirdest thing was the garlic box: it started to give off a smell—at first I thought it was the animal—but then there was no sign of it—like the smell chased it away. And I looked in the garlic and it had one of those talismans inside—"

With Vicki's arms around him Bob's sleep turned deep and dreamless, and when he woke up to the ringing of the downstairs phone he felt almost normal.

"Hello?" he answered it in the study. The clock on the rolltop desk said exactly ten o'clock.

"Good morning, Mr. Wilson," said Max Corrant. He

sounded like he was going to say something else. Then he paused.

The telephone had made a funny noise while he was talking, like a little squeak.

"This is Alvin Corrant, with Ball and Landau," Max went on. "Are you ready to look at the property we discussed yesterday?"

"What?"

"Great. I'll be by in half an hour, then. Thank you, Mr. Wilson."

He hung up.

Bob looked at the phone, then hung up too, wondering what was eating Max now.

He shuffled into the kitchen, puzzling about Max and watching little birds flutter and tumble around the feeder in the backyard. The clouds had blown away overnight and now thin, cheerful sunlight shone on a carpet of sodden brown and yellow leaves, the neighborhood quiet and peaceful. It didn't look like a place where wild animals chased you at night, mysterious old men and autistic children put Indian charms on your windows, and pubescent computer witches gave you nightmares.

And it probably wasn't, he reflected. There was undoubtedly a rational explanation for everything. On an impulse he went and knocked on Diana's door.

There was no answer.

Remembering suddenly that she hadn't been in there last night, he opened the door. The room was empty, dim and close, daylight coming faintly through drawn curtains, the computer monitor still in the same place on the bed kaleidoscoping with weird patterns. Diana's big book lay open next to it. Bob went in and picked it up curiously.

The cover was gray with plain black letters: *Principles of Thaumatomathematics*, by M. A. Al-Haq, Ph. D. The page it was open to contained a thicket of mathematical equations so dense he couldn't penetrate the first line, interspersed with short phrases in English like "Clearly, then,"

"It follows directly that," and "Thus, obviously." Bob flipped through the book. It was strange: sections heavy with incomprehensible mathematics were interspersed with sections of poetry, biology, even sections demonstrating yoga exercises, as well as glossy art prints. He studied one of the prints, a gorgeous blue, green, and pink detail from a canvass by some Impressionist. The caption read: "Note how the artist has captured regions of Type I and Type II turbulence with a complex phase boundary between. Because of the artist's deep intuitive comprehension of the behavior of real nonlinear bioaquatic systems, this rendering is an infinitely more precious subject of study than artificial, computer-generated renderings of turbulence and phase boundaries."

At the beginning of the book was a lengthy introduction. Bob started reading at random in the middle of it:

Sixty years ago Kurt Gödel and Alan Turing proved independently that no rational system of explanation can fully account for even the mathematical facts of our universe. That is, they proved that any path to Truth must leave the realm of the rational at some point. But where? And how?

Fortunately, irrationality is built deeply into human science. One need only reflect that the axioms of mathematics are based purely on intuition, and remember the testimony of many famous scientists that they were led to their discoveries by flashes of intuition and a sense of beauty. Here we begin to see an inkling of the truth: the apprehension of Truth is not the prerogative of the intellect alone; it is too great a matter for a single faculty; all the faculties must be employed to the utmost in the search for it, and all of them must be satisfied.

As we have seen, the rational intellect cannot establish first principles or primitive terms, since it relies on the prior existence of these to function at all. Is all then lost? Are the foundations of all our knowledge forever beyond our reach? I would argue that they are beyond the reach of the rational intellect.

If this is true, why have I written a *computer* book about the path to ultimate Truth?

A noise behind him made him jump. Vicki was standing in Diana's doorway in her robe, her hair tousled, looking at him with sleepy surprise. "What are you doing?" she asked.

"Honey, listen to this: 'It is because the computer is the mystical totem of the modern age. Every civilization has discovered at the basis of the universe its own most potent technology: in the seventeenth century the universe was a giant clockwork mechanism; in the age of Pythagoras and Euclid a construction of pure geometrical shapes; in the age of priests it was governed by gods and spirits. In like manner, modern observers have discovered in the universe a vast Computation. For our civilization, then, the computer has taken on the character of the shaman's drum, cut from the wood of the World Tree, which stands at the center of the universe and allows passage between Earth, Heaven, and the Underworld.'

"What do you think of that? A computer book about Earth, Heaven, and the Underworld. Doesn't it give you the creeps? Vicki, we've got to get her out of here, get rid of her. All this started when she came here; before that we were a normal, happy—"

Vicki came forward and ran a hand through his hair. "Shhh," she said. "You're still upset from that rabid dog last night, you poor thing." She kissed him. "You know, I've been thinking about that: I bet the garlic thing didn't give off a smell at all. You probably just stepped in a patch of skunk cabbage when you were running away. What do you want to bet?" She held out her hand.

He shook it slowly, staring at her.

"Where's Diana?" she asked.

"She's vanished again. Last night she—"

"I hope she's out getting some fresh air. She needs it. Do you think she sleeps? She's always working on this computer thing. All she ever *talks* about is computer stuff." She looked at the kaleidoscoping video screen, her brow furrowed.

"We've got to get her out of the house."

"Honey, it'll mess up your court case, remember? And anyway," her eyes shone, "if there *was* real magic, wouldn't it be *exciting*?"

As Bob headed for the upstairs shower, trying to think of an adequately negative response to that, she was pulling curtains and opening windows.

And she was in the basement putting some of Diana's clothes in the washing machine, and Bob had just dried off and gotten dressed, when the doorbell rang. It was Max Corrant wearing sunglasses, a tie on under his jacket.

"Go-o-od morning, Mr. Wilson," he said. "Ready to look at that property?"

"Max, what is—" Bob began, then stared at a piece of paper Max held in front of his chest. Handwritten block letters on it said: "YOUR HOUSE IS UNDER SURVEILLANCE. COME OUT TO THE CAR."

"OK," said Bob after a second. "Honey, I'm going out for a minute," he called over his shoulder, and followed Max along the front walk. The morning air was cool and clear, damp under the shade of the front yard trees. Max held the door of an old convertible Galaxy 500. The top was down and the interior was cluttered with magazines, tools, Kleenex boxes, and candy wrappers. There was a car phone tucked under the dashboard. Max got in and started the engine.

"You know an empty lot around here?" he asked. "We'll drive there and keep our cover."

"Max, what the hell is going on?"

Max slid the car away from the curb. "Check this dude in the white car as we go by. Don't turn your head to look at him, turn your eyes." A big man with sunglasses was reading a newspaper in a car by the corner. "There's another one just like him up the street on the other side." Max sounded happy and excited.

"Who are they, Wentworth's people?" Bob asked anxiously, thinking about Vicki alone in the house. "Should we call the police?"

"If I had to guess," said Max, "I'd guess they were the FBI."

"What?"

"The FBI. They mostly hire these white lawyer types. And that little beep on your phone; most people don't have the facilities to tap phones, but the FBI does."

"But why would the FBI be watching my house?"

"I don't know. You been running crack money across state lines?" He gave Bob a sideways smile. "Is there a house for sale or an empty lot around here?" he asked again. "In case we have a tail behind us."

"Straight ahead." They were headed down the hill toward Wayne. Bob guessed they could drive over to the field across from the Esterbrooks'. "But look, you must be mistaken about the FBI. That looked like a guy reading a newspaper to me."

Max drove slowly, so that the cool of the autumn air just balanced the thin warmth of the sun. He reached behind his seat and pulled out a folder, tossed it on Bob's lap.

"Those are the news stories you asked for about Armilla Robinson's kidnaping trial. You're going to like them. It caused a big sensation. Maybe the government is still interested in Ms. Armilla Robinson."

Bob leafed through a quarter-inch stack of photocopied clippings with headlines like "Couple Held in Vesperson Kidnaping," "Prosecution Charges Bizarre Rituals in Kidnaping Case," and "Torell-Robinson Trial Explodes in

Pandemonium." There were pictures that hadn't copied very well, one showing a younger Armilla Robinson and a short, haunted man with a shock of dark hair and a creased face, standing handcuffed between two large policemen. Armilla Robinson's face was scared and anguished, so beautiful it tore at Bob's insides.

"Torell was the guy she did the kidnaping with," Max summarized. "He was a doctor in this part of town so he got to see a lot of rich people's kids. He took it in his head to kidnap one of them, six-year-old adopted son of a banker named Vesperson. Wasn't a ransom thing—the prosecutor said they had some kind of child sex ring going, but it was never proved. The Robinson babe was the boy's nanny, live-in nursemaid, whatever. They never found the boy—he was presumed dead. Torell got the electric chair and the babe got fifty years as an accessory.

"She was good in court and Torell was bad. I read the reporter's notes in the newspaper files. He thought she was putting it on, but she tore the jury up. She cried, kept calling the boy 'poor little child,' and stuff like that. Torell just sat there like Frankenstein. She said he threatened her to keep her from telling the police. Torell went along with that until the very last day of the trial, when he blew up and started screaming that she had made him do it, she had hypnotized him, and that she had *eaten* the little boy—that was the word he used: 'eaten.' He was plain crazy. Result was he got fried and now she's out on parole."

There was silence while Bob looked through the clippings.

"Yech," he said finally.

"Yeah. Good, huh?"

"But it's all local. No interstate stuff or federal crimes. The FBI wouldn't be interested in it. You've been reading too many detective stories."

"Well, there's the angle about the sex ring or whatever," Max said defensively. "Or maybe she's already got herself hooked into some interstate trouble. Either way is good for us, isn't it?"

"I realize you don't have much experience with these things," Bob said coolly. "But think about it. I'm not Armilla Robinson. I'm not even representing her. They wouldn't tap *my* phone. Besides, it's illegal. Take a left here."

They slid down Pershing under big, half-naked trees. Max drove glumly. Everything was wet, glistening in the sunlight, the pavement plastered with leaves. At the bottom of the hill Bob pointed to the empty field running up the other side. Max parked across from Mrs. Wetzel's house. The Esterbrooks' old car was still missing from its driveway.

"I appreciate your concern for my telephone and so forth," Bob said patiently, wishing for the tenth time he had been able to afford a professional agency. "But you better just stick to the specific assignments I give you. Okay? Have you found out anything more than you just told me?"

"Not yet. My connection in Jonasburgh hasn't gotten back to me. But by Tuesday—"

Bob sighed. "Well, while we're down here I need to look for something I lost last night. Do you have a few minutes?"

They got out of the car. Bob stretched in the cool, washed air, relaxing. The FBI, garlic talismans, and huge wild animals all seemed impossible in this gentle suburban sunlight.

Max followed him as he picked his way gingerly into the field, hunting for dry places to put his feet. In the daylight the bushes, vines, and trees looked friendly in a tattered, frowzy sort of way, and here and there a bead of water caught the sun and sparkled like a jewel. The place had a wet, skunky, tangy smell. Skunk cabbage—Vicki was right again. After they had gone maybe ten yards, Max cursing softly as he put his deck shoes into bog holes, Bob suddenly had the feeling he had gotten the night before, of being far from civilization. There were no sounds of cars or people, and looking away from Pershing toward the woods that ran down into the Sligo Creek ravine there was no sign of the suburbs that stretched for miles in every direction. A chill went up his back as he wondered suddenly if a huge animal *could* be hiding in that tangled growth.

Then the spell was broken. A car cruised lazily down Pershing, making a sound as comfortably familiar to modern man as the sound of wind in leaves must have been to his ancestors.

"Hey, check this out," said Max.

Bob turned around. A man in sunglasses drove a nondescript car past the Galaxy 500. He paid no attention to Bob and Max.

Max swept his hand in a motion covering a big swatch of the field, moving his mouth slightly as if talking.

"Max, just because you're a detective doesn't mean everybody who drives by is watching you. Come on, I have to find my hat."

"Your hat? What's your hat doing out here?"

Bob picked his way through brambles, holding them so they wouldn't whip back on Max. "I was out here last night and a gust of wind blew it off—*there* it is."

It was cocked jauntily on a bush just as he had seen it the night before, looking good as new. A trampled place in the grass showed where Bob had run from the animal. His heart sped up, but there was no sign of anything dangerous among the tangled vines and tattered bushes. He advanced gingerly, trying to keep his feet out of the mud. Max circled around to the left where the ground looked drier. Bob shook water off his hat, turned it over a few times to make sure it was all right, and put it on his head.

"There should be a shoe somewhere around here too."

"Oh, your shoe blew off too—Gol damn!"

Max's roundabout path had brought him up behind the hat bush. Now he was leaning over and staring at the ground.

"What is it?" Bob asked, going over to look. "Holy Moses."

In the muddy ground behind the bush huge, taloned prints ran back into a dense thicket.

A clicking sound came into hearing. It was Bob's teeth chattering.

Max, who had squatted to examine the prints, looked up. "Mr. Wilson," he said. "Is there something you're not telling me about this case?"

"Let's get out of here."

They did, pulling a Florsheim wingtip out of the mud on their way. By the time they reached the car Bob had brought his teeth under control.

"Did those footprints look real to you?" he asked Max anxiously. "Like they were made by a real animal?"

"I guess so. But what kind of animal would that be?"

"That's exactly why they have to be fake," Bob argued. "It must be some kids fooling around with some fake footprint-things, see what I mean?"

"Well—"

"It's ridiculous to think it could have been real. How could a huge animal like that hide in a little patch of woods? It's impossible."

"You're right."

"Of course I'm right. Hold on a minute." Bob grabbed the newspaper clipping folder lying on the car seat, trotted across the street, and rang Mrs. Wetzel's doorbell. She opened the door with an alacrity that made him think she had been watching him and Max.

"Mrs. Wetzel, remember last night when I told you Mr. Little was trying to turn Diana over to a convicted kidnaper?"

"Mr. Little said—"

Bob thrust the folder at her. She took it eagerly.

"These are the news clippings about her trial for kidnaping, second-degree murder, conspiracy, and acting as an accessory to first-degree murder. I'll come back by and we'll talk about it."

She stared at his face as if she couldn't take her eyes off it.

"And Mrs. Wetzel," he asked, "have you ever seen animals—big animals—in the field across the street here?"

"Who is that colored man?" She was looking past him at where Max was sitting in his Galaxy 500.

"My real-estate agent."

"If you're thinking of buying lots in that field, it's old Mr. Thaxton's, and he won't sell. The developers were down again last year, but he won't even talk to them."

"How do you know it's Mr. Thaxton's?"

"It has been ever since I was a little girl," she said indignantly.

"Could it be his animals prowling around in there at night?"

"Oh, those aren't animals," she said scornfully. "The policeman told me it was some teenagers running around in monkey suits."

Back at the car, Max asked: "How's Mrs. Wetzel?"

Bob looked at him sharply, then remembered that he had studied Wentworth's file.

"She's fine. She thinks it's ridiculous to say there are huge animals running around here at night," Bob told him reprovingly.

Max sighed and started the car. Halfway up the hill Bob said: "Max, there's someone I want you to find for me. Just find, not break into their house or hide in the bushes or anything. Okay?"

Max's eyes lit up. "Who?"

"An old man named Thaxton. I don't know his first name. He lives down in the Sligo Creek area somewhere."

Max made a note in his little notebook as he drove. "What's his connection to the case?"

"There's no need for you to know that."

"Okay. Sure thing, boss." There was a trace of bitterness in his voice.

10

—

When they pulled up in front of the Wilson house, the man reading a newspaper in his car was gone.

"Come in for a minute," Bob told Max. "My wife can give you a better description of Thaxton than I can. She's seen him in the daylight."

They went up the front walk, Max straightening his tie and running his hands through his short hair self-consciously.

"Honey?" Bob called when they were inside. Then he saw a note on the side table: "Gone to get milk. Back in a minute."

"Oh, she's gone to the store," Bob told Max. "Well, I guess I can describe him—he's about so tall, with white hair, blue eyes—"

The doorbell rang.

Bob opened it, still talking.

"—a black overcoat—"

It was a very large square man in a dark suit, with sunglasses and brush-cut hair.

"Robert Wilson?" he asked.

"Yes?"

"Special Agent James Kozlowski, with the Federal Bureau of Investigation." He held a leather wallet with a badge and photo ID in front of Bob's face. "I'd like to come in and ask you a few questions if I may." The square jaw said he was coming in whether Bob liked it or not.

"Well—sure," Bob said with blank surprise, and got out of the way while he did, then watched Special Agent Kozlowski suspiciously study a widely grinning Max Corrant, who had put his own sunglasses back on.

The Special Agent ended up nodding fairly politely. "Jim Kozlowski," he said expectantly.

"Nice to meet you," said Max.

"This is Max Corrant, my—uh—real-estate agent," Bob said. "What can I do for you, sir?"

"Well, it's rather confidential, Mr. Wilson." He looked pointedly at Max.

The doorbell rang again. Special Agent Kozlowski answered it before Bob could move. Vicki, in jeans and a linen shirt, stood there holding a couple of grocery bags. She stared up at Kozlowski in surprise.

"My wife," Bob explained as she came in. "Honey, this is Special Agent Kozlowski and Max Corrant."

"Oh, the detective!" she said, flushing with happiness and excitement. "Have you found the little Indian man?"

Max didn't answer. He was still grinning.

"Won't everyone sit down?" said Vicki. "Can I get you some tea? Mr. Corrant? Mr. Kowalski? I'll put the water on."

She hurried into the kitchen.

A few minutes later they were sitting around a plate of cookies at the dining room table, drinking tea out of the best china cups.

"You can speak freely in front of my wife, of course," Bob told Kozlowski. "And Mr. Corrant is handling a case for me connected with the matter you want to discuss, if it's what I think it is." He had recovered his wits enough to puzzle it out in a hurry. And something about Special Agent Kozlowski—his size, maybe—made Bob want to keep Max Corrant around while he talked.

"I thought he was a real-estate agent," Kozlowski rumbled.

"I have my real-estate license too," said Max. "You know how it is when business is slow." He laughed loudly as if he had made a joke.

"It's Larry Abercrombie, isn't it," Bob said shrewdly. "The device I gave him to take to the Naval Lab."

Kozlowski glanced around the table, then decided to talk.

"Well, yes it is, Mr. Wilson," he said, and took off his sunglasses to show a pair of surprisingly frank and serious pale blue eyes, "and the only question I really need to ask you is: where did you get it?"

Max took off his sunglasses too. His black eyes were bright with interest.

"Are they valuable?" gasped Vicki. "Were they stolen from a museum or something?"

"You have more than one, then, Mrs. Wilson?"

"Well—yes," she said, crestfallen, looking at Bob.

"Can I see the others?"

"We have *two* others," Bob said firmly. "Could you get them, honey? Has Larry figured out what they are, Mr. Kozlowski?"

"Well, they're just what you said, Mr. Wilson: electronic devices."

"They are not," called Vicki indignantly from the rolltop desk in the study where they had put the garlic things. "They're Indian talismans. I'll show you the book that proves it."

"What kind of electronic devices?" Bob asked Kozlowski.

"I'd rather keep that confidential just for now. Suffice it to say that there's a national security issue involved."

"They were stolen from somewhere? The government?"

"No, it's not that. It's just that they're—well, very advanced devices that use technologies that aren't fully developed yet. That's about all I can tell you. But that's also why it's imperative that we find out where they came from. Now, we've done a background check on you folks, and we have no reason to suspect that you'd be involved in espionage or technology transfer or anything of that nature, and that's why I'm coming in here up front and asking you where you got them."

Bob had been a lawyer long enough to know veiled threats when he heard them; but he also knew there was no law against being cagey.

"Let's make a deal," he said to Special Agent Kozlowski. "You want to know where I got the devices. I'm dying to know what they are. That's a fair trade, isn't it?"

Max's grin was wider than ever, fixed on Bob with surprised respect, but Kozlowski's eyes were chilly.

"Let me remind you that this is an important national security matter," he said. "Frankly, your attitude surprises me, Mr. Wilson. I'd like to hear why you're so desperate to know what the devices are."

"Here they are," announced Vicki, dumping a device, a clove of garlic, and a book on the table in front of Kozlowski. His hand went to the device quickly; he took a folding magnifying glass with a built-in flashlight out of his pocket and studied it through that.

"Are there more?" he asked, looking at Vicki.

"In the garlic."

He stared at her.

Bob said: "All three of the devices came sliced into cloves of garlic."

"And look," said Vicki, holding the shaman magic book open to the picture of the talisman. "It says right here that the Indians used to use them that way."

There was silence while Kozlowski took the book and studied it slowly, then looked at the device, then back at the book.

"Do you see why we're kind of curious about them?" Bob asked.

There was more silence while Kozlowski studied the clove of garlic with his magnifying glass, found the slit in the side, worried at it with his fingernails, and looked at the book again. When he finally raised his eyes they were mystified. He said: "If I tell you something about them, I have to have your solemn word it won't go any further. Do I have that?"

They all murmured eagerly that he did.

"Not to friends, relatives, coworkers, anyone, is that clear?"

It was.

"The Naval Lab sent the device on to an advanced electronics research facility last night. They're still doing tests, but it looks like the device is an extremely advanced gain transducer."

That meant nothing to Bob, and he said so.

"A transducer is a device that transforms one kind of energy into another. In this case, electromagnetic waves into physical vibration. The device actually seems to be tuned to a specific electromagnetic signature. *And* it can amplify the output, within limits. Imagine a device that can pick up the faint waves given off by a particular person's brain, and respond by vibrating. Can you see why the government would like to be able to build a device like that? Can you see why they would worry if somebody else had built one?"

He looked around the table.

"What particular person's brain waves do the devices respond to?" Bob asked.

Kozlowski shook his head seriously. "I can't tell you any more, Mr. Wilson. I've told you too much already because I'm gambling that you're loyal citizens of this country, and because we need to get this information *now*, without a lengthy investigation. Who knows, this very minute foreign agents may be booby-trapping our country in unbelievable ways. The mischief-making potential of these devices is just about limitless."

"But they're Indian charms," said Vicki plaintively. "Look at the book."

She held it in front of his face for him.

"I don't know what that means, if it's anything more than a coincidental resemblance, Mrs. Wilson," said Kozlowski. "But you can be sure we'll check it out. Now, Mr. Wilson."

Bob talked. He told Kozlowski about the Esterbrooks, the custody case, Diana, Thaxton, and the garlic on the window molding in Diana's room.

"Could he have been trying to pass the devices to her in that way?" Kozlowski asked, writing rapidly in a little notebook. Max looked fidgety, like he wanted to write in his own notebook but thought he'd better not.

"Certainly not," said Vicki. "She's just a little girl, not a spy. And anyway, why would he leave them on top of her windows in garlic? Why not just hand them to her on her way home from school, or mail them to her?"

"Where is she now?"

"We don't know."

"Has anyone else seen the devices besides the four of you and Mr. Abercrombie?"

Bob told him about the lady in the Indian craft shop.

Kozlowski finished writing. "Can I see the room where Thaxton placed the devices?"

They led him to that room.

It was bright now, curtains wide. Vicki had tidied up and made the bed. Diana's computer sat on the bed table, the roiling hieroglyphics on the monitor washed pale and unobtrusive in the sunlight.

"A computer program she wrote," Bob explained to Kozlowski.

"I found them up there," Vicki told him, pointing. "On top of the molding above the windows."

"May I—?"

Bob pushed a chair under the window and Kozlowski

climbed onto it, started looking up and down the molding without touching it. The others stood and watched him.

"Sort of over on the right side," Vicki said.

Kozlowski got out his magnifying glass and started to look at the right side.

A sudden gasp made Bob turn. Everybody turned.

Diana Esterbrook was sitting cross-legged on her bed in jeans and a sweatshirt, breathing as if she had run up three flights of stairs. Her eyes were focused on the air two feet in front of her.

Special Agent Kozlowski lost his balance. Max and Bob caught him, helped him down from the chair. He was heavy, hard.

There was silence while everybody stared.

"Hi, Diana," Vicki said timidly. "Where've you been, honey?"

Diana gazed into the air.

"Is this the girl?" Kozlowski muttered to Bob. "Diana Esterbrook?"

Bob nodded.

Vicki went and sat on the edge of the bed next to her.

"Where was she?" hissed Kozlowski. "She must have been hiding."

He went down on one knee quickly and looked under the bed.

Vicki smoothed Diana's hair. "Are you okay, honey? We didn't know you'd gone out. You should tell us."

Kozlowski strode over and opened the closet door. Diana's green high school jacket, a shirt, and two pairs of pants hung there innocently. He went to the bed and stood over Diana.

"Were you in the closet?" he demanded.

She opened her mouth and out of it came a song. Her voice was clear, light, haunting. It was the song the lady in the Indian craft shop had sung.

"Ms. Esterbrook?" said Kozlowski. "Ms. Esterbrook, I'm talking to you."

"Diana?" Vicki smoothed back her hair. "Diana, wake up."

The doorbell rang. Bob went out agitatedly to answer it.

It was Derek and Nora Esterbrook. Nora's hair was disarranged, her face gray, eyes wild. By contrast, Derek's hair was carefully oiled and combed, his eyes bright and crafty. He had on a brown leather jacket.

"I'll give you two minutes to bring my daughter out here." He held up two fingers in Bob's face. In the chilly air alcohol reeked on him like perfume.

Bob stepped out the door and closed it quickly. "Nora, for God's sake get him out of here. If he causes a ruckus—"

"Who's causing a ruckus? *You're* causing a ruckus," Derek blustered.

"There's a *policeman* in the house—"

"Derek, honey—" Nora said in a trembling voice, putting her hand on his arm.

"Don't touch me," Derek yelled at her, shaking her hand off violently, like a little boy shaking off his mother's hand. "I know what you've been doing with him. I'm not blind. I know what you two've been doing together. And believe you me, I know what to do about it too."

His eyes protruded at Bob. "I know what you're doing with my little girl too. I know child pornography when I see it." He leaned forward and pointed at the door. "Open that door or I'll whip you like a dog again."

He started to undo his belt.

A lawyer must act at all times in the best interests of his client, say the American Bar Association Rules of Ethics. But a human being can take only so much. Bob Wilson opened his front door and stood aside.

As Derek Esterbrook swaggered into the house there was a cry from the guest room.

"Diana? Diana? Hold on, baby, daddy's coming!"

Derek roared, and his feet thumped on the carpet. Bob and Nora followed him.

As they reached the guest room, Special Agent Kozlowski was pulling Diana's sweatshirt off, leaving only a T-shirt underneath. Vicki told Bob later that he had wanted to check her for needle marks.

Derek roared and flung himself at Kozlowski.

Kozlowski reacted instantly, caught though he was caught off guard in the middle of his national security investigation. His enormous fist collided with the side of Derek's head, sending him tumbling to the floor like a bag of wet laundry. Bob, unprofessionally, felt the impact as a wild cheer he was able to repress only with difficulty.

Nora gave a rasping scream and threw herself at Kozlowski. It took a minute of stumbling around holding her arms and trying to stay away from her teeth and feet for Kozlowski to shove his ID in her face and tell her she was subject to arrest for assaulting an FBI agent. Then he looked at Bob with bitter suspicion.

"These are Ms. Esterbrook's parents," Bob introduced them.

Moaning, Derek Esterbrook pushed himself into a sitting position and began to vomit violently on the rug.

That evening was windless, the sky clear except for a few bands of clouds that caught the sunset in shades of yellow and pale orange. Crickets trilled in the chilly air. Bob Wilson stood on his back deck after dinner looking up into the deepening blue, stiff muscles in his neck and shoulders gradually relaxing. He had been heavily traumatized by the day's events, he realized, though things had ended quietly enough. After a short, murmured conference with the three other large, besunglassed FBI agents who had appeared suddenly at the front door as if psychically aware of his row with Derek Esterbrook, Special Agent Kozlowski had become gracious, almost jovial. Far from arresting

Derek, the Special Agent had expressed the hope that he wasn't hurt; then he and the others had shaken hands all around and left, taking the two garlic devices with them. Nothing more had been said about Diana, her tie-in with the devices, or her mysterious appearance in her room, but the FBI's sudden cordiality made Bob suspicious.

On the positive side, Kozlowski's wallop seemed to have sobered Derek Esterbrook up; he had sat in the living room limp and miserable, staring at the rug with anguished, guilty eyes as his wife and Vicki cleaned his vomit off the guest room floor and tucked Diana in for a nap—since, after bringing the FBI down on the Wilson household like a ton of bricks, she had decided she was terribly sleepy, perhaps from what her mother called the "shock of seeing her father beaten like an animal by that horrible man."

All in all, Bob reflected, it seemed like years since the unhappy moment when he had opened his front door on Nora Esterbrook and her family troubles. At least she had had the decency to take herself and her husband off home as soon as Diana had gone to sleep.

He took a deep lungful of cool air and went indoors. Vicki was curled up on the living room sofa, engrossed in the shaman magic book.

"I'm going for a walk," he told her. "What are people supposed to do when they're under surveillance? I'm having a terrible time acting natural. It was so easy before, but I never noticed how I did it. Now that our whole future may depend on it, I've lost the knack. I keep looking around suddenly and doing suspicious things. I just can't help it."

"Will you stop worrying?" Vicki laughed. She got up and pressed herself against him in her casual, catlike way, kissed him. "We haven't done anything wrong. If anybody's in trouble, it's your clients, not you."

"How do you think she did that?" Bob asked anxiously, lowering his voice. "Appeared in the middle of the

room from nowhere? Honey, we're living in the same
house with a—"

"Well, she couldn't have appeared from *nowhere*."
Vicki lowered her voice too. "Did you hear how she was
breathing? She'd been running. She must have run in
when we were all watching Officer Kowalski show us how
he could balance on a chair. But why was she in such a
state? It was like she was in a trance."

"Can't we get rid of her?"

Vicki began to pout. "This is the first interesting thing
that's happened to me in years, Bob. I mean, don't you
ever feel there's something missing from our lives? Isn't
there any more to life than just—this?" She gestured
around at what Bob thought was a rather nicely appointed
living room.

He went into the foyer shaking his head. A white envelope lay on the doormat. Scrawled on it were the words
"Bob Wilson."

He tore it open, heart thumping. Inside was a note:

Mr. Bob Wilson:
You and your wife and that little girl better not go
out after dark, because it's not Safe. Believe me I
know what I am talking about better than you
think. Please listen to me. Stay indoors at Night. I
am, sincerely,

> One who wants to protect you,
> Wendall Thaxton

"What's wrong?" Vicki asked when he came back into
the living room.

He gave her the note.

She read it and her eyes got big and she sat up.

"Thaxton. That's the little man, right? What does he
mean by this?"

"I don't know. I guess he's trying to scare us. We'd

better show it to the police." He looked out the window at the deepening dusk. "Anyway, I'm going for a walk."

"But he says it's not safe."

"We can't let some little nut intimidate us into staying in the house all the time, can we?" said Bob angrily. "I'm getting tired of being the powerless victim of uncanny forces. If we can't take a walk in our own neighborhood, then that little creep has beaten us. Well, he's not going to get away with it!"

11

The cricket-trilled dusk was chilly. Bob peered carefully up and down the deserted street for signs of Thaxton or the vague dangers he had warned about, then wondered uncomfortably whether he had looked suspicious doing it. No FBI agents were in evidence; though with Thaxton on the loose, having the FBI watch his house wouldn't be all bad, Bob realized.

Not that he needed protection in his own neighborhood, he thought defiantly, starting up the sidewalk. He passed the Ranellis' and the Proutmans', their resolutely middle-class front yards stolid and reassuring. He was on his home turf here, where he knew every crack in the sidewalk, every tree-shaded brick and wooden Colonial, where he was surrounded by his neighbors—though Larry Abercrombie *had* put the FBI onto him, he realized with an unpleasant feeling, as if he had discovered a chink in his armor. Larry probably hadn't had any choice, though, once the people at his lab had gotten a look at the garlic device.

Keeping an eye on the shadows behind hedges and between parked cars, Bob took a left at the corner of Shope and headed in the general direction of the Abercrombies'. He wouldn't go to their house, since that might look suspicious; but sometimes Larry took evening walks, and if they met Bob could ask him what had happened.

The sheer familiarity of the street—the unruly trees hanging over the Taylors' head-high, untrimmed hedge, the root-tilted place in the sidewalk where grass grew up, the smells of wet fallen leaves and wood smoke from a chimney, the chill, damp air—relaxed him more than any scientific refutation of the supernatural could have done. It was ridiculous to think that anything uncanny could happen in a place like this; your mind could play tricks on you, that was all, and you could imagine things if you let yourself. Like the rustling in the Taylors' hedge that had just made him jump: some small animal he had startled, probably, though you could believe you had seen a shadow move if you insisted on it.

He turned left again on Stewart, and was in the "less-kept-up" part of the neighborhood. The houses here were mostly older brick ramblers, some of their lawns unmown, and there were cars up on cinder blocks in a few oil-stained driveways. The sounds and shouts of driveway basketball came from a block away through the still air.

A streetlight flickered into illumination above him, throwing a sudden shadow across the street, for all the world as if something big had slipped over a high board fence that willow branches shaded.

Bob's scrutiny of the fence was interrupted by a figure cannonballing down the sidewalk toward him. A boy, hollering over his shoulder in a voice that made the neighborhood echo: "My mom wants me home by dark!" The sound of the basketball game had resolved itself into solo dribbling and the *thwung* of a garage-hung basket. The boy shot past Bob and was lost in the dusk.

Up ahead the street dead-ended at the finger of Sligo Creek woods that still penetrated into this part of suburbia, its cool, musky vegetation smell coming to him twenty yards away. The last house before the dead end was a small, elderly rambler barely visible in the deep dusk amid the untamed trees and bushes that seemed a spillover of the woods into its yard. Vines wrapped a rusty, leaning wire fence along the sidewalk as if to throw it down and burst from their prison.

As Bob walked next to the fence, leaves rustled in the undergrowth on the other side, as if something moved in the night darkness under the trees.

He stopped, heart pounding suddenly, eyes and ears straining into the shadows.

A growl came from the darkness behind the fence, not loud, but close, almost intimate in its ferocious desire.

Bob was frozen. He knew suburbia was right behind him, a world of streetlights and houses just ten steps backward, but he couldn't move.

The rustling in the leaves was louder now, and as he watched a shape pushed forward, breaking the surface of the darkness and leaves, and in his terror seeming to float toward him, pale eyes and lupine teeth snarling—

A roar exploded and a black shape rushed past Bob, stopping just ahead of him to hunch and bark deafeningly, its intakes of breath slavering snarls, its hackles and tail standing up stiffly.

"Rudolph!"

The spell broken, Bob ran, the neighborhood a black-and-blue blur around him pierced with lights. Rudolph ran too, keeping up with him in a stiff-legged lope, turning every few seconds to bark back at the dark yard.

When they had put three blocks between themselves and the yard, Bob stopped running, out of breath. The street behind him was empty. He squatted and hugged Rudolph.

"Am I glad to see you," he gasped, and Rudolph wagged his tail. "Good dog. Good dog."

A small, cold hand touched his. He yelled and jumped upright.

A little redheaded boy stood looking seriously at Bob's chest.

"Zachary! Where did you come from?"

"Fontina," said Zachary, and he took Bob by the hand and pulled.

Bob didn't need much urging; they went together up the sidewalk toward Shope Avenue. The streetlights showed nothing moving behind them, but each time Bob turned to look Rudolph growled, as if reminded of their mutual enemy.

"We've got to get you home, Zach," Bob said, as much to steady his nerves as anything, since you could rarely tell if Zachary understood a word you said. "Something weird is going on out here. Either that or old Mr. Wilson is losing his mind."

Yet for all the world it seemed to be Zachary who was taking *Bob* home, tugging on his hand, a serious, responsible look on his small, round face.

"It's late. Where did you pop out of, anyway?" Bob asked him again.

"Fontina," said Zachary again.

"Okay, you popped out of Fontina. Did you come to rescue me? You ought to give Rudolph a reward, Zach. He saved me from a big animal that was out to bite me back there." The same animal he had encountered in the field across from the Esterbrooks'? The thought made his heart pound again.

Walking fast, it took them five minutes to get to the Taylors' hedge. The streetlight made dark shadows of the yard beyond.

"Here we go," said Bob trying to steer Zachary up the steps leading to the cracked front walk. But Zachary resisted; he seemed to still want to pull Bob along the sidewalk. Rudolph bounded around them, whining.

"Hey," said Bob, holding Zachary back. "This is where you're going, young man. You have to go home."

"Home," echoed Zachary, pulling on Bob.

"Yes, I'm going home after you go inside. But you can't stay wandering around out here."

"Rudolph," said Zachary solemnly.

"Okay, I'll take Rudolph with me," said Bob. "Come on, Rudolph. Now you go on, Zach, and let me see you go inside."

Zachary grabbed Rudolph first and hugged him, rubbing his face into the fur of the dog's muscular shoulders. Then he went up the walk, climbed the wooden steps to the porch, opened the front door, and went in.

"Come on, Rudolph," said Bob, glad to have him along on the walk back to his house. Rudolph seemed to understand his assignment perfectly; he trotted alongside Bob with his head held up alertly, claws clicking on the sidewalk. A couple of times he stopped and sniffed the air, a low growl coming into his throat. When they got to the Wilson yard, Bob squatted and hugged him again.

"Good dog. Good dog. Go home now. Go home." Rudolph whined and batted at him with a huge paw. "I'm all right now. You can go home."

Rudolph suddenly seemed to understand. He turned and trotted away.

Bob had started up his walk under the half-naked trees when there was a flash, blinding white and silent like a hundred flashbulbs going off at once, throwing the abrupt, sharp-edged silhouette of Diana's window through the side yard.

Bob rushed inside, shouting for Vicki. She ran down the stairs wide-eyed.

"Fire in Diana's room!" he yelled. "That damn computer—!"

They banged open the guest room door.

There was no fire. The room was empty, dark and still except for the monitor on the bed, which seemed to be in free fall through endless canyons of fantastic, hallucinatory undersea shapes.

"Diana?" Vicki said, and for the first time Bob thought she sounded a little scared. "She was just in here."

They advanced slowly into the room, Bob switching on the light. Vicki looked in the closet and he checked under the bed.

"There was a flash in here," Bob said grimly. "I saw it when I was coming up the walk."

"A flash?" asked Vicki shakily. "What kind of flash?"

"A flash. A flash of light. Could she have sneaked out?"

"I guess so. What's that smell?"

They both sniffed intensely.

"Garlic," said Bob, a sudden realization coming over him. "Garlic, just like—from the box outside the window. The garlic thing."

"Bob, something weird is going on."

"No, you think so?" he said maliciously. "I think it's just skunk cabbage and some kids dressed up in a gorilla suit."

"What should we do? Call the police?" Her voice was small and breathless, like a little girl's.

"You're not getting scared, are you? Because if you are, I'm going to fall apart."

"I wish I'd married someone strong and brave," she said blankly, still in her lost little-girl voice.

They fit together easily in each others' arms, like nested spoons. He nuzzled her, rocking her from side to side.

Something caught his eye and his start made her jump. A book lay open on the bed next to the weirdly onrushing vistas of the computer screen.

"*Principles of Thaumatomathematics*," he exclaimed. "Honey, this is the book that tells her how to do this stuff. If we could understand it, maybe we could figure out what's going on."

He picked up the book and they pored over it anxiously. Vicki's brow furrowed when she saw the dense rows of equations. "She reads that? But honey, she's just a little girl."

"That's where you're wrong," said Bob grimly. He flipped to a page where there were words instead of equations. "Listen:

" 'How is it, then, that frail women can sometimes, in moments of overwhelming emotional stress, lift automobiles into the air to rescue their trapped children, that otherwise mentally deficient persons can calculate huge prime numbers faster than a computer, that others, without any training, can sculpt perfect likenesses of wild animals they have only seen for a second, that yogis can sleep naked in the subzero snows of the Himalayan mountains without ill effects? Remember that these people, as well as the likes of Newton and Einstein, who were electrified with crystalline visions of nature's soul, possess only the same 'three pounds of meat' within their skulls that you and I possess. The difference between them and us, then, can only be a difference in how this hardware is used—in short, a software difference. But software, as everyone knows, is easily modified.' "

"What is he talking about?" asked Vicki, frowning.

"Magic. Paranormal powers. Don't you see? This book is about how to develop paranormal powers using a computer. Diana said something like that before."

"Well, what are we going to *do*?" Vicki asked, looking into his eyes anxiously.

He pulled her out into the hall and closed Diana's door, held both her hands.

"She could have gone out while you were upstairs," he said. He decided not to tell her what had happened on his walk; not now.

"Yes."

"The flash could have been that damn computer screen. Who knows what she has it programmed to do? Or maybe it's malfunctioning."

"Uh-huh."

"She might be trying to scare us. I'd believe anything about her, having seen her parents."

"But why would—"

There was a sound that made them both jump: a doorknob turning. The guest room door opened and Diana Esterbrook came out, still wearing the jeans and sweatshirt she had taken her nap in. She was flushed and breathing hard, her hair disheveled.

Her eyes passed over their shocked faces and she gave them a small, distracted smile.

"Hi, sweetie," said Vicki in a small voice.

Diana went down the hall and across the living room in the direction of the kitchen. In a second there was a clink of cups and the sound of the refrigerator opening.

There was no way she could have gotten into the guest room through the windows, Bob was thinking confusedly; even if she had unlocked one, they were too high off the ground to climb into. He was equally sure she hadn't been hiding in the room.

He started to whisper to Vicki, but she said out loud: "You go on, honey, if you're tired. I think I'll have some hot chocolate with Diana." Her eyes, suddenly bright with a curiosity that seemed to have displaced her fear, were fixed in the direction of the kitchen. He tried silently to argue with her. She made shooing gestures and pinched him really hard on the arm.

It was only seven-thirty, too early for bed even if there hadn't been a witch in the house. For a while Bob sat at the top of the stairs straining to hear what was going on in the kitchen, but all he caught were the clink of cups and the murmur of voices. It seemed to be a friendly murmur, but the idea of Vicki sitting across the table from someone who might vanish with a flash made him deeply uneasy. He told himself for the hundredth time not to be ridiculous, that there was some rational explanation for everything, but even as he thought that he realized that his belief in it was slipping away, leaving him with a slight case of vertigo, as though the staircase he sat on were a steep cliff.

What about what had happened on his walk, for example? The little man in black—Wendall Thaxton—had warned them not to go out at night, and then some kind of animal had menaced him again at the edge of Sligo Creek woods. And Zachary Taylor and Rudolph had rescued him, marched him back home for all the world as if they knew exactly what they were doing.

But that could be explained without magic or monsters, Bob argued to himself. The animal was probably a stray bobcat or bear that had taken up residence in the woods; he had read of such things in the newspaper. Rudolph would certainly bark at such an animal. And Zachary might have shown up for no particular reason, which was the explanation for most of the things he did.

Bob got up and puttered restlessly around his dark bedroom. He felt strangely distant from everything, isolated, as if the second floor of his own home were a space station orbiting far out in dark regions. He considered calling Max Corrant, even the Esterbrooks, just to have somebody to talk to, but then remembered that his phone was probably bugged. He went and looked out each window on the floor in turn, trying to spot FBI agents. In charcoal-gray suburban darkness he saw the side of the Lehrers' house next door; his own shadowed backyard through a crisscross of branches; the peak of the Ranellis' house with telephone wires; and the street, framed in more branches, with a splash of greenish streetlight, cars parked along the curb. The four corners of Bob Wilson's life. Take them away and what would you have? Or drop Bob Wilson into a place where there were no streets or trees at all, no houses or neighbors or cars, only a "phase space" where equations standing for those things swirled, and what would you have? A world where you could do anything you wanted by changing an equation? Was that *this* world?

He turned away from the window trying to shake off

these melancholy thoughts, as well as his strange feeling of
loneliness. He looked at his watch. It was almost eight-
thirty. He went into the bathroom to run a bath, and was
arrested by his reflection in the mirror.

At first, out of long habit, it posed and looked intelligent, but slowly as he stared the pose wore off and he just
stood and looked at himself. Studied himself. He was getting wrinkles around his eyes, he saw, and there were faint
creases in the forehead, and small, almost invisible lines at
the edges of the mouth, though the hair was still brown.
Did the whites of the eyes seem yellower and more veined
than they had ten years ago? He looked into the eyes
deeply. Who was it, anyway? under all that flesh, under
the changes the years had wrought, and the changes the
future would bring, making him more and more wrinkled
and stooped, and finally—

He turned on the bath water, shaking himself. When
you started staring in mirrors and wondering who you
were it was time to go on a vacation, take up a hobby,
organize a dinner party.

Yet, strangely, looking in the mirror he had gotten a
feeling, just for a moment, that he hadn't had in years—for
so long, in fact, that he had forgotten its existence, the
very possibility of feeling that way. It was a feeling from
his adolescence, blowing into his mind as if someone had
suddenly thrown open the window of a musty room where
he had been sitting for years, and behold! spring was in
full bloom outside. It was a feeling of—well, it was hard to
describe. Not because it was complicated, but because of
its contrast with the familiar furniture of his mind—the
balanced, rational, self-confident feelings that had come
comfortably to surround him. He tried to articulate it, absently testing the temperature of the bath water, and found
himself thinking back on things he hadn't remembered in
years: a kid with long hair and patched jeans and no girlfriend, who slept the days away on his summer vacations

and stayed up until dawn watching late TV or reading Dostoyevsky on the screen porch as the night breeze blew.

His mind, focusing now intently on the feeling and striving to make it concrete, reconstructed a scene; reconstructed it gently and haltingly, as if from spare parts and backup files, as if it were a memory that had long ago been discarded, that had never been meant to be recalled. He had been fourteen or fifteen, and staying at his grandmother's seaside house for the summer. The house had a half basement floored with brown tile and paneled with elderly varnished pine, and small, high windows that opened close to a lawn that ran to the edge of the wooded bluff overlooking the beach, so that you could sit down there on hot summer days, the tiles cool on your feet, and hear the washing of surf and cries of seagulls and children playing on the beach, and feel the breeze faintly perfumed by hot grass and flowers and the vast, fresh smell of the ocean. And on one of those days lost in the ocean of days he had sat in that room alone, in the late morning he thought it was, and a feeling had come over him, an elation and illumination, bringing with it a vision of the space around him opening out into the vast landscape in a million directions, onto the vast, sparkling ocean, the bluff that stretched out into haze along the coast, the cedar fence hiding the driveway, and beyond it the dusty dirt road up to the state highway, and each centimeter of all that opening into further infinite directions and permutations, and in fact changing even as he watched, the trees waving languidly, the waves breaking, all exploring a limitless expanse of possibilities. Somewhere in that limitless expanse was a beautiful girl with flashing eyes like the sun on water; there were houses nestled in soft blue nights, each containing its own story; there were cities and forests; roads baking in sunlight leading to places beyond imagining—all contained in the quietness and motionlessness of that moment in his grandmother's house. It had been a feeling of the infinite depth, the infinite *directionality* of life. Somehow with the memory came a pang of grief, of intense nostalgia, as if in growing older that depth and those directions had been lost.

Baffled, Bob took a long, hot bath, the feeling ebbing as he tried to analyze it. Like the "Truths" the Thaumatomathematics book babbled about, he mused, that couldn't be grasped by the rational mind. Strange, though. He was happy here in his suburban home with Vicki, his job, and his comfortable lifestyle. Wasn't he? Strange too that after all the weird, scary stuff that had happened today he could only sit in his bathtub and have some kind of midlife crisis, grieving for his lost youth or something.

He finally dragged himself out of the bath to brush his teeth and put on pajamas. He listened at the top of the stairs again for a couple of minutes, then got in bed.

The next thing he knew someone's tongue was in his ear. He came awake with a jolt and grabbed bare shoulders.

"Honey!" he whispered, recognizing the naked woman straddling him. He relaxed back on his pillow, dark silky hair brushing his face. "Did Diana tell you anything?"

"Yes," Vicki whispered. "Kiss me."

He kissed her. "What did she tell you?"

"A lot of things. I love you, baby."

"I love you too. Like what? What things? Anything about that flash of light?"

"You're certainly romantic," Vicki said.

She studied him in the dark, then rolled off him onto her side, lay there with her head propped on one hand.

"Well, for one thing, she thinks *you're* the cat's meow," she said after studying him for another minute.

"What do you mean?"

Her shape in the dark was smoothly curved, as beautiful as the sea or the galaxies.

"You helped her with her computer program, she says. I didn't know you knew anything about that stuff."

"I don't. What do you mean I helped her?"

"She says you suggested something called a 'phase transition.' Something to do with going into a different stage or something."

"Oh, but that was—I was trying to humor her when she thought her computer was telling her she was going to die."

"Well, this 'phase transition' has made her program work a hundred times better than before, so you only have yourself to blame for whatever it does. She says it's exactly what she needed to break through to the next level—that's what she said, don't ask me what it means. The new program still says something's going to happen to her soon, though, something unusual. And that's where she starts getting all happy and flushed and secretive."

"She wouldn't tell you what she's doing?"

"She's thinking about reincarnation, for one thing. She says she's trying to remember a past life. The chant that lady in the store sang made her remember bits and pieces of it. She thinks maybe she was an Indian princess."

"An Indian princess? That sounds like one of those newspapers at the grocery store. Did she say how she made that flash of light?"

"She didn't know there had been a flash of light. She seemed very interested in it, though. She asked me what it looked like and whether there was any sound and a bunch of other things."

"Well, what did she do that she didn't know made a flash of light? Don't tell me you let her get away with just telling you she didn't know there was a flash of light."

"She wouldn't say much more. It took me hours to get that much out of her. Just that—well, she thinks she's doing magic."

"How?" His stomach tightened. "With that computer?"

"That's what she says. She launched into all kinds of jargon." Vicki frowned in the dark. "When I asked her to explain it she said there's a kind of mathematics for describing things in higher dimensions, and that kind of mathematics, when she plugs it into her computer, makes it work better. Does that make sense? It's the reason she's a big fan of yours. Because your 'phase transition' allowed her to figure all this out, or it became obvious or something. I didn't know I was married to a computer genius, but I guess it explains your disinterest in me as a woman."

He put his hands around the silky, muscular small of her back.

"Oh," she said as he pulled her toward him. "One other thing."

"What?"

"She told me who Thaxton is."

"Honey!"

"Sorry, I forgot. This is weird, honey." She sat up cross-legged on the bed. "She's known him as far back as she can remember. She's always felt guilty about it because her parents never knew. He warned her not to tell them. When she was a little girl he used to take her to his house—"

"Oh, no!"

"It's not what you think—it's almost weirder than that. I asked her if he ever did anything like that but she says no. She says he has this weird old house at the end of a little street in Sligo Woods, out of sight of any other houses—"

"Honey, what did he do to her?"

"He had her play on computers."

"What?"

"He had her play on computers. He had computers, and he had her learn to use them, play games on them, write programs for them. He was interested in her education, she said. He seemed to know all about her. He told her not to tell her parents, and that seemed natural to her at the time. She never wondered about it till later."

"He stopped kidnaping her after a while?"

"As soon as she got her own computer he rebuilt it for her and then stopped bringing her to his house. She was getting tired of him anyway. He's kept away from her ever since. She thinks he's just an eccentric old man. She had no idea about the garlic things or him watching her, but she still thinks he's harmless. In fact, she's thankful to him for having taught her about computers."

12

The next morning, full of sunlight and the twittering of suburban birds, the adventures of the night before seemed faraway and almost unreal. Bob told Vicki about his evening walk, but somehow he couldn't make it sound very serious. He had seen another big animal in the woods. She clucked sympathetically and kissed him. She seemed a little preoccupied about something anyway.

The sky was breezy and wide as he drove to the office at the tail end of rush hour, thinking gratefully about the things he had to do at work, which had nothing to do with the FBI or child custody or little men in black. He greeted Lois cheerfully, got a handful of hard mail, listened to his voice mail, read his E-mail.

He had enjoyed no more than twenty minutes of this idyllic existence when the phone rang, and a minute later Lois announced: "Barry D. Wentworth III?" with the slight sneer that meant she had never heard of him.

"Shit," he said, and picked up the line. "Bob Wilson," he said in his best soft, professional snap.

"Mr. Wilson," said Wentworth heartily. "How are you this morning?"

"Fine."

"I'm glad to hear that. A man who can keep his equanimity under any circumstances."

"What circumstances are we talking about?"

Wentworth laughed with what seemed to be real amusement. "Okay, Bob, I play cagey sometimes too. Your client Derek Esterbrook getting arrested last night for public drunkenness is what I'm talking about. No wonder his daughter is emotionally disturbed."

Bob waited, holding the phone tightly.

"Also, I had my people check out her school, finally, and they talked to one of her teachers, a Mr. Pin. Mr. Pin teaches math. Have you met Mr. Pin? He had some relatively interesting things to say about Diana Esterbrook. I guess I'm not allowed to wonder how she looked in the raw standing on top of that computer. I'm curious, though. She didn't remember anything about it afterwards. That kind of amnesia coupled with bizarre behavior is a symptom of sexual abuse, the psych expert I'm going to use at the custody hearing tells me. The child splits off a separate personality so she won't have to remember the abuse. And, of course, Derek Esterbrook fits the profile of the sex abuser to a T—adoptive father, alcoholic, unemployed, low self-esteem—"

"Wentworth, is there a jury on your extension? Or do you just need some billable time?" It came across too nasty, but Bob was trying to hide the sinking feeling in his stomach. Wentworth's investigative help was clearly better than his own, and as for a psychological expert to testify before Judge Cramer, Bob had a snowball's chance in hell of hiring one on his case budget.

"I'm trying to do you a favor, Wilson," Wentworth purred. "Or I can hang up if you'd prefer."

Bob waited.

"The way I see it," Wentworth went on, "we can either go forward next Tuesday and waste a lot of time and money on something we all know is going to turn out a certain way, or we can resolve it amicably out of court."

"Believe me, I'm ready for the hearing," Wentworth chuckled. He had a nasty, athletic, self-confident chuckle. "But my client would have no problem signing an agreement—say, this afternoon—under which your clients relinquish all parental rights to Diana and consent to Ms. Robinson exerting her natural rights."

"And what possible incentive would my clients have to do that?" asked Bob. "Since it's the worst that could happen to them in the hearing anyway."

Wentworth chuckled again. "Oh no, it's not the worst that could happen to them. Far from it. Ms. Robinson intends to initiate civil and criminal proceedings against your clients for their sexual abuse of her daughter if the hearing goes forward. At the very least they'll have to pay lawyers for years, even if they aren't eventually found guilty. But if they turn her over to her mother right now—hey, I say let bygones be bygones. What do you say, Wilson?"

"It's abuse of process. You're threatening litigation to force my clients to surrender constitutional rights."

"Oh, cut the crap, Wilson. Look at it from your own perspective. You want me to strip you naked in front of the judge again? He's likely to disbar you this time for incompetent representation." He laughed heartily. Then his voice got its dangerous purr again. "I'm making you this offer now, but it may not stay open long. My client may decide she wants the Esterbrooks prosecuted or I may decide I want to bury you just for a light workout. What do you say, Wilson? Take it or leave it."

Being a lawyer means you can't always slam down the phone if it might work to the disadvantage of your client. "I'll have to consult," Bob said carefully.

"Okay, you do that," said Wentworth. "But get back to me by nine A.M. tomorrow or the offer lapses and it's a long day's journey into night for you and your clients. Got that? Nine A.M."

Bob hung up, cursing.

His line rang. He picked it up.

"Is this the Wrench Ranch?" a gaping, benighted voice said. "My Toyota is—"

Bob slammed down the phone.

It rang again almost at once. "Is this the Wrench Ranch? My Toyota is stalled out on Route Three, and I need—"

"No, this is not the Wrench Ranch," gritted Bob.

"You sure it's not the Wrench Ranch?" said the voice, and Bob thought he caught an urgent tone in it. " 'Cause the number I dialed is the Wrench Ranch number." Bob suddenly recognized the voice.

"No, it's not the Wrench Ranch," he said slowly, wondering what was up now.

"Well, could you look in your phone book and give me the Wrench Ranch number?" asked Max Corrant. " 'Cause I need to discuss my car with them."

It occurred to Bob that Max was trying to get a phone number where they could talk without worrying about FBI wiretapping. He said the first number that came into his head.

"Thanks," said Max. "I'll call it as soon as I can find another quarter." He hung up.

The phone was already ringing when Bob ran into Wes Dalton's office down the hall. He grabbed it an instant before Wes could pick it up. It was Max.

"What the hell is going on?" Bob asked him.

"I have a couple of things to report, Mr. Wilson, and I didn't know if you wanted the FBI in on it."

Bob grunted. "Okay, tell me." Wes, gnomelike behind his big desk, was watching with puzzlement. Bob made shooing gestures at him. "But make it fast."

"Okay, three things. First, bad news. I heard from my contacts at Jonasburgh, and if you can believe convicted drug dealers, Armilla Robinson *was* a model prisoner. She was a trusty, got a special cell, got good time, and got early parole. Some of the hard girls in the wing wanted to be her girlfriend when she first arrived, but she never got into any fights, and—"

"Okay, you're right, that's bad. What's next?"

"Number two, I tracked down this Thaxton. His first name is Wendall. He lives at 523 Oakwood Court, one of those dead-end streets down in Sligo Woods, near your neighborhood."

"523 Oakwood Court," repeated Bob, writing it on a pad of paper he gestured at Wes to give him.

"Yeah, and he's been listed at that address for a hundred and sixty-seven years."

"What do you mean? How can that be?"

"I mean the land records at the courthouse list him as the owner going back as far as they have entries, a hundred and sixty-seven years. The only way I can figure it, his father and grandfather must have been named Wendall Thaxton too, and they just never bothered to change the title."

"Is your phone broken?" asked Wes.

Bob held his hand up to quiet him. "What's next? Give it to me in a hurry."

"Well, this is strange. You didn't ask me to check this—"

"Max, you promised—"

"I know, but this was harmless, just a background check on Armilla Robinson in the courthouse records. Only Armilla Robinson wasn't her original name. It was Armilla Thaxton. Wendall Thaxton is father."

"Come again?"

"Wendall Thaxton is Armilla Robinson's father."

Bob thought furiously. "Who's the mother?" he asked finally, at a loss.

"Fontina Thaxton."

"Fontina?" The name sounded strangely familiar.

"Yeah. She died six years ago. Death certificate dated October twenty-third, 1988."

"Max, I've got to go," said Bob, scribbling the date down. "Call me later at home. I don't care if the FBI hears us. I think we're going to drop the case, based on your prison information."

"Drop the case? But Mr. Wilson, what about the—?"

"I have to go, Max. Call me tonight." He hung up.

Wes was staring at him, mystified. "What the hell was that about?"

"Confidential." Bob winked at him, tore the page off his pad, and headed out the door.

Back in his office, Bob called the Esterbrooks but got no answer. It was probably in their best interests to settle the custody case, he reasoned, quite apart from the personal feeling of relief the prospect gave him. Four days of digging on Armilla Robinson had unearthed nothing but that she had been a model prisoner and that she was Wendall Thaxton's daughter. The latter was strange, but of course not incriminating.

And in fact it wasn't so strange, thought Bob with a feeling of revelation, because it gave Thaxton a motive for his obsession with Diana.

His intercom line rang. It was Emma, the receptionist. She sounded puzzled.

"There's a Mr. Fox here to see you. He says you're not expecting him."

"What does he want? What's it in regard to?"

"He says it has to do with a—magic talisman?"

Mr. Fox was a short old man with a dark, wrinkled face and the powerful nose and cheekbones of a Native American. He wore a venerable gray suit over an elderly sweater. His hair was salt-and-pepper gray, cropped close to his head. The hand he gave Bob to shake was dry and powerful, like a warm stone. "Clement Fox," he said softly, squinting up at Bob with penetrating black eyes.

"Bob Wilson. Will you come back to my office?" Bob's curiosity about the garlic devices was still strong enough to overcome his eagerness to be shut of the Esterbrook case.

Clement Fox sat in one of Bob's visitor's chairs, solid

as a stone. Bob settled himself behind his desk. "What can I do for you?"

"I'm a shaman of the Pamunkey Indian tribe down on the Eastern Shore. Probably the last one, unless some young people get the calling; but there's not many left. Shaman, that's like a spirit guardian or a spirit guide."

"I'm familiar with the term."

The old man nodded. "I come to warn you about the Eagle talisman and get it back from you."

"The Eagle talisman?"

"The one you showed the Indian woman at the store downtown. She's a woman of my tribe, my wife's cousin. She told me about what happened. She told me your daughter has already come under the talisman's power, maybe."

So the Indian Craft Store woman *had* followed them home, and then had probably gotten their names from property tax records or something like that. "Why do you feel you need to warn me about the talismans?"

"When you say talismans," said the old man, looking at Bob steadily, "do you mean you have more than that one?"

Bob thought about this. "Mr. Fox," he said. "Let's pool our information. You answer my questions about the talisman and I'll answer yours. Is that agreeable to you, sir?"

The old man nodded gravely.

"Suppose you begin by telling me why you feel you have to warn me about it."

Fox studied him for another minute. Finally he said: "The problem is, there's an invisible world that's as close to you as your own hand. You can't see it, but the roots of every living thing on this earth are planted there. Good and bad things come from there, but if you don't know the way to see them, they can hurt you. People today don't believe in that world; they think they make the good and bad things come, or that they come by themselves. Look at the mess the world is in today: it's because people ignore that world, that we call the spirit world."

"No doubt about it," said Bob. "But leaving aside the holistic philosophy, can you tell me where the talisman came from, who made it, what it's supposed to do? That's what I really want to know."

It was hard to tell whether the sarcasm had registered on Fox. He closed his eyes, and in a minute he slowly began to talk.

"Twenty generations ago Indian peoples lived in the woods all around this area, up and down the coast, and inland to the mountains, and beyond the mountains into the plains, and beyond the plains. The Indians in the woods around here were called the Powhatan confederacy, about two hundred villages of Pamunkey, Chickahominy, Mattapony, and many other Indian peoples.

"In those days the art of the shamans was still strong, and the shamans were still great healers and guardians, demon-fighters, god-talkers, and rescuers of spirits that sickness had driven out of people's bodies. In the modern day there's no one to fight demons, and you can see what has happened.

"Now there was a boy in those days living in one of the Powhatan villages. The Pamunkey say he was a Pamunkey, and the Chickahominy say he was a Chickahominy, and all the tribes claim him, but no one remembers now what tribe he was from, or his real name. The stories call him Eagle, but even the stories are almost forgotten now.

"Eagle was a sickly boy, thin and short of breath, and from the time he was eleven or twelve his mind seemed to be unbalanced: he would wander alone in the woods all day singing to himself, and at night he had strange dreams. He dreamed that spirits talked to him; he dreamed he was riding on the back of a giant who walked through the forest so that the upper leaves of the trees brushed his face; he dreamed of the forest burned and smoldering, and blood running in the streams, and sacred tobacco planted in the cornfields.

"His family decided from these dreams that the boy was called by the spirits to be a shaman, and they took him to the old shamans of the tribe to teach him."

Bob glanced at his watch, but Fox went on imperturbably, his voice slow and rhythmical.

"Omens came around Eagle. One day he disappeared from the hut of the old shaman who was teaching him. The village people searched for him in the forest and fields, but he was nowhere to be found. Finally, three or four days later, a farmer found him in the top of one of his trees, talking with the spirits. He seemed to have lost his mind, and rituals had to be done to heal him. He told the people that the spirits had taken him down into the underworld and killed him. They had cut his body into pieces and thrown away the bones and stuffed him full of magical crystals and sewn him up again. Then the crystals had carried him up through a hole in the earth, up to the sky where, in a white tent surrounded by white clouds and white winds, he had talked to the gods.

"After that Eagle was different. For one thing, he didn't remember his name or anything about his family. For another, his sicknesses were cured: he grew strong and clear-minded—"

"And this is the person you believe made the talisman?" asked Bob, no longer able to control his impatience. "Because if that's what you're getting at, I think—"

The old man shushed him with a gesture, looking a little irritated, as if Bob had disturbed his train of thought. Bob restrained himself with an effort.

"Eagle soon got a reputation for having great powers. He could do surgery without cutting people's skin, it was said. It was said he could see inside people's bodies. It was said he could reach inside rocks and pull out crystals without breaking the rocks open. It was said he could see hidden things, and walk through walls, and turn into an animal.

"Eagle lived in caves in the forest, and it was said that he spent most of his time in trance, where the soul flies away to the spirit world. He went deep into the spirit world, they say, deeper than any but the ancient shamans, and he found something there, a secret. When the Europeans came he was still on its trail. He saw the Ladder of Arrows, they say—the path for humans to return to the world as it was in the beginning of time, when everyone could talk to the gods, and there was no death, and the earth was a garden. They say all the great shamans see the Ladder of Arrows, and that is the source of their greatness and also of their despair, because once that path has been seen this world and everything in it fade to a shadow, and nothing seems real anymore. So the great shamans live in an unreal shadow-world, yet never able to reach the real forests and rivers and plains of the spirit world.

"Now at this time the Europeans came. At first there were only a few, and the Indians traded with them, but then there were more and more, and they wanted to grow tobacco. The Europeans had just discovered tobacco; but instead of using it for religious ceremonies like the Indians, they wanted to smoke it every day. So they grew tobacco on all the land the Indians traded to them, and sold it back to Europe. They tried clearing land in the forests for more tobacco fields, but clearing land was hard, and their eyes dwelled on the land the Indians had cleared over hundreds of years for their crops. They traded with the Indians for as much of this land as they could get, and when the Indians wouldn't trade any more there were wars. The forests burned and the streams ran with blood just as in Eagle's dreams. Soon the Powhatan confederacy was destroyed and the people put on reservations, where most of them died. A few hundred are left now, from only a few of the tribes. The old stories are dying out—perhaps you are one of the last to hear this one."

Fox smiled, as if at the irony of this petulant white man being one of the last custodians of his ancient legend.

"Now Eagle, he didn't want to go to the reservation. He wanted to stay in a cave that he had found that had special sacred power, that he thought was a doorway to the Ladder of Arrows. But if he stayed an Indian, the Europeans would put him on the reservation. So he changed himself into a white man."

"Come again?"

"He changed himself into a white man, or a white woman, some people say. The great shamans could change their forms and personalities. Eagle could be a man or a woman, they say, young or old, Indian or European."

"And you're saying that this Eagle made the micro— —the talisman?"

Fox nodded. "Yes."

"Mr. Fox, I believe you must be mistaken," said Bob politely. Now that it appeared all the Indian was going to give him was a lot of mumbo jumbo, he couldn't see any use in being cagey. "I happen to know—and I can't tell you how I know, unfortunately—that the object I showed the woman at the Indian Craft Store is an electronic device that couldn't possibly have been made more than a few years ago. For one thing, they're incredibly tiny."

"I never seen any of the tiny ones. I didn't know there was any such thing until the woman told me. The ones I know are bigger, about as big as a quarter. They're made of pottery and silver and quartz crystal. But it's the pattern the woman recognized: the pattern is the same. The woman knows the pattern. She has studied it."

"Well, she was mistaken in this case. An object so small—no bigger than half the size of my pinky fingernail—it would be easy to make a mistake."

"So you won't give it back?"

"I'm sorry."

Fox sighed and sat still for a minute, then stood up. Bob had walked him all the way out to the marble and gilt elevator lobby and pushed the Down button before curiosity made him ask: "This Eagle; what finally happened to him? How did he, you know, go to wherever it is shamans go?"

"Nobody knows."

"Ah."

"The stories say he split himself in pieces."

"How's that?"

The elevator slid open.

"He was powerful, too powerful," said Fox while Bob held the door for him. He seemed oblivious to deadlines imposed by things like open elevator doors. "His power kept causing trouble, drawing attention to him, so he hid from himself."

"How do you mean?"

"The stories say he divided himself into pieces, each one like a normal person, and each one looking and acting just like a person, and *believing* it was a person."

"Interesting." The elevator doors, which had been trying to close, started to buzz loudly.

"But nobody knows any more than that. The stories end there." To Bob's relief, Fox stepped into the elevator.

"Well, thanks for coming in," Bob said cheerfully as the doors closed.

13

It was Monday, so Vicki would be at rehearsal, Bob realized with a queasy feeling, driving home at dusk in heavy traffic and a chilly drizzle. Only his determination to talk the Esterbrooks into dropping their custody fight kept him from heading for a movie or restaurant to avoid being in the house alone with Diana.

The house was quiet, lamplight in the living room making everything look peaceful and normal. Diana's door was closed, but Bob thought he caught the faint click of a keyboard behind it. He hung up his coat quietly and sneaked upstairs, closed the bedroom door and dialed the Esterbrooks on Vicki's bed table phone. Nobody answered.

He put down the phone and almost immediately it rang, sending a jolt of adrenaline through him. I'm jumpy, he told himself.

The voice on the line was hollow and elderly.

"Mr. Wilson, this is Edward Taylor from down the street. How are you this evening, sir?"

"Mr. Taylor—Zachary hasn't run away again, has he?"

"No. No," said Mr. Taylor as if scoffing at the idea. "He's upstairs and his mother's reading him a story. But I did call on the subject of that same individual, to see if you and Mrs. Wilson will be able to attend his birthday party the Saturday after next. I believe Mona spoke to your wife about it."

"Oh, yes—yes, she did."

"He doesn't have many friends his own age, and he and his dog are always hanging around your house, driving you around the bend."

"Not at all."

"We thought we'd try to make it up to you and all the other neighbors who've been so kind to him by having an ice-cream social, though it's too late in the year for it."

"Not at all. Not at all," Bob said, cudgeling his brain for a polite reason to decline. "Let's see—the Saturday after next—"

"October twenty-third. Not that we're sure that's his birthday, you understand. October twenty-third, 1988's the date when he was brought to the Shady Grove Hospital emergency room."

For some reason the date touched a vague feeling of familiarity in Bob. "You don't say."

"Yes sir. A little old man brought him to the hospital at midnight. Said he had found him in an empty lot, all wrapped up in a blanket and crying. They never found out who left him there. Like a fairy story, isn't it? You still on, Mr. Wilson?"

At the words "a little old man" a chill had gone through Bob, and now he was holding the paper on which he had scribbled Max Corrant's information that afternoon, staring at the date on which Max said Fontina Thaxton had died: 10/23/88.

A suspicion was growing in Bob. It had no logical basis except that there were too many coincidences in this case, too many angles that turned back on themselves and became knots. He kept his voice casual. "That's fascinating, Mr. Taylor. Who was the old man who found him?"

"I knew once—it's been so long ago now," Mr. Taylor said. "Mrs. Taylor would remember; hold on. Mona," Bob heard him call over a muffled mouthpiece, "do you remember the name of the man who brought Zachary to the hospital? Yes, to Shady Grove, when he was born—ah, that's it. Thaxton," his voice returned to the mouthpiece. "A Mr. Thaxton brought him in."

After he had stumblingly gotten Mr. Taylor off the phone Bob sat on the bed dumbfounded, trying to make sense of what he had learned.

If it hadn't been obvious before, it was now that Wendall Thaxton was at the center of the drama in which Bob and Vicki Wilson had become unwitting bit players. Thaxton was variously the father of Armilla Robinson, the grandfather of Diana, and the man who had brought the newborn Zachary Taylor to Shady Grove Hospital on the same day his own wife had died. Could Fontina Thaxton have died in childbirth? Certainly not if she had been anywhere near her husband's age. Could Zachary be Armilla's child? His hair was red like Armilla's and Diana's, but Armilla had been in prison six years when Zachary was brought to the emergency room.

How did any of this make sense? Bob jumped up to go ask Diana what she knew once and for all, but stopped before he got to the door. What if she was gone, vanished again? He didn't think he could stand that, especially without Vicki around. He went back and sat on the bed, loosened his tie. *Think about this logically,* he told himself, *like they taught you in law school. Draw out the implications of this situation.*

He had Thaxton's address now; he could call the FBI and give it to them, let them question him. But that might not be such a good idea, he realized: it might make the FBI wonder why he had been poking around in the middle of their national security investigation, chasing down their suspects.

The best thing would be to extricate himself and Vicki from this whole situation as quickly as possible. He dialed the Esterbrooks again, let it ring twenty times. Damn. He hoped fervently that Derek Esterbrook hadn't chosen this inopportune time to quit drinking and join AA.

He looked at his watch. It was almost eight. Vicki

wouldn't be home for three or four hours. He was hungry but he wasn't going to go downstairs and risk seeing—or not seeing—Diana. On the other hand—and here a more pleasant thought penetrated the thicket of unpleasant ones that had grown up around him—Vicki kept a bottle of cherry brandy in the bedroom cabinet, in case of late-night indispositions.

He retrieved it and got a Dixie cup from the bathroom dispenser.

The downstairs telephone woke him at midnight, lying on Vicki's side of the bed in his rumpled suit. He was momentarily disoriented; then he fumbled in the dark for the extension on Vicki's night table. " 'Lo?"

"Hello, Bob? Mr. Wilson?"

"Who is this?" His mouth was dry, his voice croaking, head spinning with an incipient hangover.

"It's Max. Are you awake?" Max's voice was excited but low.

"Max . . . Of course I'm awake. What the hell—"

"I'm over at Armilla Robinson's place. I'm calling you from my car phone. I decided to keep the place under surveillance tonight."

"Max, I told you this morning we were dropping the case. I'm not going to pay you for going off on your own tangent—"

"Bob, *listen* to me for a minute! Just *listen* to me!"

Max calling him "Bob" for the second time quieted him as much as the urgency in his voice. "Okay," he said irritably. "I'm listening."

"I think we finally got lucky. There's something going on over here. I have to do another pass to be sure, but—I need you to come out here as fast as you can."

"Me come out there? But—"

"Mr. Wilson—Bob, I've got your case lying in the palm of my hand! I need your help! Please!"

"We're going to drop the case," said Bob weakly.

"No, we're not. Listen, the neighborhood out here is crawling with—witches, voodoo women—and guess where they're all heading? The Robinson woman'll be lucky if they don't run her out of town if we can get pictures of this. You can't let this pass you by; it'd be—unlawyerly or whatever."

Unethical, thought Bob. Damn! Just when he had thought he could toss the whole thing overboard. Still, it was probably another of Max's delusions. He was about to tell him to forget it, when out of the back of his mind came Barry D. Wentworth's sneering purr.

"Voodoo women?" he asked.

"Mr. Wilson, please get in your car and come over here. 607 Creek Ridge Drive, at the bottom of Sligo Woods by the creek. Don't let anybody notice you. I'm a block down, in the five hundred block. Park behind my car and stay there until I get to you. Shit, I got to go, man."

He hung up.

The drizzle outside had turned to a mist that made the street vague and smoky, like a scene from a Hitchcock movie. Bob rolled down his window, letting chill, wet air that smelled of dead leaves and damp earth finish the job of waking him up as he drove. His headlights penetrated thirty feet through the mist, then dissolved into white. Everything looked unfamiliar, and he found himself reading street signs. It took him ten minutes to make the two miles to Creek Ridge Drive.

Sligo Woods was an upscale neighborhood tucked into the swatch of woods that still surrounded Sligo Creek, so thoroughly removed by the abrupt hills and old trees from the surrounding suburbs that, except for the occasional streetlight and street sign, you could almost believe you were in a real forest. The streets were narrow and winding, and woodland growth crowded on both sides, occasionally breaking for a driveway that led up to a big house whose lights glowed dimly among the trees.

Bob crept along Creek Ridge Drive until he came to the five hundred block. There were cars parked along both sides of the street here. Halfway up the block was Max's old Galaxy, overhanging branches of a fir touching its canvas roof. Bob parked behind it and turned off his lights and ignition.

The neighborhood seemed dead. The only sound in the muffled stillness was his car's engine ticking off heat. There didn't seem to be any houses where he was parked, but half a block down on the opposite side of the street porch lights glowed on a big, dark two-story Tudor-style house set twenty feet back among the trees. Across the street from that a low stone wall with an iron gate announced another house, but this one was just a dark shape in the foggy woods.

Bob found his irritation at Max Corrant rising again. Anyway, the man's imagination had run away with him for the last time on this case, he reflected, wondering how he was going to get Nora Esterbrook to pay even Max's legitimate charges once they had decided to drop the custody fight.

Headlights angling up the street made Bob hunch down instinctively in his seat. With the muted roar of an expensive engine, a Jaguar sedan rushed by him. It rasped to a halt by the Tudor house, turned around, and surged back again. He crouched low so its headlights wouldn't hit him.

There was an empty parking space directly across from him. The Jaguar pulled into it sharply with the sound of an emergency brake being set before the car stopped moving. The driver's door swung open.

The driver was a young woman in a long fur coat. She wasn't Armilla Robinson—the hair tossed carelessly over her shoulders was thick and black. Peering over the edge of his window Bob saw a pale, pretty profile.

The woman swung long legs out of the car and her coat fell open, and Bob saw with a shock that underneath she was wearing something from the porno shop windows down on 14th Street: an exotic ensemble of lace and leather that left her crotch naked.

Then the coat swung closed and the woman slammed her door and was walking quickly up the block on spike heels. She went to the big arched door of the Tudor house and entered without a sound.

A knocking on his passenger window made Bob jump. It was Max Corrant. He grinned when Bob opened the door.

"Careful, Mr. Wilson, you don't want to get eyestrain," he said in a low voice as he slid into the passenger seat. "Not when we got work to do."

"Did you see that? That woman?"

Max nodded. "They been coming in for over an hour like that, and some of them a lot better." He looked a little shaken for all his bravado. "And they're all going into her house."

"What are they doing in there?"

"That's what we have to find out. If it's what I think it is, we'll be ready for that hearing next week."

"What do you think it is?"

Max looked at him in the dark. "Witchcraft."

"Max, be serious. This is a serious matter."

"I *am* being serious. You just got here; I been here since dark. They got the curtains drawn and blinds down, but from the snatches I've seen and heard, they're doing some kind of ritual in there."

"But—that's harmless, right? I mean, it's not *real*—"

"It doesn't matter, does it? With her just out of prison and faking a religious conversion and all, we could do something with a sex cult, couldn't we?"

"Yes," said Bob cautiously. "But how are we going to prove it? The judge isn't going to accept your or my testimony that we saw something like that, especially if it's just 'snatches.' "

"Right," said Max, with grim excitement. "We have to get pictures."

"Pictures? How?"

"We have to get inside."

"But how can we? We're not cat burglars. And they'll call the police."

"I don't think they'll call the police. I think that's the last thing they'll do. Look." He took something out of his pocket and handed it to Bob. It was a small, expensive-looking camera. "This cost three months' salary at McDonald's. You know how to work one of these? You look through here, press this to take a picture."

"What am I supposed to be taking pictures of?" asked Bob, squinting through the viewfinder. Its window showed Max's scared, excited face and ragged autumn foliage fading into fog behind him; everything looked black and grey in the dim light. Something inside the camera whirred, refocusing as he moved it.

"Anything that looks interesting," said Max. "I'm going around back and gain admittance to the residence. I want you to take up a position across the street from the front door; between those parked cars." He pointed. "I'm going to try to stir something up so that they'll come out the front, at least some of them. Try to get a shot with the house number in it; it's on a little sign by the driveway. I'll try to get some shots inside." He took another camera from his pocket.

Bob had been studying him in the dark. "You're going to 'gain admittance to the residence'? How?"

"Never mind that," said Max. "You just do your part and we'll have our case."

"Max," said Bob. "Did you get rid of that impression you made of Armilla Robinson's back-door key?"

Max looked uncomfortable. "Don't ask me any questions, Mr. Wilson, and you won't hear any lies. This way you can deny you knew—"

"It's breaking and entering, Max. Felony B and E."

"Look at it this way," said Max, and he was breathing hard suddenly, as if with some emotion. "If they really are doing some kind of sex ritual in there, and you send that young lady to live there, what might you be doing? Have you ever thought of it like that, Bob?"

"Well—"

"Take a look at your watch. In exactly five minutes I want you to go up the street and sit on the curb between a couple of those cars. Then keep a sharp lookout."

His defiant eyes gleamed in the darkness. On a sudden impulse Bob reached out and grabbed his hand and shook it.

"Okay," he said. "Okay, we'll do it your way."

"Okay." Max looked out all the windows carefully, got out of the car, and walked across the street, disappearing into the foliage beyond the parked Jaguar. Bob checked his watch. There was no sound anywhere. His heart was thumping.

Five minutes passed, very slowly. Bob got out of the car. Its door closing sounded loud in the muffled silence. He walked up the street until he came level with Armilla Robinson's driveway. Then he sat on the curb between two parked cars, holding Max's camera in his sweaty hands.

Four minutes, five minutes, six minutes he sat there squinting at the big, dark house across the street.

All at once he thought light faintly tinged the edges of two of its downstairs windows, as if a flashbulb had gone off behind thick curtains. Yes, there it was again; and again. Then darkness and stillness.

Then something strange.

A sound, or at least he thought it was a sound; yet it might have been his imagination—a horrible vomiting scream of something part animal, part metal that seemed to come from a great distance inside his head; and at the same time an earthquake movement of the ground that he wasn't sure the next second had really happened. He jumped to his feet, the camera almost falling from his hands.

Was it a trick of his fear-blurred eyes or was there a disturbance in the fog, as though it had begun to swirl around the Tudor house? There wasn't any wind—the leaves on the trees hung silent and still—and yet it looked for all the world as if the fog had begun to eddy in a large vortex around the house, like water around an open drain.

Bob started to back away, Max Corrant and the custody case be damned. Then the door of the Tudor house slammed open.

A guttural, slavering growl came from the darkness inside.

With a snarl something huge and wolf-shaped leapt from the doorway and shot directly toward Bob among the trees and bushes.

Even when its claws were clattering across the asphalt street he couldn't move, could do nothing except raise his hands in a pitiful caricature of self-defense.

His camera flashed and at the same second a voice screamed: "There it is!"

Then everything was confusion. Dizziness made the world rock drunkenly, and the ground came up and bumped Bob. He managed with great effort to sit upright, almost fainting. Another hallucinatory sound, a rapid tapping and rattling and crunching, now came all around him. He squinted to focus his eyes, and in a minute realized that it wasn't a hallucination at all, that the foggy street was full of people, of women: women in furs and scanty lace and leather and even chains hurrying from the Tudor house to their cars, and cars starting up and headlights coming on all along the street. Most of the women were young, but there were hags too, bizarre and repulsive in their S&M lingerie.

Bob drunkenly raised his camera to take pictures, but

the screeching voice he had heard before startled him. "Did you bring that animal here? Who are you? My husband is calling the police! Get out of this neighborhood right now! Is that your animal? Who *are* you?"

A middle-aged lady in a long bathrobe—the only person on the block who seemed dressed for a normal bedtime—was standing just outside the gate in the low stone wall on Bob's side of the street and yelling at the women. With vague shock he recognized Mrs. Sanzone, whose petition he and Vicki had signed.

In the distance a police siren wailed, and the hurried movement of the women became a scrambling rush, car doors slamming, engines roaring, wheels squealing.

Something touched Bob's shoulder, making him jump up and flail wildly at his attacker until he saw that it was Max Corrant holding up his hands in self-defense.

"Bob. Bob, stop hitting me, man. We've got to get out of here. Come on, man, hurry up. You got your keys?"

He dragged Bob to his car, put him in the passenger seat, and squealed away from the Tudor house, off Creek Ridge Drive, and out of the neighborhood, jostling in the panicked traffic jam of voodoo women. Bob saw vaguely out the window a few sleepy residents standing in driveways and doorways, staring in astonishment at the one A.M. rush hour.

"What did you see?" Max demanded as soon as they were far enough from Creek Ridge Drive to slow down to an innocent speed. He looked shaken. "Did you get any pictures?"

Bob shook his head. "It went off by mistake." He was surprised he could get the words out.

"I got three," Max said. "You should have seen what they were doing in there." He drove through the thinning fog, face worried. Then he shook himself as if to throw off his thoughts. "And that old lady across the street saw them all coming out."

"Mrs. Sanzone."

"You know her?"

Bob didn't answer. Max tried to read his face in the passing glow of the streetlights. "You okay, Bob? What did you see out there, man?"

"I saw—" said Bob, and his voice cracked. He tried again. "There was a sound."

"A sound? I thought I heard something, but I was busy getting out the back. I locked the door behind me—nobody's gonna figure out how I got in, or who I was."

"There was a sound, and then an—animal came. But then the lady screamed, and when the flash went off it seemed to disappear. Maybe the flash scared it."

"An animal attacked you? From the house? Was it a dog?"

"I don't know." Bob looked at Max. Talking seemed to dispel the numbness that had come over him.

Max was silent, thinking.

"The only problem," Max said finally, "is if the only pictures we have are inside the house, somebody's going to ask how we *got* inside, and when it turns out we got inside illegally, we might not be able to use those pictures. And depending on what that old lady saw, or what she'll swear she saw—Without pictures—"

"Shit," said Bob.

"Hey," said Max. "If I was attacked by an animal I wouldn't have taken any pictures either. But you said your flash went off, so maybe you got something. Anyway, there's one other angle I think we should check out. Nothing illegal," he added hurriedly. "Did you notice the license plates on the cars those women were driving? Most of them were George County."

"Meaning what?"

"Meaning George County is where the Sisters of Compassion Convent is, where Little Miss Angel says she went when she got out of Jonasburgh."

"You think—?"

"After tonight, man, I'd believe anything. If my pictures come out, you'll see for yourself. What if Sisters of Compassion isn't a convent at all but a cover for—something else? And she went there and got a letter of recommendation from the head nun."

"Hmm."

"Worth a shot?"

"As it turns out," said Bob slowly, "I think most of your ideas on this case have been worth a shot."

Max didn't say anything, but Bob thought he saw a gleam of wet in his eyes.

They had been driving through empty, streetlit avenues where suburban lives were packed now into their repetitive houses, dreaming for the night. Maybe the dreams were responsible for a vague, aimless consciousness that seemed to wander the streets as if looking for a way out. Above the heavy clouds, it occurred to Bob, stars shone.

Max headed the car back toward Ridge Creek Drive, brushing off Bob's protests. "If I go tonight, I might even catch some of them getting home. S&M porno stars arriving back at the convent. Give them any more time and they're going to put up their front again." He popped a film cartridge out of his camera. "Tomorrow morning first thing I want you to get this developed. And your picture. Then we'll see what we've got."

They reached Ridge Creek Drive. Max pulled the car over at a cross street. "Can you drive?" he asked Bob.

"Yes. What if the police are still there?"

"I'll tuck in somewhere till they leave. I've got to get my car out of there anyway before somebody takes down the license number. Don't worry about me. I'll call you at the office tomorrow."

Bob watched him recede up the sidewalk, walking with a professional slouch.

14

It was two A.M. when Bob got home. When he pulled up to the curb he noticed with surprise and dismay that Vicki's car wasn't there. The living room lamp was still burning and Vicki wasn't in bed. Bob was picking up the kitchen phone to call the Circle Theater number she had left on the refrigerator, when the sound of the front door opening made him hang up and hurry through the dining room. At the last second he lost his nerve and stopped. What if it wasn't Vicki, but Diana or—

It *was* Vicki, though, moving quietly so as not to wake anybody up. She took off her pumps on the foyer doormat, shrugged off her coat. Then she raised her hands and pirouetted with ballerina grace into the living room, face flushed with happiness, until she saw him watching from the doorway and screamed.

"Honey, you scared me," she gasped, hand at her throat. "What are you doing up? I thought you were in bed."

"You're late. I was—"

"—checking up on me? It's a good idea, darling—I feel so *alive* I could do anything. We went dancing after rehearsal tonight—first to a ballroom place, and then to a rock club, one of these places in a basement somewhere, and it was so *gorgeous*." She twirled over to him and put her arms around his neck.

"That's nice. Vicki—"

"You're not jealous? I danced with some *very* handsome men." She swooned in his arms and he staggered. She straightened up, sniffing. "Have you been drinking?"

He half dragged her to the couch. "Shhh." He glanced apprehensively toward the hallway.

"Oh, let's get her up," said Vicki. "Let's get drunk and get her drunk too. She might tell us something about—you know."

He held her wrist to prevent her from going to wake up Diana, and she came back to the couch and landed on his lap. She rested her head against his shoulder. "Bob, can I have an affair?"

"Can we talk about it later? I—"

"Talk about it later?" She turned on him, her eyes, vivid with rehearsal makeup, genuinely hurt. "You take me for granted."

"No, honey—"

She got off his lap and wrung her hand away from his with an anguish that surprised him.

"What? What is it?"

"What do you care?" she asked, turning away from him, standing with her arms crossed as if holding herself.

"Vicki—!"

"Do you want to know? Do you really want to?" she asked in a trembling voice, facing him again.

He nodded. On top of everything his wife was having some kind of psychological episode right in front of him. He felt disoriented, as if he were watching all this on TV. Perhaps the result of having to swallow too many strange things in one day.

She took a deep breath and he could see her searching for words.

"I'm going to be an old woman," she said, and tears came into her eyes. "And yet I have the sense—I *know* there's more to life than *this*," she made a gesture that took in the house and the neighborhood. "What is this place, anyway? I sleep here, then go out and show people houses, then go to rehearsal or to a show, then come back here and sleep again, then go and do the same thing, day after day, like a long hallway of weeks and days leading to—. A week ago I realized that I might go on doing this until I die—but only because I've chosen to. There are so many *possibilities*! Here, all around us! There are so many different lives you could lead, and the only reason you lead this one is because you've made up your mind to do it. There's nothing else keeping you where you are but that. That's what I realized.

"I had started picturing my life as just going on like it is now, and growing old gracefully like—like Marybel Abercrombie, for instance, and you getting old and silly like Larry, and there's nothing wrong with that, is there? —But there are so many other ways I could go—I'd forgotten that. I'd forgotten I even had a choice! I suddenly remembered that the world was big and beautiful around me—I even had a dream about it. Do you understand?" She was looking into his eyes pleadingly. "It sounds so stupid, but—do you understand?"

He nodded slowly. "I think I understand." He paused. "Because," he went on, "I've been feeling the same way. I've been getting these thoughts I haven't had since I was a kid—and dreams about something like freedom, multiple directions. Multiple ways you can go." He looked at her, wondering if she understood.

"Multiple directions," she said, savoring the words. "You've had it too?" She giggled, swallowing her tears. "I guess it's—it's some kind of midlife crisis old people get."

"Well—maybe."

She looked at him questioningly.

"Do you have time to listen to a strange story? I mean, *really* strange?"

"Is it scary?" she asked, suddenly anxious.

"It's scaring the hell out of me."

She sat down on the couch and curled her legs under her, kept her wide eyes on his face.

He sat next to her in the subdued light of the lamp and told her the story, starting with Barry D. Wentworth III's call that morning demanding that the Esterbrooks drop their custody fight, and Max Corrant's discovery that Wendall Thaxton was Armilla Robinson's father—Vicki gratified him by gasping at that. He told her about the old Indian Clement Fox and his fables, and about Mr. Taylor's claim that an old man named Thaxton had brought the newborn Zachary Taylor to the emergency room on the same night Thaxton's wife had died—Vicki gasped again. But she really gasped and her eyes got big when he told her about the Ridge Creek Drive voodoo women and the huge animal.

"There's more to this than someone—or even a lot of people—being crazy. That was my explanation until tonight. But tonight I saw something that wasn't natural. Unless I'm crazy too there's something going on that can't be explained—in the normal way. That old man Thaxton is trying to protect Diana from Armilla Robinson, I'm convinced of that, and the danger she's in is something—occult." He had to force the word out of his mouth. "But why would she bring a lawsuit, for God's sake, if she's a—witch or something like that?"

"Maybe because Thaxton's done too good a job of protecting her, so Armilla needs another way to get at her," said Vicki. "I wonder—" she ran her hand thoughtfully along his thigh. "Do you know by any chance if the little boy Armilla kidnaped was adopted?"

He looked at her sharply. "How did you know that?"

"Was he?"

"That's what the newspaper clippings said. But how—?"

"Because what if he was related to Wendall Thaxton too, just like everyone else?"

Bob thought about that. "But why would—You're saying she wants to kidnap anybody related to Thaxton? But why? And look—if Zachary's related to Thaxton, she hasn't tried to kidnap him."

"Maybe she doesn't know about him. He was born when she was in prison. What about a hot toddy? I think better when I'm drunk."

Bob heard her gasp in the kitchen as he sat moodily on the couch waiting for her to make the drinks. "What is it?" he snapped, jumping up.

Instead of answering she came out with something dangling from her hand. A chain of six dark brown wooden rings linked together.

"What is it?" he asked again.

"The napkin rings." Her voice was shaky.

"The—let's see." He took them from her. They certainly looked like the six carved rosewood rings Vicki's Aunt Sylvia had given them. Except that they had been separate then, of course.

He studied the chain closely under the lamp. The rings showed no signs of tampering, not even the tiniest seams.

"These aren't the napkin rings," he concluded. "She—she got this from somewhere and left it in the kitchen to make us think our napkin rings have gone berserk."

But Vicki was approaching the mantelpiece holding out one hand, her eyes wide. When she was almost touching it Bob saw what she was looking at.

One Christmas Bob's sister had given them an upscale version of the little Santa Claus in the globe of water that you can turn over and make the snowflakes fall. Vicki had kept it on the mantelpiece behind the other bric-a-brac in the hope that no one would see it.

Except now the little Santa had gotten out of his globe.

He was standing next to it, sack over his shoulder, a stray snowflake stuck to his hat. The globe itself was unbroken and still full of water.

Vicki handed the Santa and globe to Bob. He automatically checked the glass sphere for breaks, seams, places where it could be unscrewed. There were none. And there was no real doubt this was the Santa-in-a-globe Meryl had given them: for one thing, Bob wasn't aware of outlets where you could purchase Santa-and-globe sets with the Santa outside the globe.

Vicki said shakily: "Let's have those drinks."

Late the next morning Bob Wilson sat on a plastic chair in the tiny waiting room of Capital Photography, his head splitting with a double hangover, sleep deprivation, and post-traumatic stress syndrome. The place had the usual radiant wedding pictures on the walls and smelled of chemicals, like a hairdresser's. It took twenty minutes for the short, cheerful man who had taken Bob's film to come back, wiping his hands on a towel and eyeing Bob curiously.

"Four sets of the exposed frames," he said, putting two rolls of negatives and a manilla envelope on the counter. "I thought you said they weren't pornography."

Bob opened the envelope and took out one of inner packets. He spilled the prints onto the counter, feeling his heart speed up.

In the first three, female bodies were intertwined orgy-style on the floor of what looked like a large living room with heavy drapes over the windows. In the center of the orgy was a divan, and on the divan a beautiful female form lay, in the first two pictures prone as if asleep or unconscious, though hands reached up from the mass of bodies to clasp her in twenty places. In the third picture the reclining woman's face was raised in dizzy puzzlement, and Bob saw that she was Armilla Robinson.

But it was the fourth picture that made both Bob and the photographer stare.

It was the picture Bob had taken accidentally outside the Robinson house: the background was misty street, and the flash had even caught the little address sign near the driveway. In the foreground was a woman. Not one of the voodoo women: this one was stark naked. The flash had caught her in a sprint toward the camera, hands and feet viciously clawed, body knotted with inhuman muscles, slaver streaming from teeth bared in a gargoyle scream.

It was Armilla Robinson.

"Where did you get that?" asked the man behind the desk. "Is it from a movie?"

"Lycanthropy," said Bob. He shakily shuffled the pictures back into their envelope, paid the puzzled man, and left.

At the office he got a handful of phone messages from Lois, went into his office and called Vicki. She answered sounding hung over.

"Honey, I called to give you some good news. Armilla Robinson isn't a witch, she's a lycanthropist. I got the pictures developed, and—"

"Honey, you don't have to yell in my ear. What are you talking about? What's a lycanopist?"

"Lycanthropist. Remember last night when I told you we can't use the explanation that the people in the Esterbrook case are crazy? Well, I've changed my mind. I got the pictures Max and I took last night, and they don't show anything supernatural, just a bunch of suburban housewives doing some kind of sex ritual around a woman lycanthropist. Lycanthropy—that's a mental disease where a person believes they can turn into a wolf. It's like a delusion that you're a werewolf. It's a well-known psychological thing: I've read about it."

"A woman lycanthropist," Vicki repeated slowly.

"Armilla Robinson, of course. She's got a coven of yuppie 'witches' convinced she's the real thing. So our theories from last night are correct, with one exception: it's not real magic Thaxton is trying to save Diana from—it's the murderous delusions of his daughter. He knows that if she gets hold of Diana she'll kill her like she killed the Vesperson boy. And Thaxton's as crazy as she is, so maybe he thinks it's real magic; hence the garlic, the warnings, and all the rest of it."

"Hmh," said Vicki shortly. "And how does a crazy little old man get those super-advanced garlic devices? And what about the footprints you saw with the claw marks?"

"She wears a wolf suit," said Bob triumphantly. "She puts on fake claws and runs around in the woods at night. That's what lycanthropists *do*. As for the garlic things, who knows how he gets them. Security is lax all over this country. Or those FBI assholes could have been lying to us about what they are."

There was a discreet knock and Lois came in and handed him a note. It said: "Mr. Wentworth is holding—he says it's important."

"Honey, I have to get off," Bob said. "That Wentworth shitbag is on the other line. We're due to have a swaggering and blustering contest." The thought gave him fierce satisfaction now that he finally had something to swagger and bluster with.

"Well, don't call me anymore just to hang up in my face," said Vicki irritably. "Diana was in her room this morning when I got up."

"She'd better start going to school, or we're going to get rapped with contributing to the delinquency of a minor. Honey, I have to get off."

He pushed the button next to the flashing arrow on his telephone display. "Mr. Wentworth."

"Mr. Wilson. Do you have an answer for me on the proposal I made to you yesterday?"

"I'm afraid I don't," said Bob, and now it was his turn to purr. "I wasn't able to get in touch with my clients. I'm afraid we'll have to take some additional time." *Let's go to trial*, he thought; *and if Ms. Robinson doesn't tell you about last night, so much the worse for you.*

"As you know, letting an express time limit lapse effects a withdrawal of a settlement offer as a matter of law," said Wentworth, but Bob, listening carefully, thought the self-assurance in his voice seemed a little overdone. *She's told him*, Bob thought; *he's trying to see how much he can get out of me, playing the slim chance that it wasn't my people out there last night, or that I'll be too afraid to use evidence gathered that way.*

"Yes, I'm aware of that."

Wentworth waited just a second too long, then went on, his voice now confidential, solicitous, as if sharing a secret only two professionals would understand: "But as it happens, Bob, I spoke to Ms. Robinson yesterday and urged her to modify her position. After all, our main concern is the best interests of the child, and maintaining friendly relations among her caretakers is an important aspect of that."

"Sure," said Bob, trying to sound like he was flipping through a magazine.

"So Ms. Robinson is now offering," Wentworth went on, "to let the Esterbrooks maintain primary custody of Diana, as long as she has secondary custody rights, taking Diana for six weeks in the summer and two weeks at Christmas—just the usual type of joint arrangement," he wound up casually. "This is a settlement I don't think your clients can afford to pass up. In fact, Ms. Robinson directed that you either accept immediately or we go to trial."

There was a long silence. "Wilson, are you there?" Wentworth asked finally with irritation.

"I'm here."

"Normally people respond when the first speaker gets done talking," said Wentworth with his nasty little laugh.

"The problem is I'm never sure you're done talking," said Bob.

Wentworth let that go. *He knows I've got him,* Bob thought, savoring the feeling. "Do you have any reaction to Ms. Robinson's offer?" asked Wentworth. "It's very generous under the circumstances, especially when the judge has already pretty well made up his mind to grant custody to the biological parent."

"Well, not having talked to my clients, I can't give you a final answer," drawled Bob. "But I will tell you that I'll recommend against any arrangement that would result in Ms. Esterbrook spending unsupervised time with a person of Ms. Robinson's—character."

"More malpractice, huh, Wilson? Jesus, wait till His Honor hears this one," Wentworth said, chuckling. "Okay, this offer lapses in exactly three minutes."

"Then I guess we'll see you in court."

"Do you have another job lined up when the judge disbars you?"

"Did you have any further points to make, Mr. Wentworth?" asked Bob sweetly. "Because I have eleven phone messages to answer."

"Wilson, listen to me," said Wentworth, trying to calm himself. "Let's not waste the court's time. Let's put our cards on the table. Each of our clients may have what the court could view as—impediments to taking custody. If we litigate it's a roll of the dice, and Ms. Robinson doesn't want her daughter's future riding on a chancy proposition like that, so I'll tell you what. She has authorized me to make one last offer if all else fails, otherwise we *will* go into court—and with some pretty juicy additional allegations about your clients too. So here's the final offer, Wilson: weekend visitation, six hours of unsupervised—"

"No," said Bob, thinking of Armilla Robinson's twisted, slavering face in the photograph. You could do a lot to a little girl in six hours.

"You stupid fuckhead—" Wentworth got out before Bob quietly hung up, smiling in malicious triumph.

After that he tucked his phone messages under the paperweight, told Lois to hold *absolutely* all calls, put his feet on his desk, and took a nap.

A haze had come over the sun by lunchtime, and in the strangely still air the sounds of downtown traffic seemed to carry with uncanny clarity. The clouds didn't look heavy but the atmosphere had a lowering pregnancy, as if apocalyptic weather was brewing somewhere. Bob, who hadn't done any work all morning and didn't feel like doing any in the afternoon, went out for a long lunch with Wes Dalton and watched the sky over the plaid cloth of their window table turn a peculiar, luminous gray. It was after two when he got back, and there was a sheet of paper on his desk chair with the words "Call Vicki" written large in Lois's hand.

Vicki answered after the first ring, sounding strange. "Oh, honey," she said with a kind of careless cheerfulness. "You won't believe what's going on here. Is it foggy downtown?"

"Starting to get a little," he said, eyeing a faint gray haze that had formed at the end of the busy avenue his office overlooked. "Why?"

"Well, it's foggy here. And still—dead still. Is the air perfectly still down there?"

"Pretty still. What's going on? Are you all right?"

"Of course I'm all right. That fog is the most interesting thing, though. It kind of *crept* up the street—long *arms* of it creeping and swirling up ever so slowly along the curb, around the bushes—Mrs. Ranelli was out shopping and she told me it looked like it was coming out of the Sligo Creek woods when she drove by there, floating out from between the trees. Probably because of the creek and the dampness, and that's the lowest-lying area around here. But it absolutely looked like it was creeping silently up the street like rising water, only long *tendrils* of it reaching out ahead. It's very thick now. Isn't that strange and romantic?"

"Honey, are you scared?"

"Of course I'm not scared, silly. It's kind of exciting, though. Oh, and I think—it seems like a black limousine has been by the house three or four times this afternoon, going very slow. You know the kind with the tinted windows so you can't see in?"

"Did you call the police?"

"Of course not." She gave a little laugh. "The police can't stop people from driving their limousines around. But what I really called to tell you is that your favorite teenager is gone again, and this time *I* saw a flash. I *know* she was in there, Bob. When I saw the flash I went in her room to look, and I saw—" Her voice cracked and she was silent for a minute.

"Vicki? Honey, are you there?"

"I saw," she said, her low voice quite steady now, "something. When I opened her door. In her room."

"What? What did you see?"

"Well, it was like—maybe it was a hallucination. Can you get the DTs from getting drunk just one night? It was—everything had gone crystal, like every scene from everywhere was being refracted inward, like those faceted cut-glass Christmas ornaments do, but the other way—like inward instead of outward, you know what I mean? Like cells of—of *space*, thousands upon thousands of them, were all around me—or rather, like I was inside them, and I could see the room like—I could see every part of it equally, as if I was outside it *all around*. It only lasted a minute—then everything was back to normal. But I really saw it—I swear I did."

"I'm coming home. I'm on my way. Just hold tight till I get there."

"Oh, honey, will you?" her voice started to shake at last, and she sounded like a little girl. "You don't have too much work—?"

"I'll be just as long as it takes to run to the car and drive back. If anything funny happens you call the police, understand? Call 911."

"What do you mean, 'funny'? What do you define as—"

"Just anything—anything at all. Honey, I'm going to hang up now so I can start coming. Go next door to the Ranellis if anything seems odd."

"Okay. But hurry up, will you, Tarzan? Jane needs you."

Putting on his jacket and cramming his daytimer and phone messages into his pocket he wondered if Vicki might be having some kind of brain chemistry episode, maybe premenopausal. Of course, she was ten years away from menopause, but still—

On his way out the door the phone rang again. He was about to let it go, but then it occurred to him that it might be Vicki and he ran back and picked it up.

It was Max Corrant. "Bob, I'm glad I caught you," he said, and his voice was low and excited·and—scared, Bob thought. "I wouldn't even be calling from here, but—"

"Max, I can't talk right now—"

"No, no, no, *you've got to listen to me*," Max hissed intensely. "This place is—well, that doesn't matter now. What matters is that it seems you've beat up on the Robinson woman's attorney, so she's not going to take the attorney route anymore. *She's intending to*—"

There was silence suddenly; not the silence of a broken connection but the silence you get when somebody stops talking.

"Max? Max, are you there?"

Bob imagined he heard a quiet, calm exhalation at the other end of the line.

"Max?" A sudden thrill of fear went up his spine.

There were a couple of clicks and a dial tone.

Bob hung up and, cursing, jogged toward the elevators.

15

The further he drove, the thicker the fog got. Downtown it was just a white haze high up between the buildings, a milky mist that washed out colors. Then around Observatory Road the horizon, which had been hovering a couple of blocks away, contracted rapidly, until he was cautiously following the taillights of the car ahead of him through a pea soup. By the time he got home he was sure he had never seen fog like this.

He had his key out when the door sprang open and Vicki, wearing jeans and a floppy sweater, stepped into his arms and squeezed him tight. Her hands felt cold when he took them, and she was pale, but smiling.

"I guess you think I'm a good example of neurosis and codependence," she said shamefacedly as he shut the door, a wisp of fog coming into the foyer behind him.

"I think you're a good example of appropriate caution and making a guy feel needed."

"I suppose you practice saying nice things to your clients. How do you like the fog?"

"It's thick." He took off his coat, stood looking at her. "And in answer to your question: no, you cannot have an affair."

She pouted. "You want some hot chocolate?"

"Hot milk. But first—should we look in Diana's room?"

He thought she got paler, and her long fingers were twining together. "If you want."

"I take it you haven't looked in there since—"

"No."

"Okay. Well, you stay out here. If everything's normal I'll tell you. On the other hand, if you hear a throttled, gurgling scream—"

"*Shut up,* Bob."

He gave her a lopsided grin like he imagined detective heroes must give their girlfriends. It wasn't all bad having uncanny things happen around your house, he decided.

Diana's room was dark, the drapes closed, the computer monitor throwing a weird, shifting glow over the books, papers, and wadded blankets on the bed around it, making Bob for a split second fear he was having altered perceptions. He fumbled for the wall switch.

Then the light went on and the scene went from eerie to commonplace. With the ceiling bulbs confining the strange free-fall patterns to the screen, the room's pale pink walls, bed table, and closet greeted Bob like old friends.

He looked under the bed just in case. It was dusty under there, but the naturalness of that just made him feel better. He opened his mouth to call Vicki when there was a scream.

He bolted into the living room, heart pounding. She was standing with both hands on her heart staring at the picture window. She whirled to face him.

"Oh, God, honey, I'm sorry—I could have sworn—I could have *sworn* there was a hand, but I guess it was the fog. It looked like a hand, I swear." She seemed more afraid that he would scold her than she did of what she had seen.

"A hand?" he said stupidly.

"Outside the window. But it was just the fog. Oh, *God,* Bob, this whole thing has me on edge. What are you doing?"

He left the front door open and stepped out onto the lawn. Everything seemed uncannily silent in the fog. He could barely see the shapes of the cars parked along the street, but the azalea bushes under the picture window were thin and scraggly this time of year, and no one was hiding in them.

He thought he smelled something, though. He sniffed the wet, chill air. Garlic—it was the smell of garlic. The Ranellis probably, he told himself uneasily; they were always making smells like that at dinnertime.

He went back inside. "I guess I scared them away."

"My hero."

"And Diana's room looks okay."

They went in there, holding hands.

And watching the patterns on the computer monitor, Bob realized suddenly that he was sick of them, sick of being scared in his own house by a small video screen programmed by a teenager. Thick wires ran from the computer over the edge of the bed table. Bob squatted and yanked them out of the wall socket.

The computer clicked and, with a crackle of ionization, the monitor went blank. The whir of the computer's internal fan ran down and died.

Vicki gave a little scream. "Oh, honey, no! Don't do that—put it back on. Bob—" She jerked the wires out of his hand. "Who knows what that was for? Maybe she won't be able to get back." Her eyes were full of horror.

"Back from where?"

"From wherever she's gone. Bob, how could you? Plug those back in right now."

Reluctantly, he shoved the bulky three-pronged plugs back into the sockets, and the fan whir started up again. A loud beep from the computer made them jump, and then letters and numbers rapidly formed incomprehensible texts on the monitor that scrolled away out of sight, finally leaving a single message on the black screen: "C:> System Crash: (R)eboot, (A)bort, (F)ail."

"What does that mean?" Vicki said faintly, her eyes wide. "Is she—is it gone? It won't come back?"

"I don't know," said Bob.

"But what if she needed that on to come back from—wherever she's gone?"

There was a heavy knocking at the front door.

Bob and Vicki stared at each other.

"Who can that be?" asked Vicki in a cheerful, breathless voice. "One of the neighbors, I imagine."

They went to the door, staying close together. Vicki jerked it open so that fog swirled in.

"Yes?" she trilled graciously.

The man on the doorstep holding a monogrammed leather overnight bag with gold fittings just stared for a moment, as if surprised to see the door yanked open by two wide-eyed people. He himself was something to stare at. He had dark olive skin and a bushy black beard around thick lips, and his thick fingers wore several gold rings. On his head was a turban with a jeweled brooch, and a loose black robe edged with gold hung over his expensive suit.

He cleared his throat. "Ah. I feared there was no one at home. Dr. Esterbrook?" He had a deep, foreign voice overlaid with a cultured British accent, as if he had spent years in upper-crust English schools. He looked expectantly at Vicki.

"No," she said tentatively.

"I'm sorry. This is not 407 Cedar Street? My correspondence gave this as the address of Diana Esterbrook."

"Well—she is staying here."

"Excellent. Is she in?" When Vicki hesitated, he added: "You are undoubtedly wondering about me." He bowed. "I am Dr. Mohammed Abdeen Al-Haq."

"Oh, Dr. Al-Haq!" said Vicki brightly after a surprised moment. "How nice to see you."

Dr. Al-Haq shook her hand, holding her eyes with his hot black ones.

"And this is my husband, Bob Wilson."

Al-Haq's hand was fat and strong. Bob's mind was a whirl; he only realized that he had been debating whether or not to let Al-Haq into the house when Vicki said: "Won't you come in? Diana isn't home right now, but we—expect her back."

Did she remember that this was the man who had written the book on Diana's abominable computer stuff? Bob wondered. Though Al-Haq didn't *look* dangerous—he was smiling now, stepping into the house in a pair of surprisingly small, shiny black shoes.

"We were about to have tea," said Vicki, leading him into the living room. "Will you join us?"

"Thank you very much. I hope I am not imposing. I received a paper from Dr. Esterbrook, of the most extraordinary character. I decided to come directly and see her. Perhaps I ought to have telephoned—"

"Not at all." Vicki got Al-Haq to sit on the couch, and frowned at Bob until he sat in the armchair by the fireplace. "I'll put on the water."

She swept out of the room.

Al-Haq sat with his hands clasped on his stomach, looking around contentedly. Bob had almost quelled his surprise and misgivings enough to make a polite remark about the weather, when Al-Haq beat him to it. "Unpleasant weather."

"Foggy," agreed Bob.

"It came very suddenly, the taxi driver told me."

"Yes."

"Is the university far? How will Dr. Esterbrook get home-in these conditions?"

"She—we're talking about Diana, right?"

"Yes, Diana Esterbrook."

"She's not a doctor, is what Bob means," said Vicki, coming back with the tea things and a plate of cookies, which she put on the coffee table in front of Al-Haq. "She's just a little girl—a high school student."

"A *high* school student?" exclaimed Al-Haq. He looked from Vicki to Bob, dumbfounded. Finally he dug in an inner pocket and came out with a thick envelope, which he studied. "407 Cedar Street. Which is this address, is it not?"

"It is," said Vicki, sitting demurely on the couch.

"And there is no other Diana Esterbrook here?"

"No."

"And this—young lady engages in computer researches?"

"Yes, and she has a book by you that she reads constantly, called *Principles of* something," said Vicki.

"Thaumatomathematics," muttered Al-Haq. "A *high* school student!" He shook his head in amazement. "She sent me," he held up the letter, "a paper—an *extraordinary* paper on thaumatomathematics. I confess"—he turned to Vicki, who apparently seemed more human to him than her wooden-Indian husband—"that I am astonished. I assumed she was a professor of mathematics or nonlinear analysis or at least computer science. Well, of course Wolfram was only eighteen years old when—but still—She is at school now, I suppose?"

"We don't know," said Vicki. "She has a tendency to—pop in and out."

"Ah."

"Have a cookie."

Al-Haq picked one up daintily and held it on a napkin. "What computing facilities does she use?"

"She has a computer in her room."

"Impossible!" Then looking at their puzzled faces: "You are not nonlinear systems specialists, I take it?"

Bob and Vicki shook their heads.

"Ah," Al-Haq sighed. "Suffice it to say that personal computers do not have enough speed and memory for the kind of real-time experiments Ms. Esterbrook has described in her paper. She must have access to supercomputing facilities at—at school or—" A thought seemed to hit him. "Pardon me, you are not her parents? Your names—"

Vicki shook her head. "We're friends. Bob is her lawyer."

Al-Haq nodded gravely. "Could I," he said delicately after a pause, "hoping Ms. Esterbrook would not object, could I view the computer she uses? Just to determine whether it is possible that—" He waved her letter in the air.

"Surely," said Vicki, slipping the tea cozy on the pot. "In here." Dr. Al-Haq followed her eagerly to Diana's room. Bob came anxiously behind. Letting the inventor of thaumatomathematics near a computer seemed to him uncomfortably like bringing an open flame near a can of gasoline.

The "system crash" message was still on the monitor.

"Ah, you have had a—" said Al-Haq, fingers twitching. He took in the chaotic, rumpled room at a glance, eyes resting for a moment on the volume of *Principles of Thaumatomathematics* that lay open on Diana's pillow.

"Maybe you can fix it," said Vicki. "My husband—there was a power interruption." She looked at Bob disapprovingly.

"May I?"

"Please."

Dr. Al-Haq, in his robe and turban, leaned delicately over Diana's bed and began typing rapidly on the keyboard, pausing now and then to give the machine time to respond. "This is a—" he muttered twice, and "Ah-ha," once. Finally a list of some kind appeared on the monitor. He studied it intently, mumbling to himself and chewing his lower lip. Then he typed again and an electric-arc tree-branch shape quivered on the screen, a tense whine from the speakers changing in pitch and timber as its silvery-blue branches grew and exfoliated.

"My God!" Dr. Al-Haq exclaimed amidst a guttural burst of foreign words. He reached down to the computer box and ran his hands around under the edge of it. After some fumbling he had unscrewed something and lifted off the plastic case.

Bob and Vicki crowded on both sides to see. Inside, the computer looked like a miniaturized city with rows of flat, intricate skyscrapers on a landscape of dizzyingly complex streets and plazas.

"My God," Al-Haq whispered.

"What is it?" asked Vicki nervously.

"Where did she get this?" Al-Haq whispered.

"She won it in a school competition," said Bob.

"Impossible! This machine is—is *highly enhanced.* Look, four X7 chips with parallel logic. And the bus is obviously custom-made. And the hard disk stack must be a hundred gigabytes—" He leaned over almost double to peer sideways into something. "This could not have come from a school competition."

"Her—her grandfather knows about computers. He might have—" said Vicki hesitantly.

He turned on her in astonishment. "Her *grandfather*?"

"Shall we drink our tea before it gets cold?"

Dr. Al-Haq put the case back on the computer and followed her into the living room. He seemed dazed, accepting his tea with cream and two lumps and staring into it distractedly.

In the heavy silence the faint ring of spoons stirring tea was uncannily clear, and the rustle of Dr. Al-Haq's robe as he shifted on the couch came to Bob's ears finely delineated. Bob looked at his watch; it was only four-thirty, but the fog outside was beginning to turn a deep gray-brown, as though the house were sunk in turbid waters.

"Dr. Al-Haq?" asked Vicki timidly after they had sipped in silence for a few minutes.

"Yes?" He roused himself and said the word gently, eyes kindly and lips half smiling. He seemed to have overcome his shock at Diana's computer, and he sat contentedly again.

"Dr. Al-Haq, I hope you don't mind me asking, but what exactly is thaumatomathematics?"

Al-Haq's eyes sparkled, and his fat hands adjusted his cup on its saucer. *He's used to this,* Bob thought.

"It is a discipline designed to allow the average person to achieve the brain functioning optimization required to perceive a deeper level of reality, just as the great geniuses of history have done."

"Oh," said Vicki timidly, and after another pause: "Can you explain that?"

"Certainly," said Al-Haq. He settled himself more comfortably on the couch and began to talk.

"A number of years ago, I began to wonder why some people are geniuses and others not. A logical question, don't you think? There is no physiological difference between geniuses and the rest of us as far as science can ascertain, yet some people are electrified with intense visions of nature's workings while most others seem caught in endless cycles of boredom, mediocrity, and frustration. And that is the important point, is it not: What makes one *really alive*? What makes some people able to see beyond the seemingly meaningless appearances, the endless repetition of days, the aimless, baffling progression of events?

"I began to study these people, the Newtons and the Einsteins, to find out how they achieved their beatific visions of Truth. But here I seemed to reach a blank wall, for strangely the geniuses seemed to be as diverse a group of people as it was possible to imagine, with radically different personalities, beliefs, and habits. In fact, the single thing most of them seemed to share was an experience.

"This experience has been variously described by those who have had it as an intoxication, a deep, mystical silence, a crystalline clarity, an ecstasy, a wonderful certainty; but the more I studied, the more I became convinced that all these descriptions referred to the same thing. For one thing, for all these people this experience was the giver of meaning to their lives. It bestowed serenity, awe, a sense of mystery and destiny.

"For another thing, those who described the experience agreed that it was the bestower of Truth. None of the people who had it doubted for a moment that they had been given a glimpse of a deeper reality, and this glimpse was usually so persuasive that it became the basis for a lifelong search, a quest to recapture, comprehend, and express it. And in fact these ecstatic episodes did seem to release within these people avalanches of astonishing discoveries, making credible their subjective belief that they had somehow directly touched Truth.

"Being a mathematician, I naturally attempted to relate this 'epiphany experience' as I called it, to mathematics. I knew from my own experiences, as well as from the testimony of others in all times and places, that in the solving of mathematical problems there is often a moment—and sometimes more than a moment—of intoxication, a moment when the brain seems to secrete all the neurotransmitters of pleasure and at the same time when one's faculties are intensely sharpened. This experience has been studied by psychologists: they call it the 'Ah-ha reaction,' and it is associated with a temporary increase in electromagnetic brain-wave pattern correlation.

"My studies have led me to believe that this 'Ah-ha reaction,' this momentary exhilaration, is nothing less than a vitiated form of the tremendous brain-functioning optimization that occurs in the genius epiphany experience. I believe that this optimization facilitates the beatific perception—actually allows the subject *to see into* a part of the deep structure of reality that is closed to brains in the lower functioning 'normal' state.

"So what is thaumatomathematics? It is a method, a discipline, a practice, a path of intense personal mathematical research designed to allow the average person, by progressively solving mathematically the riddles of his own life, to achieve the epiphany and to perceive the deeper level of reality."

Al-Haq seemed to quiver, as if, thought Bob in alarm, he might rise into the air in a sudden burst of "brain-functioning optimization."

"But you're saying," said Vicki with a furrowed brow, "that just by studying science—"

"No!" interrupted Al-Haq. "Pardon me, but I am saying just the opposite. Science as taught and studied today is"—Bob could see him trying to control himself—"is anathematic to what I am aiming for. It is infected by intellectual fads, by egotism and one-upmanship, by competitions in ludicrous skepticism, by slavish acceptance of unexamined assumptions, by fossilized paradigms, by rivalries for grant money, prestige, titles, by *politics*." He spat the last word out as if it were a dirty thing he had taken into his mouth accidentally. "Thaumatomathematics is science cleansed of these impurities so that it becomes again a quest for the beatific vision. For example, the subject of thaumatomathematical research is one's own life. This makes it effectively impossible to publish the results, and also produces an intimacy and urgency that drive the mind to ever deeper levels of analysis." He smiled suddenly. "I beg your pardon. I have been studying this discipline, working to refine it for twenty years. Perhaps my perspective is a little one-sided." He seemed happy and relaxed again.

Their stares and the silence of the fogbound house did not seem to bother him. He waved a hand lightly. "I discovered many fascinating things in my study of this phenomenon, such as the striking similarity of the epiphany experience with the mystical states of religion; the belief by most mathematicians in 'mathematical Platonism'—that there is another world more real than this visible world; that those who have had the epiphany experience regard it as the natural state of our species, from which we have been banished by some accident or evil; that many who have had an intense form of it appear to have exhibited pronounced abnormal capacities—"

"Abnormal capacities?" Bob's anxiety, which had been lulled by Al-Haq's deep, rich voice, abruptly returned. "What do you mean?"

"These have mostly been exhibited by nonscientific persons such as—"

"But—but what do you mean 'abnormal capacities'? Abnormal capacities like what? The capacity to appear suddenly from nowhere? To get napkin rings to link up together?"

"Well—precognition and clairvoyance are more common," said Al-Haq, studying Bob curiously. "But why do you ask?"

"What about making—what about people around you having mental disturbances, such as intense thoughts of—of a kind of huge freedom, of multiple directions, vast numbers of possibilities?"

"Those are characteristics of the epiphany," said Al-Haq slowly. "A sense of limitless freedom, of vast numbers of possibilities."

"But we haven't been doing thaumanomathematics," Bob protested. "We—"

Al-Haq was alert, interested. "You have had such experiences while Dr.—while Ms. Esterbrook—?"

"Shh!" said Vicki suddenly. "Listen."

Bob and Dr. Al-Haq listened. There was nothing but a faint clicking that seemed to come from outside the house; a slow, tentative sound only audible because of the dead silence of the fog.

"Probably something dripping," Bob said.

"It certainly is not something dripping," said Vicki. "Would you like more tea, Dr. Al-Haq?"

"Thank you," said Al-Haq. The sounds of tea pouring and Al-Haq stirring his sugar and cream into it gently filled the room. "I was merely going to remark that the experiences you describe, Mr. Wilson, could be a contact phenomenon, a kind of broadcasting of the thaumatomathematical researcher's brain state. Increased cephalic wave-form correlation could, I suppose, increase the constructive interference between these wave-forms, and hence the chances of their being broadcast 'telepathically.' But the researcher would have to be far advanced in her program for this to be a possibility, I believe."

While Al-Haq talked Bob had heard the clicking again, closer now, like a stick tapping on the front walk, as if a blind person wandered there in the fog.

The doorbell rang.

"That's odd," said Vicki. "Who could that be in all this . . . ?"

She and Bob got up.

"Ms. Esterbrook, perhaps," said Al-Haq.

When Vicki opened the door and Bob saw the dark glasses, a wave of relief almost had time to go through him before he realized that the person wearing them couldn't be an FBI agent. She was an old, short, thick-legged lady with gray hair, holding a white cane.

"Hello," said Vicki.

"Hello," said the lady. "I'm looking for my son Alvin. Is he here?"

"Who?" asked Vicki blankly, but Bob interrupted her.

"Alvin?" he said. "Alvin Maxwell Corrant?"

"Yes, Alvin Maxwell Corrant. Is he here? If he is I want to talk to him."

"Well—no, he's not here. Is he—did he tell you he'd be here? He may be on his way, but the fog may have stopped him."

"Yes, the taxi driver told me about the fog," said the old lady. "He said he couldn't drive his car any farther—he couldn't see out the window, he said. But he gave me directions and I walked up. I been walking almost two hours." She fumbled at her wrist, flipped up the crystal of her watch, and felt the hands with her finger.

"Oh—would you like to come in?" Bob asked. She was fat, with an enormous bosom, not the kind of person who could enjoy walking for two hours. And she was Max Corrant's mother, and Max Corrant was a friend of his, he realized with something like surprise. "Come in Mrs. Corrant, and take a load off your feet."

"I don't mind if I do," she said, and put out her hand to feel the door frame. Bob took the hand and conducted her inside.

16

Mrs. Corrant had stood in the living room less than a second before she turned toward Dr. Al-Haq. "Hello," she said.

He stood up politely. "How do you do? I am Dr. Mohammed Abdeen Al-Haq."

"Iris Corrant. Are you having tea? That smells wonderful."

"You sit down, Mrs. Corrant, and I'll get you a cup," said Vicki.

"Thank you, darling," said Iris Corrant, and sighed. "I couldn't really afford a cab anyway."

Bob took her coat and scarf and conducted her to an armchair.

"You're Mr. Wilson, aren't you?" She turned her dark glasses toward him.

"Yes." He sat down in the other armchair again.

"Alvin has told me the nicest things about you. He says you're a wonderful person to work for."

"Thank you," said Bob, surprised at the sudden lump in his throat when he thought of Max lying to his mother about his work situation.

"Bob thinks the world of your son," said Vicki. "Two lumps? I met him myself, and I thought he was a very intelligent and well-spoken young man. And *handsome*."

"Give me four lumps, darling. He's out to better himself, and that's good. After he got out of prison, I told him—"

"He was in prison?" exclaimed Bob, thinking with anxiety of his credibility as a witness.

"Yes, but he's ashamed of it, so I knew he wouldn't tell you, even though he said he did. I told him this private eye business was just more of his wildness and that it would lead him wrong again, and now he's in trouble—"

"In trouble? Did he call you? What happened?"

"He gave me your address and telephone number and told me to contact you if anything ever happened to him, but your telephone isn't working, did you know that? I wouldn't have come all the way over here if it had been."

"Mrs. Corrant, what's happened to Max?" Bob could feel his friendly sentiments for Max Corrant evaporating. If his jailbird private investigator had been arrested illegally entering a convent or committing some other crime, Barry D. Wentworth III would be able to neutralize the Robinson photographs, and might even be able to use them as evidence of a pattern of illegal activities.

"That's just what I came to ask *you*," said Iris Corrant, holding the cup and saucer Vicki had put into her hands. "Where is he, Mr. Wilson?" Her voice shook suddenly. "Yesterday he told me he was going to do some—something. 'Vaylance' or something like that—"

"Surveillance."

"That's what it was; and he didn't come home last night and he didn't call me. But something has happened to him, I'm sure of it, and I'm afraid, terribly afraid."

"Why do you think something's happened to him?" asked Vicki.

"I've been blind since the day I was born, child," said Mrs. Corrant, touching her temple with a fat, dimpled hand. "But sometimes the Lord gives other gifts to make up for what we lack. This afternoon I *felt* something happen to my boy. I *felt* it, just like you feel heat if you put your hand over a flame. And I know something's happened to him."

"Oh. Well, I talked to him this afternoon," said Bob, relieved. The basis of his worries was just an old lady getting psychic vibrations. Yet as he thought that he remembered uncomfortably how Max had stopped talking in midsentence on the telephone. "He was just up visiting a convent today, so I don't think anything can have happened to him." Unless the convent wasn't a convent, as Max had suspected, Bob thought, his uneasiness growing in spite of himself. "What was it you thought you—felt?"

"It was as if something"—she gestured—"came into him, into his chest. I stopped breathing at that moment. But I could have been mistaken; sometimes I am. Are you sure he's all right, Mr. Wilson? He went up to a convent, you say? That doesn't sound dangerous."

"I'm sure he's all right," said Bob guiltily. "It was just a last detail we needed to wrap up our case."

"Praise God," said Mrs. Corrant, and drank her entire cup of lukewarm, syrupy tea at once. Then she sighed. "I've got to put him in the hands of the Almighty. There's nothing I can do anyway, an old blind woman. Well," she said, starting to get up, "I'd best get on my way."

"Certainly not, Mrs. Corrant," said Vicki over Bob's own protest. "You sit down. As soon as the fog is gone we'll drive you. You shouldn't be out in weather like this."

Mrs. Corrant laughed, her large bosom shaking. "I know just where I'm going, child. I've learned to walk in the dark. The fog is no bother to me."

"Sit down, Mrs. Corrant. A fog like this can't last too long. And I want to hear more about your 'second sight' or whatever you call it."

Iris Corrant lowered herself back into her chair. "You can call it that, honey, if you want to," she said. "I've had it since I was a child, and so did my brothers and sisters—but as they got older each of them lost it. No, they didn't *lose* it, they stopped paying attention because they had so many other things to see. Me, I had nothing else to see, so I was left alone with my 'second sight.' "

Dr. Al-Haq's eyes were bright with interest.

Iris Corrant sat still then, head cocked to one side as if listening. "Lord have mercy," she said softly after a minute.

"What is it?" asked Vicki.

"There is something strange going on around your house," said Iris Corrant slowly. "I would have noticed before, but I was so worried about Alvin."

"Something strange?" asked Bob.

"I've never felt it like that," Iris Corrant murmured. "Something trying to get in. And something else keeping it out, plucking it away time after time. There's danger outside," she blurted. She seemed to scan the room with her dark glasses, head moving back and forth. "And there's something else—in there."

She pointed in the direction of Diana's room and her voice was suddenly astonished. "Do you have a *voudoun* living in this house?"

"A voudoun?" asked Bob anxiously. He was picturing Diana Esterbrook appearing in the hallway. He knew he would have a heart attack if that happened.

"A magician, sorcerer, you might call it. Someone who can work in the other world."

Dr. M. A. Al-Haq leaned forward on the couch, eyes burning.

"If you please, Mrs. Corrant," he said softly, "what do you sense in that room?"

Iris Corrant turned her head toward him as if something in his voice had caught her attention. "Magic," she said almost in a whisper. "Power."

"Ah!" said Al-Haq, also in almost a whisper.

It was so quiet then for a minute that Bob could hear the blood rushing in his ears, could feel the creak of his joints as his tense muscles shifted him in his seat.

"Mrs. Wilson," said Al-Haq. "Would it inconvenience you greatly if we moved our little party into Ms. Esterbrook's room? It may be that this is a most providential meeting for me and for my studies. I had never considered consulting the impressions of a psychic regarding thaumatomathematics, yet now Mrs. Corrant has pointed out Ms. Esterbrook's room quite spontaneously, without prompting from anyone! I would like to discuss with Mrs. Corrant her impressions of that room and what has taken place there—if she is willing, of course."

"But what is in that room?" asked Iris Corrant distractedly. "What are you studying, Mr. Hawk?"

"Thaumatomathematics, madam. A kind of homemade magic."

"All magic is homemade, Mr. Hawk. Is that what you've been doing, Mr. Wilson? Magic? Have you gotten my boy Alvin mixed up in magic?" Her voice shook.

"Certainly not, Mrs. Corrant," said Bob, fixing Al-Haq with a disapproving look. "A fourteen-year-old girl has been staying in that room. She hasn't been doing any magic, just playing with a computer."

"The shaman's drum," murmured Al-Haq. "I hope it would not be an inconvenience, Mrs. Wilson?"

"Of course not," said Vicki, remembering her manners. "Would you gentlemen help me bring in chairs from the dining room? Bob, the card table is in the basement."

They unfolded the table inside Diana's door, and Vicki dusted it and put a white tablecloth on it. Dr. Al-Haq sat next to the bed table with the computer on it. Mrs. Corrant was to his right with the back of her chair against Diana's bed, which Vicki had tidied up for the occasion: she seemed subdued, even dazed; it was hard to tell what was going on behind her dark glasses. Bob faced Mrs. Corrant, the back of his own chair a couple of inches from the wall; at his left, by the door, sat Vicki, curious, attentive, and a little scared.

It was like a B-movie séance except that in place of a

crystal ball in the middle of the table were a large china teapot and a plate of cookies.

Al-Haq turned his benign smile on Bob and Vicki. "I have adopted the working hypothesis that Ms. Esterbrook's thaumatomathematical researches may be connected with certain odd phenomena in and around your home. I hope you will not think it intrusive if I ask you to recount more fully the history of Ms. Esterbrook's visit."

"Some of that is privileged," growled Bob.

"Ah," said Al-Haq pleasantly. "Could you tell me the part that is not?"

Bob started off slowly and cautiously with Diana's story. Then Vicki interrupted him, and he interrupted her, and it went on like that for much longer than necessary, Al-Haq interjecting questions now and then. By the time they were done Bob realized with chagrin that, privileged or not, they had held very little back from Dr. M. A. Al-Haq.

"Yet you did not discover the linked napkin rings or the little Santa Claus taken out of his glass until last night?" he asked Vicki.

"No."

"Tell me," Al-Haq went on after a short, meditative silence. "Has Ms. Esterbrook ever shown signs of confusion between right and left? Such as getting directions mixed up or not being able to tell her right from her left hand?"

"Not that I know of," said Vicki slowly.

"Have you ever seen parts of her body floating in the air, apparently dismembered?"

"Now what does *that* mean?" snapped Bob, frustration and puzzlement finally getting the best of him. "Do you think we're crazy? What do you mean, have we seen parts of her body floating in the air?"

"I mean that I may possibly have the solution to some of the mysteries that have been afflicting you. But this solution opens up further mysteries of its own."

Bob was silent, determined not to give the man the satisfaction of an eager audience.

Al-Haq again pulled his letter from an inner pocket and held it up. "The paper Ms. Esterbrook sent me brilliantly proposes using higher-dimensional mathematics to build thaumatomathematical models. In particular, she suggests *mappings to higher-dimensional nonlinear differentiable manifolds!*"

"What does that mean?" asked Vicki faintly.

"It means that, while life events may seem unpredictable and incomprehensible when viewed in three special dimensions, Ms. Esterbrook has presented evidence—preliminary as yet, but evidence just the same—that these events may become understandable if they are mapped onto—that is, roughly, expressed in—spaces of higher dimension. On the face of it, it seems inconsistent with heterotic string theory, but do you see the implications?" His voice shook with excitement.

"No," said Bob.

"What if," said Al-Haq, "our real lives take place in higher-dimensional space? What if the reason life seems incomprehensible is because our perceptions are arbitrarily limited to three dimensions? So that the patterns and relationships we see are arbitrarily limited? It would be like trying to discern the activities of a group of bathers while being able to see only the paper-thin silhouettes where their bodies intersect the surface of the water. Yet if you were able to rise above the water and watch them playing—" His burning eyes seemed to look off into higher-dimensional spaces of their own.

"The fascinating thing," he went on after a minute, "is that the feats you say Ms. Esterbrook has performed might be possible for a person having access to higher-dimensional space."

Bob and Vicki stared at him. It was hard to tell whether Iris Corrant was listening behind her glasses.

"For example, linking napkin rings. In three-dimensional space this is impossible, of course. But it is easily done if you have access to four spatial dimensions!

"Think of a string," he went on to their puzzled faces. "There is no way to knot a string in two-dimensional space because you cannot lift one end of it over the other. 'Lifting up' implies a third dimension to lift up into, which is unavailable in a two-dimensional, or flat, space. So an unknotted string will remain forever unknotted in two-dimensional space. But it can easily be knotted in three-dimensional space.

"Similarly, while two unbroken rings cannot be interlinked in three-dimensional space, they can easily be interlinked in four-dimensional space. Since Ms. Esterbrook has apparently managed this trick, it suggests that she has learned how to operate four-dimensionally, perhaps through her higher-dimensional thaumatomathematical model.

"Likewise with the little Santa Claus. While in three-dimensional space he is destined to stay forever inside his globe, in four-dimensional space one could easily reach in and take him out without breaking the glass.

"So too with Ms. Esterbrook's apparent disappearances and reappearances. Someone moving from three-space into a higher dimension would look to a three-space observer as if she had disappeared, except that parts of her body might still be visible if those parts happened to intersect with the three-space."

"Dr. Al-Haq," said Vicki suddenly, "what would four-dimensional space look like? Would it—would it seem like you could see everything all at once, and the insides of things, and things outside the place you were in, as if there weren't any walls?"

Al-Haq opened his mouth, but the voice that answered wasn't his.

"That's what it looks like, child," said Iris Corrant, her voice slow and heavy. "You see the insides of things, and everything all at once. And when you move you see different inside sides, just like you were walking through the things you were looking at, but around them at the same time."

"Yes," whispered Dr. Al-Haq, his eyes intent on Iris Corrant. "You can *see*, Mrs. Corrant."

"Sometimes," she said, nodding. "If I look in the right direction."

"Can you look in that direction now? In this room?"

She shook her head. "No. It's hard. I can't remember how. I can only feel feelings in this room."

"What do you feel?"

"I feel—a hole. There's a hole in this room—I can feel wind blowing in."

"Where is this hole?"

"I don't know. If *you* can't see it, it must be in—that other direction."

"What would help you see it? How can you find that other direction?"

"If I could turn toward it. I've done it before. But it's hard."

"Perhaps I can help you," said Dr. Al-Haq, and he switched on Diana's computer. Its fan wound up to a dull whine in the silence. "I believe," he said, "that in this computer's memory lies a description of *that direction*, and *how to turn in that direction*. I believe Ms. Esterbrook has used her thaumatomathematical model to reach a deeper level of reality just as I intended, but, unknown to me, that level resides in higher-dimensional space. If I can translate the mathematics of Ms. Esterbrook's model into a set of instructions for you, Mrs. Corrant, it may help you turn in that direction, which we call the 'fourth spatial dimension.' Are you willing to try?"

Iris Corrant nodded. "I am willing to try," she said, and her voice trembled, "because on that wind I smell my boy. On that wind I smell a trace of my boy Alvin."

The computer beeped loudly, making Bob and Vicki jump.

Al-Haq got up and switched off the ceiling light, then put the computer monitor on the card table in front of him. He put the keyboard on his lap and typed on it.

The monitor was the only source of light in the room now, throwing dramatic shadows across Al-Haq's beard and turban, making Iris Corrant's face even darker and more unreadable. The light shifted and colored as patterns played across the screen.

A pattering, scratching sound came at the window, and for a moment Bob thought it had started to rain, but the sound stopped with an unnatural suddenness, and a minute later there was the faint smell of garlic.

Bob and Vicki exchanged a look, but neither Al-Haq nor Mrs. Corrant seemed to have noticed anything. Al-Haq typed sporadically, eyes riveted to the monitor. He seemed almost to have gone into a trance; he mumbled from time to time in a voice too low to understand.

Finally he muttered, a little louder: "Let your feelings guide you.

"That is the best way. Just as you *feel* the space around you in our world, *feel* the higher space. It is all around you too, though I can't point to it."

His voice was rhythmic, hypnotic. Listening to him, Bob's eyes began to close. That was all right, he told himself. He was tired. He could let himself rest for a few minutes, ride the lull of Al-Haq's voice, relax—

"It is 'above' our world in every direction, but in no direction you have ever looked," Al-Haq went on. "To go there is a step, just one step, but in a direction you have never taken. But remember a dream where you felt a vast freedom, an exhilaration, infinite possibilities: that is it."

Bob had had such a dream; he had swum in a vast clear ocean, the edges tinged with the mist of distance, his old life left behind—

"You can change your left hand to your right hand just by turning around in the higher space. The whole world shifts around you, changing its orientation as you move in the higher space. It's so simple. *Feel* yourself turn that way, not up or down, left or right, forward or backward, but at right angles to all those directions, into a vast freedom where there is no right or left, outside everything and yet looking into the heart of everything . . ."

As Al-Haq continued to talk, giving instructions in his deep, hypnotic voice, a breeze began to stir in the room.

At first Bob tried to ignore it, block it out so he could keep sinking into the deep, relaxed concentration induced by Al-Haq's intonation. But the breeze, which was chilly and damp, got stronger. Someone had left Diana's window open, Bob thought vaguely, and now the wind was rising outside. He expected someone to say something, to get up and close it; he kept his eyes shut waiting for them to do that so he could keep sinking into the exquisite, resonant silence—

But no one did, and the breeze was uncomfortably insistent. Still, it was an effort for Bob to pry his eyelids open and turn his head toward the source of it.

When he did he found himself looking at something unrecognizable.

Nothing like it had been in the room before. It was a six-foot sphere of what looked like polished silver, like a giant Christmas tree ornament. In some strange way it seemed not really to be in the room at all, but somehow superimposed on it like a bad photographic collage.

Bob got out of his chair and went toward the thing very slowly. And after that nothing was ever the same for him again.

After he had taken a few steps toward the sphere thing, Bob turned around to ask the others what it was.

And got the shock of his life.

He found himself looking at something he didn't at first recognize, a dull, faintly buzzing chaos hanging somehow below him in a wide space. His first thought was that his eyes had gone out of focus or that he was hallucinating. But then the scene fell into place, and he wished he were insane or had never been born.

A bomb or some kind of destructive force had gone through the guest bedroom, hacking everything to pieces. Al-Haq, Iris Corrant, and Vicki, *his own Vicki,* were mounds of bones and organs oozing from their chairs, everything around them torn open, the walls blown away.

Bob staggered backward, turning to look away from it. Get away. Go die somewhere without thinking about it. His stomach rose into his throat.

But there was something peculiar.

In the split second when he moved, the scene changed. All the objects in the room *rotated their insides at him.*

He fainted.

When he came to, dizzy and sick, he was still looking down at the blown-up room, and in that room—He stared. Something that couldn't be was happening. The shapes, the burst-open shapes of his wife and one of the others *were moving.* He was terrified now, and he made another move to get away, run as fast as he could from the animated corpses, but he stopped again at once, realizing that it had to be a hallucination. Al-Haq had hypnotized him with that voice of his; that had been an hypnotic induction—

Again, as he moved, everything in the room bubbled with internal detail.

It was horrifying yet fascinating. Hesitantly and slowly he moved again, stopped, then again, watching closely. It was dawning on him that the effects of his movements were not random; it was as if they caused the things below him to scroll through a series of internal images of themselves. And abruptly he saw that the room *hadn't* been blown apart: all the objects—and to his inexpressible re-

lief, the people—were unbroken, still maintained their
shapes—*but he was seeing the insides of them.*

At that same instant he realized that the vague buzzing he had been hearing was *voices,* voices yelling in shock
and calling his name. Two of the three cutaway meat-and-
skeleton people below him had moved from their cutaway
chairs, one opening the cutaway door of the cutaway room
and running out into the cutaway hall.

Their voices were like the tinny sounds from a cheap
radio. "Bob! Bob! Where are you?" "Mr. Wilson? Mr. Wilson, sir, respond to me!"

He didn't answer. Because through his fear and confusion and relief and guilt another feeling had burst like a
volcano: a vertiginous exhilaration. *He had entered another
world,* he realized with overpowering shock. *He was there,
looking down at earth! He could see the insides of things!*

Had he died? he wondered numbly as he glanced
around, restricting the movement of his head so as not to
see too much at once, not to succumb to the vertigo and
dizziness. He didn't see his own body below him as he had
heard you were supposed to when you had a near-death
experience; and anyway, the cutaway, internally rotating
Vicki and Dr. Al-Haq were looking for him wildly all over
the house, one of them running up the stairs and the other
into the kitchen. He could see them even though there
should have been walls in the way, and indeed there *were*
walls, but standing at an angle he had never imagined before. It was as if he saw them, as well as the rest of the
house and the insides of everything in it, from no particular angle and yet from every angle, so that he was all
around the house and it was all around him, and yet he
was removed from it, above it—though *above* was not the
right word: he was removed from it in some inexpressible
way. It was like imagining a house, not from any particular
angle, but just imagining it in general—except he was *seeing* it that way. And outside the house the neighborhood
stretched away in the same cutaway condition, all the

houses, trees, cars, everything revealing their insides to
him, and rotating their internal images at him as he or
they moved; but the farther away the object the less internal detail he could see, until in the far, fish-eye distance
things looked almost as they had for all his normal life,
except stretched out "below" him in seemingly infinite
perspective.

The fourth dimension. He was in the *fourth dimension*,
he realized from what Dr. Al-Haq had said. His body
burned as adrenaline poured through it, heart pounding as
if it would burst. He closed his eyes to calm himself, careful not to move. If he moved he might accidentally step
back down into the third dimension, where he had lived
all his life, and he didn't want to do that, not yet. When
you were forty-one years old with a house in the suburbs
and a job that would last until you retired and nothing in
particular going to happen between now and the time you
died, you couldn't afford to pass up something like this.
He knew he could go back to the lower world anytime he
wanted—it was just a step away: he could see it! But what
if, when he got there, he couldn't find the way up again?

He opened his eyes, and after a minute of gathering
his courage, raised them to look "upward," to see what
was beyond the world he had always known.

And almost immediately lowered them again, trembling and gasping.

He had seen pictures of the Himalayas and the Andes,
mountains with country-size gorges and dizzy overhangs
so high that the distances below seemed as misty and endless as the distances above; he had flown on business trips
among thunderheads like the towering, black, and roiling
castles of heaven; but looking up timidly from his new
vantage point he saw a space whose every centimeter fell
away in vast perspectives wider than any he had known,
so vast that in the high distances they seemed to curve into
time itself. Yet he did not fall; the monstrous spaces approached him tenderly and he stood upon them; he felt as

he had when a little boy and walking at sunset in a wide field of new-mown grass, the evening light and utter stillness of the air making the sky a cozy infinity through which the distant sounds of children playing came with perfect clarity. He could not have described this place or formed an accurate image of it; but forever after the impression that came when he tried to remember it was that of a mountain path, or rather an infinity of them leading in different directions, the mountains themselves many ranges superimposed on one another, some upside down and others sideways, so that yawning chasms and peaks spread above and below and on every side.

Because the fourth dimension wasn't just another direction like up, forward, or sideways, he realized, squeezing his eyes shut as tears streamed from them. It was like an infinite number of three-dimensional worlds folded into each other. *There was no end to the directions you could go!* In such a world, instinct told him, there could be no death.

His head swam. Yet he knew he would look up again. He had to look up. His whole life revolved around looking up into that space.

A chilly breeze distracted him.

He glanced around to see where it was coming from and again noticed the silver sphere.

It seemed to hang in the higher space at the same "level" as him, just "above" the guest bedroom of his house, perhaps touching it imperceptibly.

Bob approached the sphere. Somehow he was able to move in this space, he realized belatedly; he would have to consider this wonder in its turn, but now the sphere had his attention. It was bearable to look at, unlike the deeps "above"; it seemed in fact just a shiny, three-dimensional ball, except that it didn't reflect his image. Instead it seemed to display another image, a picture of a house, distorted on its curved surface just as a reflection would have been. An ordinary, slightly dilapidated house nestled among trees in what looked like a heavy mist. And out of this picture came the breeze.

Bob leaned forward to touch the sphere, but its solidity was an illusion. His hand encountered no resistance; he lost his balance and fell forward into it.

17

~

Inside, the sphere was ashen-dark and suffocating, as if he had fallen into a grave. With the panic of claustrophobia he lunged backward to get out.

He went back a dozen feet but the darkness and narrowness persisted. He turned and ran, whimpering with fear. A tree branch hit him in the chest and he fell onto hard, muddy ground, breath knocked out of him.

He thought he knew what had happened but he didn't want to believe it. If only he had stayed away from the sphere—

He ran wildly back and forth through misty forest now looking for the "hole" that had dropped him into the lower world, and through which maybe he could climb back up. He stumbled on roots and brush, branches tearing at his clothes and scratching his hands and face. There was no sign of a hole or any other unusual thing. Finally he sank to his knees on a blanket of wet fallen leaves and started to sob.

After a while his sorrow turned to dull despair. He stood up again. He felt like a flat man in a comic strip. But a man who had tasted the freedom of the higher space—the endless depths, the infinite directions, the heavy, full luminescence of the light—only to be banished again to this moribund ashes-world.

Yet he had gone to that space once, he realized. He

could go again. He could get Dr. Mohammed Abdeen Al-Haq to do another mathematical hypno-séance on him, suggesting to his receptive brain the "direction" of the higher space, where he would gladly die if they had no food he could eat or water he could drink—though the hunch came to him again that there could be no death there.

Bob turned around to orient himself, find his way back home, find Dr. Al-Haq—

There was a house, he realized now, nestled among some trees twenty feet away, just visible in the fog: not his own house—this one looked like a run-down Victorian with moss on the roof and paint peeling from the siding. It was the house he had seen in the silver ball, he realized. It now occurred to him that the silver ball had been one end of a "tunnel" running through the higher-dimensional space; he thought vaguely that he had heard of such things, perhaps in the science fiction books he had read as a teenager.

And now, his mind slowly clearing, he recalled that Diana Esterbrook had been disappearing mysteriously from her room over the past few days. Had she disappeared through the "tunnel"? If so, this house was apparently where she had been disappearing *to*. He suddenly wondered whose house it was.

He went toward it cautiously, aware now of the silence of the fog, in which his footsteps rustling dead leaves sounded loud. The house was dark. There were no other houses in sight. An uneven walk of moss-grown brick led to a front door. The street number was painted on one of the pillars supporting the portico: 523.

523 Oakwood Court was Wendall Thaxton's address, Bob remembered with sudden clarity. And Diana had told Vicki it was at the end of a street in Sligo Woods, out of sight of any other houses. Wendall Thaxton's weathered front door was unlocked.

Inside, the house was dark and dead still. Bob stepped

in and closed the door behind him without noise. He wasn't afraid, he noticed. After seeing the higher space it would be hard to be afraid of anything in this paper-cutout world, he guessed.

The house smelled of old furniture and cold fireplace ashes. He could hear nothing over the internal sounds of his body. His fingers felt a door frame and old, crackling wallpaper beyond it.

As his eyes got used to the dark, vague shapes showed themselves, humps and angles of furniture. A doorway outlined itself beyond them.

He felt his way silently to the doorway. There were steps going up. He climbed them as carefully as he could, but they creaked. He froze and listened, but the silence was undisturbed.

When he got to the top there was a hall, and in the first room off the hall someone sighed.

Bob stood scarcely breathing for a minute, two, three. The house was utterly still. He crept to the door. The room was pitch dark, but the air was heavy with the smell of sleep.

He found a light switch, flicked it.

The dim ceiling bulb seemed blinding. He was in a small bedroom with faded flower wallpaper, a dark antique bureau, a sagging bed. A shade was drawn over the window. In the bed Diana Esterbrook lay fast asleep in her clothes.

After a moment of shock, Bob moved toward her.

"You won't be able to wake her," said a voice behind him.

He jumped high enough to hit the ceiling.

Wendall Thaxton stood in the doorway. He was wearing his black overcoat but not his ski cap, and his white hair was wild. He looked at Bob from under scraggly eyebrows, hands hanging at his sides.

"I've given her sleeping pills," he explained.

"You," gasped Bob. "You kidnaped her. I'm going to call the police."

"Please don't," said Thaxton. "It would destroy any chance we have, she and I, of—doing something we have to do."

Bob was much bigger and younger than Thaxton—he was sure he could overpower him. Yet Thaxton was studying him with a calm, grave expression; not the look of an apprehended criminal.

"How did you get here?" he asked Bob. "How did you protect yourself without one of the talismans?"

"I'm going to call the police," Bob repeated. But as he said the words something shook loose in his brain, something that had been suspended, turned off, interrupted by the overwhelming experiences of the past few hours.

How *had* he gotten here?

The utter strangeness—craziness, really—of his experiences: what was the most likely explanation for them? Had stress or hypnotism caused him to have hallucinations, a delusional episode? He tried desperately to think, to recollect some solid criteria of reality against which he could measure what he had seen.

Wasn't a hallucination the most likely explanation?

If he had been hallucinating then he might be crazy, but worse than that, much worse, *there was no higher space:* it had been an illusion. There was no escape from this flat, ashen, pointless world where you had to die after all, no vast, luminous perspective that penetrated the insides of things, no infinite ways to go.

Yet he was here, he told himself desperately, at Wendall Thaxton's house, and Diana was here. And the things that had happened over the past week couldn't all have been hallucinations, because Vicki had seen them too.

Whatever the explanation, Wendall Thaxton was at the center of it. If there really was a higher space, odds were Wendall Thaxton knew about it.

"Tell me," he rasped hoarsely at Thaxton, who was still standing motionless, watching him. "Tell me what's going on—what's going on here."

"Will you come down to the kitchen, Mr. Wilson? Let's have a cup of—"

"No, tell me here."

"It's a long—"

"Tell me here."

"All right." Thaxton sighed. He bowed his head and seemed to think. "How much do you know already?"

"I don't know."

"All right." Thaxton's eyes were abstracted; he raised his hands; they were long and narrow. *A sorcerer's hands,* the thought came to Bob, unbidden.

"A long time ago," Thaxton began, and his eyes were distant, "a long time ago this land was quiet. It was a quietness you can scarcely imagine in this age of clamor: the stillness of woods and meadows and hills that had always been. There were few people then, not enough to disturb more than a few small patches of countryside. The wind rustled the trees and the sun shone and the crops grew silently in the fields and dogs barked in the villages. In those days you could sit in a cave in the cliffs to the east of here and all around you was silence.

"There was a boy living near here in those days. His family were farmers and by every expectation he should have been a farmer too, but there was something wrong with him. He first began to feel it when he was twelve or thirteen. It was the quietness that seemed to disturb him. It seemed to him that something hung in that quietness, something just beyond the reach of his senses, like something waiting to materialize from thin air. The wind in the trees had a voice he could almost hear, the light of dusk seemed to be the glint of an eye, the rain a gateway to another world. The boy walked in the forest day and night, listening. The sense of it—the feeling that there was something just beyond the reach of his hands—tormented him.

"His family worried about him, but finally they saw that there was nothing to be done. So they arranged for him to enter an occupation where his impairment wouldn't matter much, and by the time he was twenty he was supporting himself meagerly. But he still spent most of his time alone in the forest. By then he had learned how to sit still and listen. That is a lost art today." Thaxton smiled at Bob.

"Sitting and listening for days at a time, many things came to the young man. For one thing, he became convinced that there *was* something lurking in the silence just beyond the reach of his senses, something numinous, something he and every other person he knew seemed to have been looking for since they were born. He began to believe that as embodied in this world both our minds and bodies are incomplete, fragments of something greater lying in deeper spaces outside those we can see."

"Deeper spaces," said Bob hoarsely.

"Yes," said Thaxton.

"Have you seen them? Have you been there?"

"I don't remember."

Bob stared at him. "Who are you?"

"Ah," said Thaxton gravely, "now you are beginning to understand. It's just that you don't yet have the sense to wonder who *you* are."

In a minute he went on. "Those days were long before the modern idea developed that mind and consciousness are made up of mindlessness and unconsciousness, so it was natural for the young man to suppose that in such deeper or higher spaces might reside a higher Mind, and that humans might be exiled fragments of this higher Mind, something like repressed complexes residing in a twilit, dimension-poor subconscious realm of this Mind—though of course those concepts hadn't been invented yet either.

"Imagine how it feels to be a repressed complex, a fragment of mind-stuff trapped in some kind of neural feedback loop that can never contact the enormous mental space outside itself. Cut off from a source it can't imagine, bounded, small—fearful, perhaps; unable to remember but perhaps intuiting a state of being part of something much greater. In this Eagle thought he saw—"

"Eagle?"

Thaxton watched him carefully. "You have heard of Eagle?"

Bob nodded.

"Then you know the old stories. You have heard this before."

"No."

Thaxton studied him closely. "You haven't heard how Eagle decided to invade the realm of the higher Mind? How like an obsessive complex he determined to disturb the higher Mind until it took notice of him, how he vowed to reopen the connection between Earth and Heaven by curing the higher Mind of its repression of the contents of our world?"

"No."

"And you don't know how Eagle's plans were frustrated, how war of a kind he had never seen before descended, breaking the crystalline silence that had allowed his perceptions, his cognitions, his travels? How the enormous neural energy he had built up for his task became not only useless but dangerous, how he had to—"

"No."

Thaxton's eyes became distant again, pensive. "It was a mistake," he sighed after a minute. "A simple failure in planning. He thought the war between the settlers and his people would be like the Indian tribal wars before it, soon over, leaving the land to its silence. He didn't realize that the roar of great machines and the babble of millions of people would soon fill the land, that in that cacophony and profound disturbance of the natural world the silence he needed to cross to the higher spaces would disappear.

"But not knowing that, Eagle took what seemed the wisest path. He devised a method to disguise himself until it should be safe and quiet enough for him to begin to work again."

Bob knew what was coming next. Clement Fox had ruined him for this. He took a deep breath. "So you're going to tell me he divided himself into pieces and turned into a white man. You're going to tell me that this Indian shaman turned into half a dozen white men, right?" While he was having trouble right now deciding what to believe and disbelieve, he still knew enough to disbelieve this neolithic fairy tale.

"Not half a dozen," said Thaxton. "Five. That was roughly how much energy Eagle had accumulated, enough for five people. And they weren't all men. Not all the time. Men and women. And children."

So that was what he had to believe if he wanted to believe in the "higher space." Despair and anger and fear of this crazy old man jostled each other in Bob's brain.

"The current incarnation of one of them," Thaxton said, "is lying on that bed behind you."

"The woman you know as Armilla Robinson is another," Thaxton went on. "The little boy Zachary Taylor is the third, and another little boy you never met was the fourth. She doesn't know," he gestured at Diana again. "She has hardly any of the memories; just whatever deep structures are needed to support her portion of the personality. Most of the memories are held by Zachary and me."

"You!"

"Of course. Is it really such a surprise? Good; I'm relieved the disguise is so effective. One of the fragments needs to have enough memories and continuity to watch over the others. I'm the only one who doesn't cycle from youth to age. I've lived in this house and this body for over three hundred years, trying to be as inconspicuous as possible."

"This is insane. This is—"

"And yet you've seen the higher space, haven't you?" said Thaxton shrewdly.

Bob stared at him, his brain a jumble.

"How did you get to it? People don't just stumble into it; not normal people."

"I—" said Bob, head spinning. "A man—hypnotized me. I looked up and saw—"

"A man? Who?"

"His name is Mohammed something—Al-Haq."

Thaxton looked shocked. "Al-Haq?" he demanded. "You saw him? Where?"

"He—he came to our house. He wanted to see Diana."

Thaxton's skin had gone gray; for a moment Bob thought he would faint. But instead he mumbled: "This is it, then. *This is it.*" His eyes focused intensely on Bob. "Can I count on your help?"

"No! I'm going to the police—"

"There isn't time for that," Thaxton snapped. "The reintegration will have to be done *tonight,* before Armilla wastes the rest of her energy. And Al-Haq is right under our noses! It has to be tonight. *Tonight.*

"Please, listen a few more minutes before you decide," he interrupted Bob's opening mouth. "Though I don't remember everything—Zachary has the memories of the higher space. Eagle made that fragment mute; it would be impossible to be inconspicuous if you could talk about those things. Though his memories make it possible for him to help me in my work at times.

"I lived many years in despair after I finally realized that the silence had disappeared forever. If Eagle were remade he would never be able to fulfill his plans; he would have to hide in the vanishing forests, or more likely be imprisoned or hospitalized as a freak or lunatic. I watched helplessly as his other fragments live out their fifth or sixth incarnations as maladjusted freaks. It wasn't until the 1940s that I finally saw a glimmer of hope: the invention of the electronic computer. It occurred to me that someday perhaps these buzzing, humming, clicking monstrosities might be able to use the higher-dimensional mathematics invented in the nineteenth century to mimic the enhanced kinesthetic sense Eagle had developed to guide himself through the silence and into the deeper space.

"I taught this fragment "—he gestured to the sleeping girl on the bed—"which holds most of Eagle's powerful reasoning capacity—everything I could find out about computers. As I had hoped, she had a strong affinity for them. I let her play on the most advanced machines I could build, and gave her books about the mathematics I thought might be needed to reach the higher space. One book was particularly exciting: an eccentric genius—Mohammed Abdeen Al-Haq—was developing mathematical techniques for changing states of consciousness—and seemingly unbeknownst to him, the changes he aimed for appeared to be those that allowed perception of the higher space!

"Then disaster struck.

"It was too much of a strain on me to keep the other fragments always in my household as my 'wives,' 'children,' and 'grandchildren': the fragments are for obvious reasons socially dysfunctional. The most troublesome has always been 'Armilla'; she holds most of what you might call Eagle's temperament—his appetites, drives, sexuality, egotism. As Armilla's 'father' I was put to trials I do not envy natural humans; I sent her out to live on her own as soon as I could, with her 'daughter' Diana, and arranged for her to work as a nanny in a household where one of the other fragments had been adopted.

"That was a mistake. The little boy fragment—Travis—held much of Eagle's magical aptitude.

Without the formulas in the mute Zachary's memory and the analytical aptitude held by Diana, Travis could never become an actual shaman; rather, he grew lifetime after lifetime into a sickly, melancholy, quixotic person. An aura of dark mysticism hung around him.

"Unfortunately, growing up with me and my books Armilla had developed a preoccupation with magic. As soon as she moved into the Vesperson household she became obsessed with Travis. She developed the intuition—in a normal context it would have been a psychotic fixation—that she could gain great powers if she could somehow absorb or be unified with him.

"Finally she arranged with a local man to kidnap him. I have no idea how she accomplished the reintegration. I devoutly hope she did not literally dismember and eat him, as her coconspirator testified at their trial. But the result was exactly as she had hoped: she now commanded twice the neural energy of a normal human, plus a good deal of magical aptitude.

"I met her at the gate on the day of her release from prison. She laughed at my offer to take her home. Instead, she took a bus to a town where there was a coven of self-styled witches. She demonstrated her powers and they lavished worship and money on her. With their help she made a beeline for Diana Esterbrook. The intuition had come to her, again correctly, that she could increase her powers even more if she 'devoured' her 'daughter.'

"I built in my basement tiny copies of a talisman Eagle had designed three hundred years before in silver, quartz, and pottery. I put them around Diana in cloves of garlic, just as the original version had been used. That is what your wife found me doing in your house a week ago. I apologize for frightening her, but the talismans have undoubtedly saved you from attempts by Armilla to enter your home.

"Armilla's extravagant use of her powers—especially the making of this fog—is an enormous drain on the energy Eagle so carefully saved up. I cannot let that continue. At the same time, it appears that Diana has found the way to the higher space. The time to reintegrate Eagle is *now*.

"I need to gather the fragments together. Diana is already here and Zachary will come if I ask him, but Armilla hates and distrusts me; after all, I am her 'father.' Yet she must be brought before she wastes all her energy, or damages Al-Haq or Diana's computer model. You must bring her to me—tonight."

"You must be—this is insane!" Bob burst out, his agitation finally overcoming his disorientation. "You—you're asking me—Look," he tried to calm himself, think rationally, "let's assume what you're saying is true—"

"You know it is. You've seen the higher space."

The two of them stared at each other.

"It's exhilarating, isn't it?" Thaxton went on finally. "And there's a yearning I remember faintly—as if once having seen it, he couldn't rest. That was *real life*, Eagle's peripheral memories say. This," he waved his hand, "is a counterfeit, a pitiful fake."

Bob was hanging on his words.

"There," Thaxton went on, "there is no death. The way out of death is as easy as the way out of a locked room. You can move across time. Please help me," he said to Bob. "If you do, I'll make sure Eagle takes you there, shows it to you again. I promise. What do you say?"

Bob opened his mouth to say *no*, but Thaxton's words had touched something in him, reminded him of what he had seen. He said slowly: "Let's assume you're not crazy. If there's anything to your story, Armilla Robinson is one of the most dangerous people alive. What's to keep her from killing me?"

"I'm glad you asked that." Thaxton dug in the pocket of his overcoat and held something out to Bob in the palm of his hand. It was a clove of garlic. "These talismans have no power in themselves. When they detect shamanic auras—what we would call 'augmented neural energy'—they vibrate. The vibration atomizes the garlic, which gives off a characteristic smell. That's all the talismans do.

"But they work. They've saved Diana from Armilla several times, and may have saved you. Yet I believe they're just markers. I speculate that once Eagle gets into the higher space, he will return to the places and times in our space where intervention is needed to ensure that the chain of events leading to his reintegration is unbroken. I believe that from the parts of the higher space that allow movement in time, our space looks flat, dark, confusing. To find his way to events in our space where his intervention is needed, Eagle must have markers, like the intense smell of atomized garlic.

"The fact that Diana, you, and I are still alive, indicates that Eagle has come back to the events marked by the talismans—that is, that he will come back and help us—is already helping us. That means we will succeed in reintegrating him! So don't be afraid. Concentrate on your reward. The higher space! Your last visit there was a fluke, a one-in-a-million accident. *You will never see it again if Eagle doesn't help you.*"

Bob opened his mouth to say no, to shout at the little man that he was crazy, a psychotic kidnaper—

"All right," he heard himself say shakily instead. "I'll try. You promise about the—the higher space?"

"I promise," said Thaxton. "I promise."

18

It wasn't until an hour later that Bob realized that even if he was fated to be a conduit for Eagle's successful reintegration, it didn't necessarily mean that he himself would survive.

But by then he and Thaxton had split up and Bob was in his own neighborhood, the night eerily silent, impenetrable except for occasional street lamps like disembodied spheres of light floating in the fog. He stumbled once over a misplaced garbage can and another time over a tricycle left on the sidewalk. He saw the glow of windows a few times, but mostly he walked through a solitary, purgatorial landscape planted with street signs from an earlier life, which he practically had to climb to read.

He walked as fast as he could, cold, wet breath of the fog wafting over him. Numb though he was, he was anxious to get home and show Vicki he was still alive. Thaxton had not told him how to find Armilla other than an ominously vague instruction to "walk around"; he guessed this qualified.

He had reached Shope Street when out of the fog from two or three blocks away a bloodcurdling howl rose, the exultant scream of a huge animal on the scent of blood.

Bob Wilson scuttled in the direction of his house, hands held out blindly in the fog, breath sobbing in his throat. He ran full into a planted sapling, stumbled off a curb, careened off a parked car.

When the howl came again it was deafening, so close he could feel the vibration of it, hear the slavering intake of breath.

The fog was a silent chaos of blindness, his heart thundering, a scream trapped in his throat, hands scrabbling in his pockets for the garlic thing Thaxton—

—*hadn't given him,* he remembered suddenly—*he hadn't taken the garlic thing from Thaxton*—

His stomach surged into his throat and the ground heaved under him like a boat in a storm.

Then, strangely, his fainting fit and terror were gone, replaced by an icy clarity in which he saw that he would either lose his life or save it in the next minute. It was the same feeling he had gotten the first time he had ever stood up in court.

"Ms. Robinson?" he said into the blank gray of the fog. "Armilla Robinson?"

A huge, deep-chested growl came from only a few feet away.

"Ms. Robinson, I know where Diana is. She's not at my house. She's somewhere safe, but without my help you'll never find her."

Bob felt a movement of air and the heat of a great body.

"Think about it, Ms. Robinson. You don't get Diana unless I help you. And someone told me your power's going to run out soon, so you may not have long to find her."

Armilla Robinson emerged from the fog two feet from him and stood smiling in the darkness.

"Who told you that?" she asked.

She was wearing more than in his photograph of her, but not much more: a brief leather outfit designed for support rather than modesty, and there were leather thongs on her feet. Her skin glistened with sweat and her eyes were full of a wild exultation. The fog swirled around her as if she gave off some kind of field that disturbed it.

"Who told you that?" she asked again.

"I'd rather not say."

"Don't play lawyer with me, little man. That part of the game is over."

"Then don't you play werewolf bitch with me, little lady. You want my help, we'll talk. You don't want my help, you can—eat me up or whatever you're going to do and never get to Diana, and run out of the power you got from Travis, and end up a housewife in the suburbs around here." He was breathing hard.

He couldn't tell if she looked more shocked at his mention of Travis or the word *housewife.* "Where did you hear about that?" she snapped. "Have you been talking to my father?" Then with growing revelation: "Ahh! So *he* has Diana, that meddling old bastard. Well, it'll be a pleasure to pay him for that, after I take you."

Her eyes were blazing but Bob already had a perplexed look on his face. He had done enough negotiations in his time to know that a shrewd guess by the other side was just that—a shrewd guess.

"Your father? What are you talking about?" he asked with puzzlement. Then irritation: "Are you kidding me? Okay, screw you—I'm out of here."

He moved to walk off but her steel-hard hand held him. "Don't lie to me," she snarled through gritted teeth. "You won't like the result."

"Oh, your super powers tell you when people are lying too, huh? Then I guess it's no use trying to fool you any more. Think of me when you buy your washer and dryer, and when you start getting wrinkles in that beautiful face."

"Prove you're not lying."

"Trust me."

Her hand felt like it would crack his arm bone, and raw hatred passed over her face. "I should kill you right now," she said through gritted teeth, "just for being a big shot bastard. Just for being able to live in this filthy world."

In spite of everything he felt suddenly sorry for her. Good; compassion could be a tool like anything else. His voice trembled a little as he said: "Armilla, I know what you've gone through. I know more about you than you do yourself. You need to get to Diana. You need Diana more than you realize. I want to help you. Come with me."

She looked suddenly into his eyes with the anguished indecision of a child.

"Come with me," he said gently.

He disengaged her hand from his arm, which tingled as blood ran through it again.

He led her down the sidewalk until a deep voice snarled: "Freeze right where you are!"

A big man in a trenchcoat emerged from the fog pointing a gun at them with both hands. FBI, it flashed on Bob.

Armilla backhanded the man and Bob saw a glimpse of his feet, then heard his gun rattle on the roof of a parked car. He turned to her in horror. She smiled. "Your house is right here, if that's where you're taking me. And now that I have you," she got her vise-grip on him again, "you can get me past whatever it is you have guarding it. A charm of some kind, right? Did my father give you that as well?"

"Your father again. Maybe you need a psychiatrist instead of Diana."

He shuffled up the path to his front door, carefully disguising his eagerness. As they got near he heard a tiny, shrill whine, so high it was nearly inaudible. The intense smell of garlic came to him—not a cooking smell, he realized now, but a raw garlic aerosol. The most beautiful smell in the world, if only it meant what Thaxton said it did.

"That's it," said Armilla nervously, stopping. "That's the charm. Turn it off. Turn it off, you understand?"

"I can't turn it off. Come inside. Don't worry, it won't hurt you."

He pulled her forward, confidence blooming in him. Apparently she had had some unpleasant experiences with the talismans. That thought made him a little more comfortable about letting her into his house.

The front door was locked and he didn't have his key: the consequence of having left by an unusual route. The thought intensified the lifting feeling in his chest: *the higher space was real!* He knocked.

The door flew open and Vicki stood there, face red with crying. When she saw him she sobbed and fell into his arms. Her arms were very tight around him.

He lifted her and carried her inside.

Dr. Al-Haq was standing in the foyer.

"Mr. Wilson!" he exclaimed. "We feared—" He stopped as Armilla Robinson stepped into the foyer and closed the door behind her.

Now Vicki was looking at her too. Her arms went away from Bob and she stood on her own feet. "And to think I was worried about you," she said casually.

"You're not going to believe what I'm going to tell you," Bob said breathlessly to her and Al-Haq.

"Try us," said Vicki coldly, wiping her tears with her hand. Armilla had a sardonic smile on her face.

"Mr. Wilson, we saw you disappear—!" Al-Haq blurted. "May I ask you, sir, what was your own experience? Was it something that could have been consistent with—"

"—the higher space. Yes," said Bob. He was dizzy with excitement and happiness now. He took Vicki's hands and looked from her worried, perplexed face to Al-Haq's flushed one. "You saw me go?"

"Yes, just before Mrs. Corrant went. Did she come back with you?" Al-Haq stared at Armilla Robinson as if to satisfy himself that this was not Mrs. Corrant. Armilla was listening curiously.

"Mrs. Corrant? She went up too? No, I didn't see her. She might have gone in a different direction. There are a million different directions!" Bob was so happy he could barely think. *The higher space was real!*

"But Bob, how did you—" Vicki's voice broke and tears rolled down her cheeks, her eyes wide and scared, as if he were still missing.

That sobered him. He took her in his arms and rocked her, and for a minute they were all alone.

"I thought you were dead," Vicki whispered into his ear. He stroked her hair. "I decided not to die without you," he whispered back.

"Where's Diana?" Armilla demanded. "I can watch TV if I want to see this kind of stuff. Where's my daughter?"

"Okay," said Bob, holding Vicki with one arm and turning awkwardly in the foyer so he could look at the others. "I'll explain everything later. Right now we have to go somewhere. To Diana," he answered Armilla's suspicious, angry look.

The telephone rang.

Vicki went into the study agitatedly to get it. "It's Agent Kozlowski," she called.

"Have you left your house tonight?" Kozlowski demanded abruptly when Bob got on the phone.

"What do you mean?"

"I mean have you walked out the door of your house tonight," said Kozlowski angrily.

"No, I haven't," said Bob truthfully.

"You didn't meet a woman on the sidewalk in front of your house? Didn't talk to a nude woman on the sidewalk in front of your house?"

"No."

"Let me give you a piece of advice, Mr. Wilson. Don't go out tonight. You go out and you could get mixed up in a criminal conspiracy, maybe even treason. Is that clear?"

"It certainly is, Mr. Kozlowski."

Kozlowski hung up.

"What is it?" asked Vicki. Everyone had come into the study, Vicki and Al-Haq curious, Armilla tense and suspicious.

"Kozlowski says to stay home," said Bob. "But we have to get to Diana tonight, now, and then *I get a ride to the higher space.*"

"Oh, no," said Vicki. "Not again. You set one foot in Diana's room, Bob Wilson, and I'll divorce you."

"The FBI is probably watching our cars," said Bob, thinking furiously. "Do you have a car?" he asked Armilla.

She studied him before she nodded.

"But you can't drive in this fog," said Vicki. "And they'll arrest us. Bob——"

Out in the fog, it struck Bob that maybe his plan wasn't so brilliant after all. The little plastic box he had taken from over his bedroom window, though swathed in many layers of kitchen wrap, gave off a stench that could probably be smelled a block away. At the same time, the rustling of leaves as they pushed through the Ranellis' hedge, murmured ejaculations by Dr. Al-Haq in his mother tongue, and Vicki stumbling over roots should be enough to alert every FBI agent in the neighborhood to their presence.

"One more house over and then across the street," Armilla whispered, her lips to Bob's ear. She gave him a little lick too. Her mood had improved as soon as they had left the house, her eyes shining as if they were on some kind of adventure. Troublesome, Thaxton had called her, but 'perversely unpredictable' was a better description. And this was Eagle's personality, Bob thought worriedly; and then was shocked at himself all over again for believing in Eagle.

Cold water from the hedge trickled down his neck. He pulled on Vicki's hand, hoping she still had hold of the invisible Al-Haq, who was carrying the computer box. He tried to make himself remember Thaxton's argument that Eagle would be reintegrated, but thinking about it gave him a feeling of unreality, as if he were walking in a dream. He banged his head solidly into a low branch on one of the Ranellis' trees.

"This way," Armilla licked into his ear after they had crossed most of the Proutmans' yard. She seemed at home in the fog. She changed direction and Bob felt pavement under his feet. In a few seconds he heard the click of a car door opening.

"In," Armilla breathed. He ducked into the rear of a limousine, a black, bus-length vehicle with two sofalike back seats facing each other. Bob sank into one of them and pulled Vicki next to him. Al-Haq stumbled in with a guttural exclamation and thumped Diana's computer down on the floor.

Armilla shut the door quietly and sat next to Al-Haq, facing Bob and Vicki.

"Now what?" she asked. "I'll give you, say, thirty minutes to get me to Diana. After that there's going to be trouble."

"Well," said Bob, not knowing how to break it to them. He fumbled in his pocket, pulled out the little box, and unwrapped it. The smell of garlic became violent. All three of the others protested simultaneously.

"Is the key in the ignition?" asked Bob. He was wondering how he would explain this if it didn't work. Because now that he was actually doing it, it seemed certain that it wouldn't.

"Honey, what are we *doing* here?" Vicki demanded, sounding close to tears again. "Did you bring us here just to suffocate us? What if we get arrested?"

Al-Haq, after fighting it for a minute, broke into a long, wheezing cough. Bob's own eyes were watering.

"You stupid bastard," Armilla choked.

Bob held the garlic box out on the palm of his hand.

He could feel it vibrating, the talisman's transducer triggered by Armilla's brain waves. "Eagle," he said solemnly, aware of how foolish it sounded, "we need—"

The limousine's starter turned over and the engine roared to life.

There was no one in the driver's seat or in the front seat at all. But looking over his shoulder Bob thought he had seen a blur by the ignition key; and now another one moved the automatic transmission selector to Drive.

Two blurs appeared on the steering wheel.

Vicki, Al-Haq, and Armilla barely had time to open their mouths and eyes in panic before the big car squealed away from the curb.

Vicki and Armilla screamed. Al-Haq sat bolt upright, clutching the armrest.

The astonished face of a trenchcoated man flashed by the passenger window, and then the big car picked up speed, nothing visible out the windshield but onrushing billows of fog.

Bob gripped the door handle as the car fishtailed around a corner, holding desperately to the mental model he had made of this, picturing himself looking down onto a two-dimensional foggy street. From the third dimension he would be able to reach down and operate a car in that flat space while still being able to see "above" the fog.

Armilla Robinson was at him now, powerful fingers clawing at his throat, terror-stricken face screaming: "What is it? What is it?"

The car took another corner and she was upside down by the door, long legs flailing. A dozen parked cars flew by six inches away. As the limousine accelerated into a straightaway Bob thought he heard faintly an explosion in the street, as if someone had fired a gun.

Thirty more seconds and another turn and the car screeched to a halt that tumbled them all into the backward-facing seat.

"What's the matter?" Bob asked in a trembling voice.

However fast they had been going, they couldn't have reached Thaxton's yet. "Eagle? Eagle, what is it? This isn't the place."

The car sat still, engine idling.

"I better get out and see," Bob quavered to the others' shocked faces. "Maybe we have a flat."

He had walked around the car twice looking for damage before he noticed the cracked sidewalk and the tall hedges looming out of the fog.

Eagle had brought them to the Taylors' house.

Something had happened to Thaxton, it flashed on Bob. He hadn't been able to get Zachary. So Eagle had stopped by to pick up Zachary.

Through the fog several blocks away Bob heard a shout.

He said through the limousine window: "I'll be back in a minute." The Taylors' yard was pitch dark and damp, smelling of wet earth and vegetation. Rudolph's booming bark came from inside the house.

He climbed the creaking porch steps, fog a smoky yellow from the bare bulb above him, and knocked at the door.

Old Mr. Taylor opened it fast enough to have been waiting there.

"Mr. Wilson, thank heavens. Did you find him? Did he run down to your house in all this—?" Mr. Taylor's weak eyes behind his glasses seemed to be searching the fog around Bob.

"Zachary? Are you talking about Zachary?" Bob blurted. So Thaxton had gotten to him after all. Then why had Eagle brought them here?

"Yes, yes, Zachary. You haven't seen him then?" He turned and called over his shoulder: "False alarm, mother. No, it's not Zachary." Then back to Bob: "Mrs. Taylor's worried sick, of course. But I told her—Come in, Mr. Wilson, come in."

"I-I know where he is," Bob stuttered. It had suddenly

occurred to him what Eagle might be wanting—peculiar, yet in its own way logical. "I came to take you and Mrs. Taylor to Zachary."

"Ahh!" Mr. Taylor's eyes brightened and he turned around once more. "Wrong again, mother. Mr. Wilson's got him and's going to take us to him. He's all right, isn't he?" He turned his worried eyes back on Bob.

"Oh, yes, he's fine," Bob said. He had one ear out for the yells down the block.

"Well, come in, sir, come in, while we get our coats—"

"Thank you, Mr. Taylor, but I'm in a terrific hurry. My driver, you know—the fog. Could you and Mrs. Taylor possibly just come as you are?"

"Oh, you *drove*. My eyes are so bad I couldn't even walk in this weather. Just a moment. Mona! Mona! Never mind about the coats: he has his car. Come on, sweetie, we're going to get our little boy."

Mrs. Taylor appeared at the door looking out of breath and worried, wearing an old tweed coat and tying a transparent rain scarf over her hair. She threw a ratty sweater onto Mr. Taylor's arm. "You put that on," she ordered him. "It's damp."

"Yes, mother," he said, winking at Bob. He took a battered hat from a hook and put it on. "Lead on, Macduff," he said cheerfully.

While Mr. Taylor was helping Mrs. Taylor down the porch steps, clucking at the treacherousness of the footing, Bob heard voices and saw the beam of a powerful light sweeping through the fog from down the block.

"Please hurry," he hissed.

"We are. We are," Mr. Taylor said merrily. "Old folks go a little slower, sir. We'll be right with you."

Bob helped Mrs. Taylor down the cement steps to the street with agonizing slowness, in the process almost upsetting Mr. Taylor, who was helping her on the other side, and opened the rear door of the idling limousine.

"Is this a new car?" asked Mr. Taylor, holding Mrs. Taylor's hand as she stiffly got in. "This is quite something, Mr. Wilson. And a chauffeur! You lawyers make one—oh!" He had caught sight of the nearly naked Armilla Robinson. Mrs. Taylor, seated next to Vicki, was already staring at her in dismay.

Feet ran down the sidewalk at Bob's back and a voice yelled: "Freeze! Stay where you are!"

Bob piled in on top of Mr. Taylor and swung the door shut against the centrifugal force of the car peeling away from the curb.

There were definite shots this time, but Mr. Taylor's hat and glasses had fallen off and Mrs. Taylor had been caught in Dr. Al-Haq's arms, and in the confusion nobody else noticed.

"Quite an engine," Mr. Taylor said as his belongings were restored. "You'd better put on your seat belt, Mona dear. Don't you think he's going rather fast for conditions, Wilson?" As he talked he was slowly and clumsily shrugging and pulling his sweater off, and then he held it out to Armilla in his old, tremulous hand. "Here, my dear, put this on. You'll catch your death in this weather."

To Bob's surprise Armilla took the sweater with a shy smile.

"Thank you," she murmured, dropping her eyes.

And she put it on, buttoning it up all the way, its baggy, tattered tweed covering her like a minidress.

"Is that the young lady that has been staying with you and Mr. Wilson?" Mrs. Taylor murmured to Vicki.

"No. Her mother." Vicki, looking numb, was not even bothering to turn around to see the car steering itself.

But Al-Haq spoke up, his voice thick and shaky. "Mr. Wilson, some explanation—"

There was a shocking bang that shuddered the car, and an orange-and-white sawhorse with the words "Police Barrier" flew off the hood. Then there were rotating red and blue lights, and the limousine swerved terrifyingly back and forth. Sirens wailed, but they and the lights were quickly lost in the fog.

"You're going too fast!" Mr. Taylor yelled angrily into the empty front of the car. "Any ticket your chauffeur gets will be charged to you, won't it, Wilson?"

"I hope not."

Al-Haq said in a choked voice: "Excuse me. I think I am going to vomit."

Mr. Taylor pulled off his hat and held it out to Al-Haq, and Al-Haq took it and threw up into it over and over, until even with the windows quickly cranked open the sound and smell, together with the fast, wild motions of the car, made Bob feel seriously queasy too.

"That's an old hat," said Mr. Taylor.

"Would you mind throwing it out the window if you're done?" asked Armilla. "That's the most disgusting thing I ever witnessed."

Al-Haq looked questioningly at Mr. Taylor, and at his nod tossed the hat and its contents out the window.

"I am deeply, deeply sorry," Al-Haq said humbly, wiping his mouth on his sleeve.

The car screeched to a sudden halt, but everyone had their seat belts on this time.

Again it wasn't Thaxton's; there was no sign of overhanging trees or a hill. But Bob thought he knew where they were. He thought he knew now what Eagle was doing. He opened the car door and got out hurriedly. "One more pit stop."

"I'm coming with you," said Vicki, her voice near panic. Halfway up the narrow walk she caught his arm and turned him to face her. "Bob."

She was trembling and her eyes were big in the dim glow from the windows of the house up the walk.

"Bob, *what is going on*?" she sobbed. "Am I crazy? *Who is driving that car?*"

"An Indian in the fourth dimension," he said, and she slapped him hard across the face.

He barely felt it. "Honey, get hold of yourself." He took her gasping body in his arms. "You were right! Indian magic, and Diana is an Indian princess, sort of . . ."

She pushed herself back so she could read his face. "I guess I don't like magic as much as I thought I would," she quavered.

"Try to keep an open mind—shit."

A muffled crash and a bellow had come from the house up the walk.

"Derek Esterbrook," said Bob grimly to Vicki's questioning look. "And I don't think we can leave without him. Look, you go back to the car."

"I'm staying with you."

"Honey, he's obviously drunk; he's uncontrollable when he's drunk—"

"What if that car takes off before you come back? I'm not going to lose you again."

"It won't. Eagle wants everyone's parents there to say good-bye to them, I guess. He's old-fashioned."

"Who?"

There was another crash and a woman's scream.

"I've got to get them before they kill each other." Bob started up the walk again. "You can come if you want, but stay outside."

As they got closer, brightly lit windows glowed through the fog with a kind of celestial radiance. A man's and a woman's voices were screaming insanely inside.

Bob rang the doorbell. There was another crash, followed by Nora's wild sobbing.

"The poor thing," Vicki whispered in dismay.

Bob rang the doorbell twice more, then opened the door, trying to keep Vicki back out on the stoop. She came into the house an inch behind him.

The living room was a mess. Broken glass covered the floor; the television was smashed upside down in a corner. A bookshelf was overturned, books and brick-a-brac scattered everywhere. Nora Esterbrook sat on the sofa with her face in her hands, crying convulsively. There was no sign of Derek.

"Oh, you poor thing," Vicki gasped, shocked, and pushed past Bob to go to her. Nora was looking up now in astonishment and horror at the Wilsons; she opened her mouth to say something.

Derek Esterbrook, wearing his brown pants and grimy undershirt, appeared in the kitchen doorway with an armload of dishes.

"Special delivery!" he crowed, then stopped dead, staring at Bob standing by the front door.

"Who the hell invited you?" he demanded, and dropped the dishes on the floor at his feet, smashing most of them. Nora screamed something incomprehensible.

"Where's my daughter?" Derek screamed in sudden, maniacal rage. He advanced on Bob, brown shoes crunching on broken crockery. "You sex pervert, where's my daughter?"

Bob was too worried to be scared. "Right out here," he said, opening the front door. "Derek, I want to take you to your daughter right away." Derek's rage-swollen face was an inch from his, gusting alcohol-breath. "I have a car to take you and Nora straight to her."

There was a violent screech of tires in the fog, and the sound of a powerful engine receded fast up the street.

"Hey!" Bob yelled after a moment of stunned incomprehension, jumping out onto the stoop. "Hey, come back!"

A large, hard hand closed over his wrist and dragged him back into the house. Derek Esterbrook slammed the front door, still holding on to him.

"Don't you *ever* do that," Derek snarled in his face. "Don't you *ever* stand on my steps and yell like that. You want to disturb my neighbors? Huh? Then I'll disturb *you*."

He lifted his free hand, but a flying dish hit his head with a solid *clunk*, cutting his scalp open just above the ear and bouncing off to shatter on the wall.

Derek let go of Bob and turned drunkenly. Nora stood by the kitchen door where he had dropped the crockery, her thin, gray face twisted with rage.

"Oh-ho!" crowed Derek eagerly. "Ha-ha! Ha-ha-ha!" Blood was running down the side of his head, dripping off his ear. Holding his hands out from his sides like a wrestler, he advanced on his wife, doing tricky little sidesteps as if to confuse her.

She opened her mouth and there was a sound, but it didn't come from her. An enormous, crackling, electronic voice made all four people in the Esterbrooks' living room jump.

"Occupants of four twenty-two Pershing Drive, this is the FBI. Come out with your hands up. Drop your weapons and come out with empty hands held above your heads. This is the Federal Bureau of Investigation. You are under arrest. Come out with your hands up," blasted the bullhorn, rattling the windows.

Derek turned around, eyes full of shock. Bob realized now what had made Eagle take off. Of course the FBI had been watching the Esterbrooks'. And of course you couldn't sneak up on Eagle, looking down as he did from the higher space.

"Come out immediately with your hands over your heads," crackled the bullhorn. "If we have to come in after you there may be serious consequences."

"But I'm a—" whispered Derek in horror, then began to scream: "I'm a patriotic citizen of this country! I'm a patriotic citizen of this country!"

Vicki's wide eyes sought Bob's, and he held out his hand. She came across the living room and he pulled her toward the door, telling her to put her hands up in the air. He was numb, his regret for having failed Eagle abstract and distant.

Then he heard something. The roar of a powerful engine.

With a wrenching crash the far end of the Esterbrooks' living room exploded in dust and debris.

Bob's first thought was that the FBI had opened fire, but then through swirling dust he saw the black limousine, steam hissing from under its buckled hood, backing away into the darkness of the side yard from the gaping hole it had torn in the flimsy wall and floor of the house.

Yells came from outside. The bullhorn gave an inarticulate honk.

"It's now or never. Now or never," Bob babbled, starting across the littered, tilted living room toward the hole. "Come on!" he screamed into Derek Esterbrook's ear, grabbing his thick wrist and yanking him along.

Derek staggered forward without resisting, squinting stupidly as if not sure what he was seeing. From the corner of his eye Bob saw Vicki dragging Nora.

The rear door of the limousine was open and Armilla Robinson, flushed and grinning, helped Bob drag the three others through the jagged hole in the house and into the car. One of Bob's feet was still on the lawn when the car took off.

They churned through grass, ran down a fence, jumped a curb, broke through a sawhorse barrier, sideswiped a police car, and then were roaring uphill in an impenetrable darkness full of sirens, Mr. Taylor yelling: "No sir, I won't be quiet! I demand that you stop this car!"

The limousine's wild careening shook its eight passengers violently, but only for a few more minutes. Then a clanking grew in its engine and there was a smell of burning. It shuddered, losing power until, with a final choked rattle, the engine seized and the car slid to a stop with a ratcheting of gears.

19

Bob was the first one out of the car. In the sudden silence his ears rang, and his feet tingled against the solid ground. Dripping leaves hung from the darkness and the street sloped upward.

"The very first thing I'm going to do when I get to a telephone is call the police!" came Mr. Taylor's furious voice from the backseat. "Someone's going to be arrested, and it's not going to be me! Mona, doll, are you all right?

Bob strode anxiously up the street. The fog seemed to be thinning now. After a dozen steps a mossy brick walk led to the hazy outline of a house with a few lit windows.

The front door flew open two seconds after Bob knocked on it.

"Wilson! Did you bring—" Thaxton started, silhouetted in the light of the doorway, then gasped as he saw the other limousine passengers straggling up the street. "What is this? What are you—?" He stopped again as Armilla emerged from the fog. Thaxton cringed, seeming to try to shrink behind Bob. "Armilla, dear. I have something for you, did Mr. Wilson tell you? And the professor is here too. Dr. Al-Haq, I presume? Come in, come in. Is that Ms. Esterbrook's computer you are carrying? Excellent."

Thaxton turned to Bob and held out his hand. "Wilson, thank you for your help. I wish I could visit with you and these other fine people, but I have a project to finish up. Let me help you with that, Dr. Al-Haq. Has Mr. Wilson explained—no? Well, I think this may be of interest to you in your researches."

"Is this where Zachary is?" asked Mr. Taylor, limping up the front walk angrily. "Where is my little boy? You take me to him right away. Right away, do you hear?" Mrs. Taylor burst into tears.

"And my daughter!" screeched Nora Esterbrook. "I'm going to call the police!"

Thaxton turned to Bob with a sick look. "Why did you bring them here?" he hissed desperately.

"Eagle drove us. He insisted on picking up the Taylors and Esterbrooks," Bob whispered urgently. "I'd guess he wants them to have a chance to say good-bye to their kids. There's no time to waste, Thaxton: the police and the FBI—"

Voices yelled from the fog: "Nobody move! Put your hands in the air! Hands in the air! *Now!*"

Everyone spun around as black-clad figures with black grease-painted faces ran out of the darkness. Bob saw with shock that they were carrying assault rifles, even pointing them.

"Everybody against the wall!" they yelled. "Hands on the wall, feet apart! *Now!*"

"Terrorists!" yelled Mr. Taylor. "Arabs! Get the police!" One of the black-clad men dragged him to the house, planted his feet in a bedraggled flower bed, and shoved his hands against the wall.

Mrs. Taylor screamed and fainted.

"Stay back! Hands in the air!" yelled another of the men as Vicki and Dr. Al-Haq made a move toward where she lay on the mossy lawn.

"Terrorists!" yelled Mr. Taylor, struggling vainly to stand away from the wall. "Mona? Mona, love, speak to me!"

"This is the FBI," said another voice—a deep, serious,

dramatic voice Bob recognized. A large figure in a gray trenchcoat had walked out of the woods behind the commandos: Special Agent Jim Kozlowski. "All of you are under arrest."

Bob was working to recover his wits. Thaxton seemed to have lost his; he stood staring, holding on to his front doorjamb as if to keep from falling.

"Then we'll take our Miranda warnings now, and each of us would like to talk to his or her lawyer," Bob called over his shoulder as he was hustled toward the wall to be frisked.

"You shut up," said the large, stone-hard man hustling him, and shoved him extra hard.

"Your men are using excessive force, Kozlowski," Bob called. "I've got nine witnesses here. You've roughed up an eighty-year-old man, rendered his wife unconscious, and you're about to commit second-degree sexual assault by frisking those women." FBI commandos were leading Vicki, Nora Esterbrook, and Armilla Robinson toward the wall too.

"Hey, Bob!" yelled Armilla to him. "You want me to kill these guys?" She sounded excited and happy.

"No!" yelled Bob in panic. A couple of the FBI men laughed.

Bob had no idea what was going to happen next or even what he wanted to happen, but like a good lawyer he kept talking. "Assault and battery," he called to Kozlowski as the snarling commando frisked him. "False arrest. Infliction of severe emotional distress. Sexual assault. Trespassing."

"I said *shut up!*" bawled Bob's commando in his face.

"Yeah, do that, Wilson," said Kozlowski, but he mumbled something to one of the other men, who began yelling the Miranda warning: "You have the right to remain silent. Anything you say can and will be used against you in a court of law. You have the right to a lawyer—"

Bob was trying to think, another thing lawyers are

supposed to do. His commando was done frisking him. Thaxton was standing two feet away slack-jawed, having just been frisked himself.

Bob leaned toward Thaxton and opened his mouth, but before he could get anything out a blow to the side of his head knocked him against the wall, and the landscape went blurry.

"You shut up until somebody tells you to talk," the commando who had hit him snarled.

Through rage and dizziness, though not yet pain, Bob saw Kozlowski come through the thinning fog to stand over him, hands in the pockets of his trenchcoat, lip curling. "I didn't figure you for a spy, Wilson," he said. "You had me fooled pretty good. But don't think you can get away with it any more. Another wrong move and I'll have Patch here lay you out. That clear?"

"I want to talk to my lawyer," gasped Bob, feeling the side of his head. It was numb, and there was blood on his hand when he took it away.

"I'm appointing you everybody's lawyer." Kozlowski smiled. "I can't have you phoning out and alerting your co-conspirators. But the law says everybody gets a lawyer, and you're a lawyer. Pretty neat, huh? I bet the Bureau can make it stand up in court too. Especially when we tell them how you volunteered." He and the commando laughed. "For starters, counselor, here's my search warrant." He pulled a folded piece of paper from an inner pocket.

Bob put out a shaking hand to take it. A plan, vague and with lots of holes in it, was coming into his mind.

"If I'm their lawyer, they have the right to consult with me," said Bob thickly past a cut inside his mouth. "Do you want to consult?" he asked Thaxton, who had been watching this exchange with horrified fascination.

Looking into Bob's eyes as if trying to read them, Thaxton nodded nervously.

Kozlowski looked from one to the other of them, then shrugged. "Let them talk," he said, and walked away.

Bob was vaguely aware that Derek Esterbrook was screaming, two agents restraining him. With a contemptuous look at Bob, the commando who had hit him moved a couple of steps away.

Bob whispered to Thaxton: "What do we do now?"

Thaxton was suddenly coherent, urgent. "The four of us need to get all together, touching each other. I've prepared Zachary and Diana—and I'm warning you, they won't recognize their parents or be able to function naturally. But we need to get together—"

"Thaxton, this is all on the level, isn't it? You're not a spy or—"

"You saw the higher space!" Thaxton hissed intensely at him. "You *saw* the higher space!"

Bob thought about it. "Okay," he whispered finally. "I'll give it a try."

"Kozlowski!" Bob called. His commando looked like he wanted to hit Bob again but couldn't think of an excuse. Kozlowski came striding back through tatters of fog, chewing gum.

"Mr. Thaxton wants to make a confession," said Bob, ignoring Thaxton's horrified look. "But he has a couple of conditions."

"What are they?" said Kozlowski, face hard, jaw working.

"He gets to have his family around him when he does it," said Bob. "The Robinson woman, the redhead over there, is his daughter. And his two grandchildren are in the house here. He wants them next to him when he confesses."

Kozlowski moved his hard gaze onto Thaxton, who nodded, trying to smile.

"Confesses to what?" Kozlowski asked finally.

"You'll find out when he does it," said Bob. His head was starting to hurt now, and his rage was resolving itself into vindictiveness, a burning desire to thwart the FBI any way he could, including turning their treason suspect into a fourth-dimensional Indian shaman.

Kozlowski chewed a little more. "Okay," he said finally. "We found the kids; they're on drugs or something. You got a winner of a client here, Wilson." And to the two commandos standing nearby: "Bring everybody inside. Bring the kids down." And to Thaxton: "You're doing this on advice of counsel. We're going to have a tape recorder going when you talk."

Thaxton nodded again, eyes abstracted as if thinking furiously.

Derek Esterbrook had been subdued and was now crying, protesting that he was a proud American. Nora was white and silent; Dr. Al-Haq dark and silent; Mr. Taylor and the revived Mrs. Taylor leaned on each other, looking suddenly very old and fragile. Armilla Robinson's cheeks were flushed and her eyes bright, looking around as if hungry to know what was going to happen next. Bob sought Vicki's eyes and she smiled at him, and his heart dropped as he imagined her for the first time in a jail cell.

With the lights on, Thaxton's living room was large and antique and worn, with old wooden chairs, smoke-darkened portraits, a hearth of gray stone, and a threadbare rug on a stone floor. A single shabby armchair sat near the fireplace next to a small table covered with papers and books. There was a moth-eaten sofa against the opposite wall. Thaxton went to the armchair, and the FBI commandos crowded the four women and Mr. Taylor onto the sofa. Dr. Al-Haq and Derek Esterbrook stood nearby.

Bob's commando put his gun in Bob's way when he tried to join Thaxton, but at a nod from Kozlowski let him go. Thaxton's long, nervous hands were toying with his chair's armrests as if the familiar feel of them gave him comfort. Through an arch at the other end of the room there was a creaking of stairs, and two commandos appeared leading Diana Esterbrook and Zachary Taylor. The children walked without stumbling, but their faces were blank, intent, as if they were watching TV.

There was a shriek and Nora Esterbrook pushed past all the guns and agents to kneel in front of Diana and take her in her arms and rock her back and forth. The Taylors struggled off the sofa to go to Zachary. Mrs. Taylor picked him up and Mr. Taylor held his hand and they crooned and soothed and clucked as he looked blankly into space.

"Okay, Mr. Thaxton," said Kozlowski, "we're ready anytime you are."

"When he gets his relatives around him," said Bob. Kozlowski glowered at him for a few seconds, then waved a hand wearily.

"Okay, get the kids next to him," said Kozlowski. "And Ms. Robinson. Hold hands with him or whatever he wants, and just for the record, your confession is completely voluntary and on advice of counsel, Mr. Thaxton, is it not?"

"Yes," said Thaxton.

Armilla Robinson got up hesitantly, looking at Bob. He nodded to her. She shrugged, tossed her head, and came across the living room to stand next to him by Thaxton's chair, beautiful and wild-looking in her tweed sweater and tousled hair. Thaxton didn't look at her. He was licking his lips nervously, watching the FBI agents separating Diana from the hysterical Nora Esterbrook and Zachary from the indignant Taylors.

Then the two blank-faced, docile children were led over to stand by their "grandfather." All eyes were on the sobbing and protesting parents, but Bob saw Thaxton gesture to Armilla, and her hesitantly lean down, and he whisper something in her ear.

She quivered then, and at that instant Bob's ears rang dizzily, as if Armilla were a gong Thaxton's whisper had hit. By the time he had shaken the feeling off Armilla had straightened up again, but now her face was as blank and distant as the two children's.

Thaxton gestured to Bob next.

He leaned over apprehensively, but all Thaxton whispered was: "Get away now. Go stand with the others."

Bob did that. He walked across the room and stood by where Vicki sat on the sofa. She took his hand. He remembered later that her hand was ice cold.

"Now," said Kozlowski.

Thaxton cleared his throat nervously. "I want first to say," he said, "thank you to everyone who has helped us, and especially to those who have taken care of—these young ones. Without your love, this would have been a hard world indeed. I—we will never forget you. Even though I never thought of it this way before, it is in part for you that I—we are going to do—what we are going to try to do. If you knew what that was, you would wish us success. I'm no good at making speeches, as you can see, but I hope Eagle will be satisfied with that."

Bob glanced at Kozlowski, but he was just staring stolidly at Thaxton, his jaw working rhythmically.

At a word from Thaxton the three young people around him, who Bob suddenly saw looked extraordinarily alike, joined hands with him and each other in a single movement. Thaxton mumbled something else and closed his eyes.

Then a light came, a glow that seemed to emanate from the four people at the armchair, blurring their shapes. It flared suddenly, enveloping them in a blinding glare.

For a split second a figure seemed to form in the glare: the figure of a man; but before Bob could be sure an ear-splitting bellow dashed the light to pieces in smoke, splinters, and screams.

When the two commandos who had fired lowered their assault rifles, four bodies lay twitching and shuddering by the fireplace.

"I was *dead*, man," said Max Corrant, cookie forgotten in the hand he rested on the white cloth of the Wilsons' dining room table. "That convent bitch was a professional; she knew right where to put that blade. Then my body wouldn't do what I wanted; it just kind of sighed and lay down real clumsy, still holding the phone, and my last thought was, why did I have to be so smart? Why did I have to prove I was Sherlock Holmes, sneaking into the place and using the phone and everything? I felt bitter. Then I was gone.

"I don't know how long it was, but the next thing I heard was my mother's voice. It was the most beautiful sound I ever heard. I had forgotten everything, and I felt like a baby just waking up in her arms. Don't ask me how she got there or where she pulled me out of or how she did it, but she did it. She's a—well, you know. She pulled me out into this place—I can't describe it, don't even ask me to try." His eyes were suddenly distant, wet. "It was—like—" he waved his arms.

"Deep," said Bob, sitting across the table next to Vicki, sweat breaking out on him as he listened.

"Deep," agreed Max. "My mother had me by the hand, and it was as if we were—flying, like, and I was looking down, and—" He stopped, looking helplessly into the eyes of the other three people at the table.

"Where does your mother say you were? What is her description of that place?" asked Dr. Al-Haq, hands clasped excitedly on the table.

"She won't talk about it," said Max. "She tells me to hush and someday maybe I'll learn for myself. Anyway, as soon as I could think again she was putting me in bed at home and giving me a cup of chamomile tea with milk, like she used to when I was little."

"Tell us," said Dr. Al-Haq, "whatever you can about that place. That deep place."

"Well—" said Max, and his voice trembled. "It was like—it felt somehow like I was finally *home*, really *home*, though it was so strange. I looked down into the place my mother had pulled me out of, and I thought: 'Oh, that's death, but look, it's as easy to get out of as—as a tomb.' That sounds funny, but in that world you could get out of a tomb just as easy as walking, see what I mean?"

"The higher space," whispered Al-Haq.

Vicki held Bob's hand tightly under the table, her dark eyes wide.

"And the other thing," Max went on chokingly, "was that I looked down and I saw people! But seen from there we are so free! I can't describe it, it's like nothing you ever experienced. But it was like—as if all the people, all the living beings were—were, like *raindrops* falling across a countryside from a huge thunderhead above, and each of them perfect, crystalline, silent, reflecting everything inside themselves, *everything*! I don't know," he said in frustration. "I can't describe it." He seemed to notice his cookie then, because he put it in his mouth and chewed it.

"I hope death is like what you said, that you can get out of it in that world" said Vicki, and her voice was shaking too. "Because those poor children—"

Kozlowski had resigned from the FBI in the scandal over the shooting, and was under criminal investigation a month later. The agents who had done the actual firing faced indictments for second-degree murder. The FBI, the congressional panel that had been formed to investigate the shootings, and the press had concluded that Thaxton had merely been a brilliant, eccentric inventor who had built the garlic devices in his basement along with some high-powered computing equipment. No evidence of espionage had been found.

The congressional panel had not been impressed by the FBI agents' testimony that Thaxton had tried to use some kind of laser weapon against them. The public wanted blood to follow the blood of the old inventor, his beautiful daughter, and the two innocent children, and the thing had turned into high political theater. Heads would roll, and Bob wasn't happy about it.

"I guess I thought the four of them would kind of melt together like protoplasm and form into Eagle," he told Vicki, Max, and Dr. Al-Haq for the tenth time. "But even though they didn't, I don't think the FBI committed murder. Those bodies must have been empty shells by the time they were shot. Because if Eagle wasn't awakened, reconstituted, whatever, then who came back in time to protect Diana and the rest of us from Armilla? And who drove the limousine?"

"Make sure you do not confuse higher spatial dimensions with the time dimension," Al-Haq cautioned, also for the tenth time. "They are not necessarily symmetrical. Even someone who could traverse the higher spatial dimensions could not necessarily 'go back' in time."

"But it had to be Eagle! Who else could it have been?"

They had had little time to talk about it; they had been giving testimony to investigators, prosecutors, grand juries, and members of Congress, dodging the press, consulting with their own lawyers (Bob had hired Wes Dalton for himself and Vicki), and giving depositions. They had all corroborated the FBI agents' story of a bright light coming from Thaxton and the others, but this had been dismissed by the investigators as an optical illusion perhaps caused by an electrical surge that had made the lights in Thaxton's living room momentarily brighter.

"If only," said Al-Haq, his own voice trembling now, and his eyes moist with emotion, "if only Diana's hard disk had not been damaged by the federal agents! We might have the answers to all these questions! As it is, I will have to continue my researches. And I will! I have her paper still in my possession, and I watched some of her graphic displays. I will devote my life to it! And you good people will be the first to hear if and when I succeed."

"I—I kind of feel like going to church," Vicki said.

"Though it'll be weird; I haven't gone since I was a little girl."

"I already went. With my mother," said Max quietly.

The three of them looked at Bob. But he was wondering how Eagle, if he still existed, was getting on in his quest in the higher space, and whether he would succeed, and whether they would know if he did. One way or another, Eagle still owed him a trip up there. He had promised.

ABOUT THE AUTHOR

JAMIL NASIR was born in Chicago, Illinois, of a Palestinian refugee father and the American daughter of the inventor of the fork-lift truck. He spent much of his childhood in the Middle East, where he survived two major wars, hiding in cellars and storerooms with his family. He returned to the United States and started college at age 14, studying hard sciences, philosophy of science, English literature, psychology, and Chinese literature and philosophy, finally graduating from the University of Michigan in Ann Arbor with a Bachelor of General Studies.

Between college stints he hitchhiked extensively over much of North America, working as a carpenter, assistant gardener on an estate, shop clerk, warehouseman, apple-picker, and paralegal, among others. He finally found himself back in Ann Arbor, where he got a law degree in 1983. Since then he has been employed part-time at Swidler & Berlin, a major Washington, D.C. law firm.

He has sold science fiction stories to *Asimov's, Universe* (vols. 1, 2, and 3), *Interzone, Aboriginal SF,* and a number of other magazines and anthologies, including Steve Pasechnick's 1990 best-of-the-year anthology *Best of the Rest,* and Dozois' and Dann's *Angels!,* a reprint anthology. He won a First Prize in the 1988 Writers of the Future competition.

Mr. Nasir meditates three hours a day, likes to cook, listen to music, play computer games, read, and walk. He lives with his wife and two small daughters in the Maryland countryside 25 miles outside Washington. His first novel, *Quasar,* was published in 1995.

And be sure not to miss

Q*U*A*S*A*R

BY

JAMIL NASIR

THIS BRILLIANT DEBUT NOVEL by an acclaimed master of short fiction takes us from the squalid depths of a biologically ravaged Earth to the dizzying heights of the artificial environments mankind has erected as the last bastions against chaos. And in this nightmarish landscape, one man must face the darkness of a woman's private, mental hell. On one hand lies tarnished stability, and on the other a mad fever-dream of epic scope. Now if he can only survive long enough to make the choice. . . .

_____56886-8 $5.99/$7.99 in Canada